TWO WHITE PILLS

kelli thalman

Grateful acknowledgment is made to Charlotte Perkins Gilman for the excerpt from "The Yellow Wallpaper" © 1892

Grateful acknowledgement is made to The Bangles for lyrics from their song, "Manic Monday" © 1986

Author photo by Sheri Mueller
Cover design by Blue Water Books

ISBN 978-0-578-66578-8 (paperback)

For those who always believed in me and those who never did—
because of you I never gave up. Thank you.

CHAPTER 1

MOLLY

Some days are good. Really good. But then there are the bad days. The days I dread. The ones that make me wonder if life is worth living.

That's why every day of my life begins with two white pills.

A gulp of water chases them down. Discreetly, I return the pill bottle to its secure location in my jewelry box, and I'm set for the day. Ready to take on the world.

Grabbing my backpack, I slip my arms into the straps and glance around the apartment to be sure the lights are off. Leaning slightly to the side, I strain to see if the toaster is still plugged in, then stop myself. Clearly the pills haven't kicked in yet. Shaking my head, I force myself out the door without looking back.

In one swift motion, the door is closed and locked, my hand lingering on the cold metal of the doorknob. If this is a sign of things to come, this is not going to be a good day.

A brisk wind hits my face as I turn the corner from my apartment and head for the stairs, my flip-flops echoing off the walls of the complex as I walk toward the wrought-iron gate. The air is thick with marine layer, leaving my lips salty and my skin sticky. I swear I can feel the volume of my hair increasing and am pretty sure I'll look like a poodle by the time I reach my first class. Running my hands through it, I attempt to smooth it down, but my attempt is futile—my hair is rising faster than bread dough.

Feeling through my backpack, I locate my sunglasses and slip them on, glancing at the sky long enough to see the sun attempting to break through the fog. In a few hours, this small off-campus town will be filled with students heading to and from classes on foot or by bike. It'll be the complete opposite of the ghost town it resembles this early in the morning. No one else is dumb enough to schedule classes at this unholy hour, but I've come to love the peaceful early morning walk. The fewer people, the better.

* * *

ADAM

I immediately regret my decision to change to the day shift.

Nights keep me on my toes—it's the only time this sleepy city really sees any action. I used to thrive off of that shit—the slightly faster pace of things, the intermittent chaos. But then things changed. I just need to get over this damn irrational fear so I can function again and get back in the game.

Jamming the nozzle into my gas tank, I press a few buttons and hear the telltale gush that confirms my car is filling with gas. Even during the most boring part of the day here in Small Town, USA, I have to be on guard, which is why my eyes are up, scanning the gas station.

Silver Mercedes. Late-model, maybe ten years old. Young female. Brown hair, navy-blue tank top, white miniskirt, flip-flops. It's easy to spot the college girls.

Red Ford F-150. Brand-new. Two men in dirty white T-shirts and blue jeans, work boots, dark hair. One pumps gas while the other walks inside the convenience store. Twenty bucks says he's buying coffee—heaven knows I could use some caffeine myself this morning.

The gas pump pops, shaking me from my thoughts, and I replace the nozzle at the pump, taking one last look at my surroundings before I slide behind the wheel of my patrol car.

There's very little chatter on the radio, which makes me wonder if everyone else on the road this morning is as checked out as I am. It's not that I'm ungrateful things move at a slower pace around here, but a little action would be nice.

Feeling a vibration in my pocket, I dig out my phone to find a text from Dawson, a college roommate from my freshman year. I haven't seen him in a few months.

Party tonight at Jill's. You in?

I stare at my phone for a few seconds, considering the invitation. I'm not one for parties, especially after the accident, and for the past two years, I've been able to use work as an excuse—definitely one of the perks of working weekend nights.

I have two options here: one, I go with Dawson to this party; two, I get harassed for the millionth time about never going out anymore. And unfortunately, getting off at five o'clock means I have absolutely no excuse not to go.

Not up for it tonight. Maybe next time, I type, then quickly erase it.

No, thanks. Catch you next time. I erase that too.

I'm in. What time? I click send before I can give my fingers enough time to delete the message.

It's been awhile since I got back in the saddle. Tonight could be good for me.

I can't help but laugh out loud. After all, who am I kidding? Tonight is destined to be a train wreck.

* * *

MOLLY

All morning I can feel it building. The dizziness and nausea.

The feeling that things just aren't right. Thankfully, I make it to the bathroom inside the library before it gets out of hand.

Locking myself in the farthest stall from the door, I lean my back against the polished tile wall, hoping the shock of the cold ceramic will do something to cool my skin—it's on fire. But nothing helps. I'm too far gone.

My breathing is fast and shallow, and I'm pretty sure my heart is going to burst from my chest. Although I'm doing my best not to panic, I can't help it. My forehead is wet with sweat, and my hands are shaking uncontrollably. No, my whole body is shaking uncontrollably. Like a leaf holding tight to a tree, I hang on for dear life, praying my heart won't explode and I can remain steady on my feet.

Breathe. Breathe in—one, two, three, four. Breathe out—one, two, three, four.

By now, my head is spinning out of control and I think I might fall over. Somehow I've gained about a hundred pounds in the last five seconds.

Breathe in—one, two, three, four. Out—one, two, three, four.

Leaning all of my weight plus the extra hundred pounds against the wall, I let myself slide to the floor.

Knees to my chest, I drop my head forward and cradle it in my hands, the vise continuing to tighten its unrelenting grip on my lungs.

In—one, two, three, four. Out—one, two, three, four.

If I can slow my breathing, I can beat this thing, but in the midst of hyperventilation there is a much better chance I'll just pass out. Yeah, pass out. I'm definitely going to pass out.

Focusing everything on my breathing, I zero in on every word.

In. One. Two. Three. Four.

Out. One. Two. Three. Four.

My breaths slow ever so slightly, and I pray the worst is behind me.

With a creak, the door opens, and someone enters the bathroom. The echo of heels hitting the floor bounces off every hard surface in the room. I think my head might explode.

"Hello?" a voice asks timidly from beyond my stall door. "Are you okay in there?"

She must hear me gasping for breath. I'm sure it sounds like I'm dying. And who knows? Maybe I am.

"Okay," I manage to squeak out amid hurried breaths.

"Do you need some water?" she asks.

"Nnnnn," comes my nearly inaudible response.

"Okay," the voice hesitantly says. "Um, I hope you're okay."

"Thanks," I whisper. I hope I am too.

And with that, the door creaks and I'm alone once again. On the floor. Under the blinding fluorescence of the overhead lights.

It feels like an eternity before can I muster the strength to lift my head. Glancing at my watch, I can see I've been here for thirty minutes. Thirty whole minutes. Thirty minutes of my day gone. Why does this keep happening to me?

Panic attacks were never a part of the package deal until recently. I still can't identify my triggers, so these horrible events come on out of nowhere, for seemingly no reason. They usually happen when I'm alone in the safety of my apartment, but this is the second one I've had on campus this past week.

While I definitely had issues in high school, I'm grateful the panic attacks waited until college to make an appearance. High school was brutal enough without them.

I'm suddenly very aware that I'm sitting on the floor of a public restroom. Unsure of my strength, I slowly stand, wishing I could jump up, wash my hands, and burn my clothes. It figures this is where I'd end up—on the floor in one of the filthiest environments on the planet. Wonderful.

My feet seem pretty steady, so I take a test step. If not falling over is a good sign, I think I'm okay.

Retrieving my backpack from the hook on the dingy green door of the stall, I carefully carry it out and set it on the countertop. One pump of soap just doesn't seem like enough, so I pump five times, wash my hands, then pump five more and repeat the process.

Avoiding my reflection in the mirror, I watch my hands closely as I attempt to scrub the bathroom floor from them.

They're abnormally small, my hands. I've been teased about them pretty much my entire life but never really paid attention to them until this moment. It's like I'm seeing them for the first time. It's hard not to laugh. This is certainly the least of my worries right now.

Splashing some water on my face, I finally allow myself to take in my reflection. My face is pale but not green, so that's a plus, right? Always looking for that silver lining . . .

I try to force a smile but just can't. My face is numb, and I really don't have the energy.

Retrieving my water bottle from my bag, I take a swig and focus on the way the water feels as it slides down my throat. Cool, clean, calm—everything I'm not. My throat opens and closes instinctually, welcoming the crisp water into my exhausted body.

The chime of bells rings out, signaling the start of a new hour. One o'clock. I have one more class this afternoon, but there's no way I'm going to make it. I can't.

My pulse hammers at the thought of being seated in the middle of an auditorium. That will only work if I'm willing to risk giving my entire class a front-row seat to my panic attack, which, obviously, I'm not. These attacks typically don't come in pairs, but lately they've been so unpredictable I really don't trust myself to not have another.

Facing my reflection in the mirror again, I survey the young woman in front of me. Against the pale backdrop of my face, my smudged mascara looks like smoky eye gone wrong. And this is exactly why I always keep a mini makeup bag in my backpack— as long as I maintain an exterior of perfection, people can't see the tornado of destruction swirling around inside me. Too bad

I'm not a little better at the perfection side of things.

It takes my phone buzzing to shake me from my thoughts.

Party tonight at my house! XO, Jill

I watch my reflection frown under the fluorescent lights of the bathroom. This is definitely not the face of a girl looking to party it up tonight.

I don't know if I can make it. I hit send.

Seconds later, her reply comes through. *You're joking, right? You HAVE to come!!!!!*

I'm just not feeling well. Send.

What kind of party will it be without my Molly?? Plus, Dawson is coming and you HAVE to meet him!! I need your opinion!!

Crap. Dawson is the new guy she's been seeing the past month. I'm not sure why she cares so much about my opinion of him, but I try to take the request as a compliment.

Tonight just isn't going to work, J. Sorry.

My thumb hovers over the send button. Hitting send will not be the end of this discussion—is it really worth getting Jill worked up when I know she'll beat me into submission anyway and I'll end up at the dang party?

The air whooshes out of my lungs in a long, exaggerated sigh.

What time should I be there?

YAY! We'll pre-party at 9 and people should start showing up around 10. Get here early!!

Great. See you at 9.

Shoving the phone into my bag, I grab my water bottle, slide my backpack on over my shoulders, and slowly make my way out the door, jamming my sunglasses on my face before I reach the exterior doors. It's like I'm hungover, only without any of the preceding fun. An anxiety hangover.

Yep, just living the life.

CHAPTER 2

ADAM

I'm late getting home, thanks to the lady who yelled at me for fifteen minutes about her speeding ticket. Twenty over the speed limit warrants a ticket—it's technically reckless driving. *When did you getting a ticket become my fault? You're right, ma'am. I spent my whole day waiting for you specifically to drive by so I could harass you.* Letting out a sigh, I drop down onto the couch.

This duty belt feels like the weight of the world on my hips, but I'm too tired to get up and change.

Instead, I just sit in silence, staring at the framed pictures across the room. I'm not one for keeping pictures, or really decorations of any kind, around my house, but I like to keep a few of my favorites on display to help me remember the good times.

Mom, Dad, Jake, and me standing in front of an erupting Old Faithful, arms around each other, smiling like we don't have a care in the world. I vividly remember this trip. Stopping to watch moose on the side of the road, wishing I could take a dip in one of the bright-blue hot springs. Bubbling mud pots that looked like they belonged in some fancy day spa my mom frequented rather than the wilderness. But Old Faithful. Man, that was something else. Jake couldn't get enough. We stood in front of that geyser at least seven different times that trip, Jake bursting with glee at the first signs of hot water erupting into the air. He was six. That was the summer before our lives changed in the most finite way possible. It's just not fair to have your life taken from you in the blink of an eye.

I haven't thought about that trip in years. It was all so long ago.

Shaking my head, I pry myself up from the couch and head back to my bedroom, making a quick pit stop at the fridge. The smell of cold pizza greets me as I open the door, surveying my choices. Cold pizza, a few premixed protein shakes, and a jar of olives. Cold pizza it is.

Getting out of my uniform is really a job in itself. I have to remove everything, hang my gear, put my guns in the safe, and hang up my uniform. But the vest. There is nothing more satisfying than taking that vest off at the end of a long shift. *Rip, riiiiip,* goes the Velcro, then a huge sigh of relief. Can anything feel better than this moment right here?

Throwing on gym shorts and a T-shirt from the dresser, I lace up my running shoes as I cram the last bite of pizza into my mouth.

Earphones in, music blaring, and I'm out the door, jogging at a steady pace toward the beach. I can't seem to crank this heavy metal up loud enough to block out my thoughts, so I increase my pace. Down the never-ending stairs that take me from the bluffs to the sand, and I'm off, pushing myself harder and harder, trying to silence the chaos in my head.

Did my earbuds just die, or are my ears ringing? I can't turn this song up loud enough.

He was so young.

I'm so sorry for your loss.

Yellow roses. Hushed whispers. Uncomfortable stares.

I feel the tears well up in my eyes but force them down and run faster still. Faster and faster until I'm not sure if my legs or my lungs will give out first. It's like a competition—go until something stops working. Run until my body stops.

My knees hit the sand with a muffled thud. I'm exhausted in every way possible and know there's no sense in trying to stand. I sit here on my knees in the cold sand, my head in my hands. Why fight it any longer? *What the hell is happening to me?*

I want to scream. I want to yell. I want to wave my arms and stomp my legs and throw a toddler-style tantrum. But instead, I just sit here. On my knees. As the sun drops lower and lower in the sky, finally extinguishing itself in the cool water of the ocean.

* * *

MOLLY

Cara works part-time at the coffee shop on campus and always comes home from work smelling like little drops of caffeine heaven. If I were her, I would never wear perfume, just the delicious aroma of coffee. What better way is there to a man's heart than the comforting perfume of a cup of joe?

She's taking a shower as I stand in front of the closet, scouring my wardrobe for an outfit that speaks to me. Fall has finally hit in our small town, and the nights are getting colder, so a dress is out of the question—I don't want to be uncomfortable *and* frostbitten.

Tossing three tops onto my bed, I step back and survey the scene. How am I feeling tonight? A little sassy? Flirty? *Absolutely uncomfortable.*

"Oh, wear the black one," Cara says as she walks into the room wrapped tightly in a towel, hair tucked up in a shower cap.

"I'm not sure," I say, pulling a face. I'm not sure I'm feeling up to sassy with a side of slutty tonight.

"You don't have a choice—black it is," says Cara, gathering up the other tops and tossing them into my closet. They fall into a crumpled heap on the floor, but I fight the urge to pick them up. She's made her point.

Cara steps into the closet and comes out a few minutes later looking absolutely flawless in a little black dress. Her skin is the color of warm mocha, her long black hair in tight ringlets around her face. She has this sashay as she walks that commands attention, and deep, dark eyes and full lips that can't be ignored.

She twirls a 360 and asks if she looks okay, nibbling her plump bottom lip as she doubts her outfit. Seriously—if her dreams of becoming a biology teacher don't work out, she should consider modeling. She's got legs for days, and I'm sure any agency would be happy to scoop her up and plaster her flawless face all over the world.

"You look amazing," I tell her. I should be jealous. She is stunningly beautiful without even trying, yet I just can't help but love her. Even if sometimes I'd like to punch her. Or maybe lock her up at home so she can't steal the show like she does every time we go out.

We finish getting dressed and expertly apply makeup to our faces, tousle our hair a bit, and are ready to go. Excusing myself to go to the bathroom, I stand in front of the mirror, staring at my reflection—the reflection that only a few hours ago in the library bathroom was pale and exhausted. Here I stand looking beautiful. Flawless, even. Cara was right—the thick braid across my forehead is the perfect addition to my fit-just-right jeans and black tank top. Throw in some four-inch heels and I'm the picture of party-girl perfection.

I've got this.

With a deep breath, I burst from the bathroom to show my enthusiasm for the night—fake it till you make it, right? Cara squeals with glee, and we're out the door and into the thick, humid night air.

CHAPTER 3

ADAM

Dawson steps out the front door as soon as I pass through the gate into the yard. I've driven past this house several times (truth be told, I've probably arrested a few people in front of this house) but have never really taken it in, what, with the patrolling and being focused on other things and all. The house is tiny, dwarfed by the bougainvillea climbing up the fence and lighting up the yard with its bright-pink flowers. It's just what you'd expect from a house in this tiny town—beachy-blue siding, four cars jammed into a driveway big enough for two, and white twinkle lights strung throughout the yard. This house is obviously inhabited by girls.

Bass from the sound system booms through the night air before Dawson even opens the door. I could hear it all the way down the street where I parked about a half a block away. As Dawson opens the door, the sound of a dozen voices spills out over the front lawn, along with the tune of a song that clearly has everyone inside dancing.

Dancing. Crap, I hope they don't expect me to dance. I haven't been to a party since I was in college, so I feel a little out of touch even though it's only been four years. Have I seriously aged into a grandpa at the ripe old age of twenty-five?

"Adam!" shouts Dawson a little too loudly. My guess is he's already drunk. I glance down at my watch to check the time. Nine thirty. Sounds about right.

"Hey, man," I say, extending my hand to give him the usual handshake. Slap, bump, shake, "Hey-o!"

Dawson lets out a deep, throaty laugh. "Glad you could make it, man! Come inside. The party just got rolling!"

Firmly grabbing my shoulder, Dawson pulls me inside.

It's loud. I'm not a fan of loud. When did I become such an old-timer?

I hear pieces of conversations as I make my way toward the back of the house with Dawson.

Hey, baby!

Can you believe SHE showed up?

I'm going to be making some bad decisions tonight!

From the exterior, I never would have guessed the house was this large inside. The front room is packed with at least forty people, all obviously college students. *Why am I here again?*

"Hey, Adam," comes a singsong voice from somewhere ahead of Dawson. Leaning around him, I see a girl I assume is Jill. A little over five feet tall, long brown hair, pretty face. Yep, this has to be her—she fits his girlfriend profile to a T.

"Nice to meet you, Jill," I say, extending my hand. We exchange a few pleasantries, and she seems nice enough, but I'm still feeling seriously out of place.

A new song starts blaring from the sound system, and a collective shout comes from the front room.

"This is my favorite song!" Jill yells over the noise. "Dance with me, D!" And with that, Jill leads Dawson into the front room, her hands high above her head, hips moving to the beat.

It takes me a few seconds to realize I'm now standing alone in the middle of a kitchen in a house I've never been in before. So much for playing it cool.

Scanning the crowd for familiar faces, I turn toward the front door just in time to see it open and a dark-haired supermodel enter the room along with a flash of blonde hair behind her.

* * *

MOLLY

Dancing bodies bump into us as we walk through Jill's front

door, and I recognize the song blaring throughout the room. It's one of my favorites. Cara and I look at each other and start shouting out the words, hands in the air, hips swaying. The earlier events of the day have melted away, and now it's just us and the perfect soundtrack to a Friday night.

We push our way to the center of the room and let loose, bodies moving in rhythm with everyone else crammed around us. Yes, this is what Friday nights in our small coastal town are made of.

"Jill!" I can barely hear Cara's voice, even though she's standing right next to me.

Turning, I see Jill dancing all over some guy. It has to be . . . Devon? David? Dawson! Yeah, Dawson! He's her current flavor of the month. She doesn't see us, so Cara grabs my hand and pulls me farther into the house until we're close enough Jill finally spots us.

"Molly! Cara!" Jill is clearly drunk. She's slurring her words, and her eyes are only half-open. Oh, Jill. I do love this girl, but sometimes I worry about her.

"Are you having fun?" asks Jill, leaning forward, tipping her cup just enough that brown liquid spills out onto our feet. "Ooops, sorry!" she laughs.

"Great party!" shouts Cara, seemingly unfazed by the drink Jill's just dumped on her.

"Hey!" Jill yells much too loudly for how close we're standing to her. "Dawson's cute friend is unattended in the kitchen! You should go keep him company." She gives us an over-exaggerated wink as she turns back to Dawson and dances away.

Cara and I exchange a glance. I shrug, and we head to the kitchen to find this mysterious friend.

* * *

ADAM

Using my height to my advantage, I peer over the heads of most of the partygoers and search for the girls who just walked through the front door, but they seem to have vanished.

This isn't my scene, and I'm exhausted after the long workday and subsequent run on the beach. *One, two, three, go.* I force my feet to start moving as I make my way toward the front door. There must be twice as many people in this room as when I arrived just minutes ago. This has to be some kind of fire-code violation. *Yep, and that right there is why you're known as a buzzkill.*

Giving the kitchen one last glance, I turn back toward the front of the house in time to crash square into someone passing through the breezeway.

"Oh, shit," I mutter. "I'm so sorry—I didn't see you there."

"Watch where you're going!" the tall one says.

The short one is looking at her feet. Maybe she twisted her ankle when we collided?

Short blonde hair. And the tall friend . . . It's the girls from the front door.

* * *

MOLLY

I'm pretty sure one of my shoes just broke, but nothing looks out of place on my feet. With how hard this guy slammed into me, I can't believe a strap didn't pop. My toes ache.

I can feel him staring at me, watching for my reaction.

Contorting my face into the ugliest scowl I can manage, I glance up at the freight train that just about took me out. And there he is. Military-short brown hair. Steely-blue eyes. Broad shoulders. Strong face that looks like it's taken a few hits.

"I'm really sorry," he says, reaching down to touch my arm, extending the proverbial olive branch. He continues saying something else, probably an apology of some sort, but all I can feel is his warm hand, large and strong, on my bare arm. By the feel of his hand, I can see why crashing into his chest just about took me out. He is clearly built.

Wearing a gray T-shirt with blue jeans, he sure doesn't look like the guys you meet at house parties here on the weekend. He's not drop-dead gorgeous by any means, but it's obvious there's something more to him.

"It's okay," I sputter as I stare at him. "I wasn't watching where I was going."

There is this twinkle in his eye and an electricity in his touch that makes me hope he's in no hurry to take his hand back.

And just like that, as if he's read my mind, he removes his hand from my arm and extends it toward me. "I'm Adam."

"Molly," I say, grasping his hand and returning the gesture. I honestly can't remember the last time a guy shook my hand at a party. Usually they just dance up on you and drop their name in some douchebag move they clearly think is working for them.

"Well, I was just on my way out," says Adam. I feel him hesitate as he searches my face. Is he hoping I'll beg him to stay?

"Uh, okay," I say. And with that, he's brushing past me, making his way toward the door. I'm tempted to go after him and ask him about himself. I can't explain it, but there's something about him that makes me want to know more.

Pushing past the dancing bodies, he makes his way toward Jill and Dawson.

"What say we find this cute friend?" Cara says, bumping me toward the kitchen.

Dawson and Adam exchange a handshake. Could this be the cute friend?

"Um, I'm pretty sure that guy we ran into was the friend," I say, motioning toward Dawson and Jill.

"The guy who about knocked us over? No way!"

Keeping my eyes on Adam, I watch Dawson lean in and say something to him, then see Jill pointing in our direction. In an attempt to be discreet, I turn away just as Adam looks over at us. That's definitely Dawson's cute friend. My face burns with embarrassment as I replay our encounter in my head.

In an attempt at nonchalance, I glance over in the general direction of Adam, Dawson, and Jill to find just Dawson and Jill dancing. No sign of Adam. With a perfectly timed spin, I scan the rest of the party. Still no Adam.

"Shake it, girl!" shouts Cara.

A new beat starts on the sound system, and I let myself get caught up in the music. I doubt I'll see Adam again, but I'm not going to let that ruin my evening. After all, this is what a college Friday night is all about, right?

CHAPTER 4

ADAM

So, my return to the party scene didn't exactly go too well last night, and this bowl of cold cereal isn't much of a consolation. With each bite, I see her face. Sweet, pretty. Why didn't I stay and try to talk to her more? And to top it all off, she's friends with Jill, which makes me feel like even more of a jackass about the whole thing.

Scooping up my bowl and spoon, I drop them into the sink beside all my used dishes from yesterday. The perks of living alone—no one to nag you about doing the dishes.

It's six o'clock in the morning on a Saturday, so there is

absolutely no movement anywhere on the street in front of my house. Giving my patrol car a once-over, I confirm that everything is in working order and climb behind the wheel. I shift into drive and pull out of my driveway. *Bring it, Saturday.*

The freeways are just as quiet as my neighborhood, as is just about every other street in town. Seeing that everything is in order, I head back to the office to finish up some paperwork from my last shift.

Paperwork. I never realized how much I'd be required to do as an officer. I mean, sure, I figured there would be some, but, damn, I feel like I'm constantly drowning in paperwork.

I spot only one other patrol car in the station parking lot and breathe a sigh of relief as I recognize the badge number—it's Hernandez.

"Hey, Hoffmann," calls Hernandez as I walk into the office. This whole building is seriously outdated, with fixtures and paint colors that were no doubt all the rage in the 1970s. Orange Berber carpeting lines the floors and hallways, and off-white paint covers the walls. Most of the photos hanging around the office haven't been updated in probably just as many decades, making a stroll through the halls like a trip back in time.

"What's up, Hernandez?" I say as I cross the room to my locker.

"A whole lotta nothing," he says. His dark eyes are always intense, but he is by far one of my favorite people to work with. Given the length of his brown hair, I'd guess his wife buzzed it for him last night. He has one of those smiles the ladies can't get enough of, and I swear there are women in this town who speed just so he'll pull them over.

"Same here," I say, digging through the mountain of paperwork filling my locker. I'm far from the messiest person in the department, but I'll be damned if I'm not somewhere near the top of that list. I keep telling myself I'm going to be a responsible adult and get organized, but really, I'm pretty sure I'm just a lost cause.

"You going to Sarge's house tonight for the BBQ?" asks Hernandez, turning back to his own mountain of paperwork.

"I was thinking about it," I say, trying to remember where the hell I left off yesterday on this accident report.

"LT said he wants us all there, so you'd better show this time," Hernandez says, smirking.

There have been at least four other get-togethers in the past year, and every time one pops up, I find a reason not to go. I love these guys and trust them with my life, but the thought of having a conversation beyond small talk right now is still unbearable.

"I know," I say, keeping my eyes on the accident report. "And yeah, I'll be there tonight."

"Rumor has it even Sergeant Carlson is coming," he says, eyes widening at the mention of the name.

Sergeant Carlson has been with the department for as long as anyone can remember, maybe thirty, thirty-five years. No one seems to know exactly how long. He tends to keep to himself, but even still, there's never a shortage of gossip going around about him. I guess back in the early days of his career he was a bit of a badass, taking down dirtbags and giving them the business. It seems like all his rough edges have only been sharpened over time, and he is one of the most gruff, tough, and disliked officers in the department.

"Well, that should be interesting," I say.

We have a 10-56 on Cherry Lane and Hillcrest. A blond male, early twenties, shouting at cars was almost hit by passing motorist.

Hernandez and I look at each other, but I beat him to the punch.

"Tango 587, show me 10-17," I say into my radio.

Copy, Tango 587 10-17 Cherry Lane and Hillcrest at 0658 hours.

"Be safe out there, Hoffmann," Hernandez calls after me as I jam the pile of paperwork back into my locker and hurry out the door. "Seven o'clock at Sarge's house. Be there."

I wave my hand behind me as I open the door, brushing him off and thinking how much better I'd feel if I was waving him off with my middle finger.

My car starts up fast, and I'm out of the parking lot. I still get an adrenaline rush every time I key up on the radio or press my foot firmly on the gas pedal, lights flashing, sirens blaring. Time to make sure this drunk idiot doesn't get himself killed.

CHAPTER 5

MOLLY

I'm not feeling up for much today, so Cara and I are headed to the beach to work on our tans and get some studying done. Honestly, who needs the library when you have the beach at your disposal?

I will never get tired of the weather here. It's the start of October, and although much of the country is starting to see winter weather advisories, I'm walking across the warm sand in my bikini, getting ready to lie out under the shining sun. How people survive in the colder parts of the country, I will never understand.

Sliding my sandals off, I drop down onto the large red blanket Cara has laid out on the sand and retrieve a simple blue notebook from my bag. This notebook has been my constant companion the past few months—it's where I keep all my important notes, thoughts, and musings.

Flipping three pages in, I find what I'm looking for: the list of items needed to apply for a writing distinction in my English degree. Only a handful of students receive this honor in each graduating class, and I'm really hoping I can be one of them. Earning this distinction will make finding a writing job so much easier when I graduate because it's a well-known fact that this prestigious title is reserved for only the top students within the major. My future is counting on this. My entire college career has been preparing me for it.

Slipping my earbuds into my ears, I select my most inspirational playlist, "Get Some," and start jotting down notes.

To Do:

Request copy of transcript

Talk to Profs. White, Henderson, and Kazinsky about Letters of Rec

Write letter of introduction

Gather 5 writing samples

Tapping my pen against the page, I wrack my brain to see if I'm forgetting anything. I feel like I am.

"Molly!" I hear as I feel a hand slap my arm.

"What the heck?" I ask, pulling out my earbuds while rubbing my arm.

"Sorry," Cara says unapologetically, "but isn't that Todd?"

Her eyes get wide, and a smile creeps up her cheeks as she motions toward a group of surfers heading in from the ocean. It takes me a whole second to see exactly who she's pointing to and recognize that walk. It's Todd.

I'm lying on this blanket fully exposed, with nowhere to hide. I might as well be sitting here naked.

Todd is, well, Todd. He and I dated on and off for the first three years of college until I finally wised up and dumped his sorry butt two months ago. Even though our college town is tiny, I have somehow managed to avoid him. Until now. But here I am, laid out on a blanket on the beach with no way to avoid an encounter. Maybe if I run fast enough I can get up the bluff before he gets here. Or I can claw my way through the sand and be in China before he sees me.

"Molly!" I hear a male voice call out. It's a voice I know all too well, and just hearing it again makes me want to punch someone. Crap, I'm too late. There's no turning back now.

As casually as I can manage, I glance up at Todd and offer a forced smile as I say hello.

"You guys go ahead," he says, waving his friends on. Mother eff. He's going to try to talk to me. Eff, eff, eff, eff, eff . . .

"Hey," he says in a tone that's so sweet it makes my teeth ache. Todd is a smooth operator, that's for sure, but his charm has lost its effect on me and now really just makes me want to puke.

"Hey," I say, returning his greeting. Maybe a big wave will wash up and swallow me whole. I would give my right arm to be anywhere but here right now.

Todd bends down, and for a second I think he might try to kiss me. Instead, he gives me an awkward hug. Rolling my eyes, I sit there, limp as a dead fish, arms at my sides.

"I haven't seen you in so long, Molly," he says, "Too long." He sounds genuine, but there is no way I'm getting sucked back down this rabbit hole.

"Yeah, it's been awhile," I say, looking down at my notebook in an attempt to hurry him along.

His surfboard hits the sand with a thud as he drops down beside me. He's so close our knees are touching. Who the heck does this guy think he is?

I glance sideways at Cara, who's shoved her earbuds into her ears and is pretending like she can't hear us, but I know her well enough to know she's not listening to a dang thing on that iPod right now. Catching my look, she muffles a giggle. She's loving every moment of this. Cara was always "Team Todd," and I know she's praying to everything holy right now that I take him back. Not an effing chance.

Todd leans in close to me. Amid the saltwater and sunscreen, I can smell his signature musk and am instantly transported back to the first time we met.

Todd and I were in the same dorm. He lived in the hall above mine, to be exact. We had several mutual friends during our freshman year and spent a lot of time together. I will never forget the first time I saw him walking through the halls of our dorm flanked by Shawn and Spencer. They were the three hottest guys in our building, and for me, it was love at first sight. I was like a deer in headlights, or maybe more like a ship caught in his tractor beam. Whatever I was, I'm sure I looked stupid. I just stood there, frozen, watching this gorgeous guy float by as I stared at him like an idiot, an overloaded basket of laundry in my arms, in total awe of this guy who was so out of my league.

"Hey," he said as they passed, flashing that perfect smile at me and leaving a trail of his musk behind. His cologne may as well have been called Pheromone, because after that, I couldn't resist him.

"Uh, hi," I stuttered back. He was so cool and collected, and I was an anxious, nerdy mess.

Todd's hand on my knee snaps me back to reality.

"I've been thinking about you a lot lately," he says, leaning in dangerously close. *There is no way you're going to let this douche weasel his way back in. Be strong.*

"Oh, have you?" I say in my most uninterested voice.

"Yeah, I have," he says, leaning in even closer. I can smell the sweet mint on his breath and feel the heat from his skin. How the heck is he radiating heat when he just stepped out of the ocean a minute ago? *Be strong. Be strong. Be strong.*

"I'd really like to get together—maybe get lunch or dinner one day. Coffee. Soda. Ice cream—you know, whatever you want."

He smiles that deadly smile and gives me a wink. Crap, crap, crap, crap, crap . . .

"You know, I'm pretty busy with my classes," I say, forcing myself not to lean in toward him. It's like he's the earth and I can't break free of his gravitational pull.

"Too busy to give me a few hours of your time?" he asks with mock hurt and disappointment. I can't believe this crap ever worked on me.

"What is this Todd?" I ask in a tone that's a little more direct than I intend.

He leans in close again, closing the gap between us. There's nearly no space from him to me, and I feel like I'm breathing in his breath and vice versa. Feeling my heartbeat quicken, I start to realize that the sensation I'm experiencing is not my heart racing the way it does when you long for someone, but rather the way it does right before I have a panic attack. I'm going to have a panic attack right here in front of Todd and Cara. I'm going to hyperventilate and die, and this is how I'll spend my last moments?

Focus on your breathing. Focus on the ocean and the way it ebbs and flows. Match your breathing to its movement.

Praying no one can see behind my sunglasses, I squeeze my eyes closed for several seconds and focus everything I have on my breathing.

"Babe," he says, his voice a seductive whisper. What kind of game is he playing?

Pushing myself backward, I stand, not realizing how quick and rigid my movements are until I see Todd tense up and scoot back. Cara about falls over, not anticipating the sudden movement. I'm not really sure where to go from here. That was anything but smooth, and I'm afraid if Todd sticks around, I'm going to have a full-blown panic attack.

Todd quickly stands up beside me, reaching for my hand. In an attempt to make him go away, I stand still, praying he'll just leave.

He's so close now his lips are brushing against my ear as he speaks.

"I was stupid before. I know I was. It was my fault, and I take full responsibility for it. Please say you'll consider my offer. Please give me another chance."

"Okay," I choke out, hoping that will shut him up and get him out of here.

A smile spreads across his face, a look of triumph.

Seeming to sense something going on in my head, he hurriedly grabs his surfboard, kisses me on the cheek, and says he'll call me. He's moving so fast I'm sure he's trying to get away before I change my mind.

He turns back just once as he makes his way to the bluffs, but once is all it takes. What the heck is wrong with me?

"Oh, my gosh!" squeals Cara, hitting at my arm. "I knew you'd get back together with him. I just knew it!"

"I am definitely *not* getting back together with him," I say. How on earth am I ever going to explain what just happened? My heart slowed significantly the second Todd turned to walk away, but I'm still on edge, wondering if this panic attack is going to disappear or come back twice as strong.

"What do you mean?" she asks incredulously. "You just said you'd go out with him. It's inevitable."

There is no way I can talk to her about the near-panic attack. She doesn't even know I take antianxiety medication. I can't let her know there's something wrong with me.

"I know what I said," I explain. "I could tell he wasn't going to drop it unless I agreed to go out with him, and I really just wanted him gone. You know I can't be around him. Not after what he did last summer."

Just saying those words makes me sick. Todd and I started out innocent enough—a crush that turned into first love. It didn't take long, though, for his true colors to come out.

Glancing at my bare belly, I remember all the times Todd told me I should work out. How I didn't want to gain any weight. He was always reminding me how good he was for me. Maybe I was naive, or maybe he's just that good, but he sure had me fooled, and by the time I realized what he was doing to me, it was too late and I was in too deep.

"Earth to Molly!" shouts Cara.

"Huh?" I say, trying to shake the thoughts plaguing my brain.

"Holy hell, Molly, I said your name about a thousand times. What gives?"

She's clearly trying to figure me out by how hard she's staring at me.

"Sorry," I say, trying my best to fight the flush heating up my cheeks. "I was just thinking about Todd."

"Yeah, you were!" she shouts in a teasing, I-told-you-so way. Before I know it, she's making kissy faces and saying things like "Oh, Todd!" and "I've been waiting for this for so long!" Cara can be a real lady douche sometimes.

"Whatever," I say, refocusing on my notebook. Cara was there through everything. She is the only person who knows what really happened. I will never understand what the heck she sees in Todd that makes her think he and I are so great together.

By now, Cara is dancing around, singing some song she's just made up about Todd. "Eyes like mountains, skin like the sand, everywhere he's tan, tan, tan! But no one knows this, oh, by golly, better than our very own little Molly!"

Kill me now. No, seriously, kill me now.

An hour later, Cara is still singing her new favorite song. I must already be dead because this is definitely hell.

CHAPTER 6

ADAM

Being off work at five o'clock gives me no valid excuse to miss the crew barbecue tonight. Maybe I'll spontaneously become sick. Or my toilet will overflow. Or my car won't start.

Dammit. Everything goes smoothly from the moment I step inside my house until the one before I lock the door behind me and head for my car, a twelve pack of Coke under my arm.

Sarge's house isn't far from mine, so it takes only a few minutes to get there. The street is relatively empty, with just a few cars parked in front of his house. I've only been here a handful of times for yearly barbecues and Christmas parties, but it would be easy to spot Sarge's house without knowing his address.

Much like Sarge, the exterior of his house screams order. Hedges form a fence around his yard, and I'd bet anything if you took a ruler to them, they'd be the exact same height the entire way around. Bird of paradise line the walkway to the front door, and there is always the crisp scent of clean laundry wafting from his home, making you want to let yourself inside and get comfortable.

Sarge's wife, Erin, answers the door within moments of my knock.

"Adam," she smiles, "come on in. Everyone is out back. Go ahead and go through the house and out the back door to the patio."

"Thanks," I say, smiling back at her. Erin is perhaps the most genuinely nice person I've ever met. She must be the yin to Sarge's yang because they are polar opposites. Where she is warm and friendly, he's often harsh and rather stingy with his emotions. Don't get me wrong. He's a great sergeant, and I like working for the guy, but he's a man of few words and even fewer compliments.

Sarge's house is the complete opposite of mine. One step in the door and it's obvious that my house is a bachelor pad— couches facing the TV, flanked on either side by mismatched end tables covered in takeout containers. A large flat-screen TV mounted to the wall, a handful of picture frames intermingled with old college textbooks and a few Sherlock Holmes novels on a beat-up bookshelf, and a bistro table set up in what should be the dining room. It's pretty pathetic, but it's home. Sarge's house, on the other hand, looks like it belongs on the cover of a home-and-garden magazine, complete with perfectly matched couches and the most intricate built-ins I've ever seen, which are also filled with books and pictures, only the pictures in his house are from this decade and show a happy family, while the books on his shelves are like passport stamps to every interesting place he's ever been.

Making my way to the back of the house, I open the French doors and locate the rest of my crew in the backyard. Hernandez and his wife, Alicia, are here, which isn't a surprise—they're always the first to arrive at any event. Alicia is model gorgeous, with waist-length dark hair and creamy tan skin. Her belly is just beginning to show, and she looks happier than ever. Hernandez lucked out when he convinced Alicia to marry him, and we make sure to remind him of that every chance we get.

"Hoffmann!" Hernandez calls from across the lawn as I step out onto the porch and set down the twelve pack of soda. "Nice of you to join us!"

"And who is this beautiful woman beside you?" I ask, motioning toward Alicia. "She must be a saint accompanying a guy like you to an event like this."

Alicia winks and gives me one of her traffic-stopping smiles. How the hell did he win her over? Note to self—find out

Hernandez's secret and follow suit.

"It's great to see you!" she says, leaning in for a hug.

"You too," I say, returning the gesture.

"I honestly didn't think you'd show up, man," says Hernandez, shaking my hand.

"I honestly didn't think I would either," I say mostly under my breath. "Hey, have you seen LT? I want to make sure he sees me before I cut out early."

"I heard he had some family emergency come up at the last minute," says Hernandez. "That or he got called out on something. You know—it's always something."

"Yeah," I say, biting my tongue. While I absolutely respect LT, something always seems to come up, preventing him from attending these social events. When I use that excuse, I get a reprimand. The joys of the law-enforcement hierarchy.

I'm really not one for social situations like this. Last night was a perfect example of that. I found the most beautiful girl in the room and damn near plowed her over. Now, here I am, surrounded by people I genuinely like, and I have absolutely nothing to talk about.

"Hoffmann!" comes a booming voice from behind me. I turn around in time to see Sarge barreling down the deck steps, headed straight for me.

"Hey, Sarge," I say, shaking his hand. "Thanks for inviting me."

"Well, thanks for finally showing up to one of these," Sarge says, slapping me a little too hard on the back. His hands are strong and perhaps the most obvious sign of his time in the Marines.

"I like to keep people guessing," I say, half smiling. I've never been good at small talk. Hopefully someone starts talking about a recent arrest or traffic stop so I feel a little more in my element.

"Is everyone here?" asks Sarge, turning around in a circle, taking inventory of his guests. There's Hernandez and Alicia; Franklin, his wife, Chloe, and their twin boys; Zamora and his girlfriend, Janessa; and then there's the new guy and his wife. Or girlfriend. I honestly can't even remember his name. Street? Stone? Smith? I'm pretty sure it's Smith.

"All right, Sergeant Carlson called and said he'll be late, so let's get started."

I shoot Hernandez a look that is quickly reciprocated. So Sergeant Carlson really is coming tonight. This should be interesting.

We load our plates with hamburgers, chips, salad, and cantaloupe, then retreat to the outdoor dining area to eat around the oversized table. Everyone is sitting toward the far end of the table, so naturally, I plop down in a seat at the opposite end. There's nothing like showing up solo at a party to find out everyone else brought someone. Not that I have anyone to bring. If I'd known it was going to be like this, I definitely wouldn't have come.

Hernandez ends up on my right, and there's an empty chair

to my left serving as a constant reminder that I'm the only one here without a significant other.

Biting into my hamburger, I keep my eyes fixed on my plate, using eating as an excuse to remain silent. I hear bits and pieces of conversation from all around the table and gather Zamora and Janessa are house hunting; Franklin is planning to spend a week this fall hunting in Colorado, much to Chloe's dismay (I can see why—their boys are a handful); Sarge is talking about a DUI stop he made last week; while Hernandez and Alicia are talking close together, touching her stomach and letting out little squeals of joy every few seconds.

"Hey, Hoffmann," says Smith, dropping down a chair away from me. *It's Smith, right?*

"Hey," I say, swallowing a large bite of salad.

"We haven't met yet," he says, extending his hand toward me, "I'm Sam Smith."

Smith—I was right. Nailed it!

"Good to meet you," I say, taking his hand. His hands are smooth, and his handshake is a little weak, both of which catch me totally off guard. What kind of police officer has smooth hands?

"Sammy," comes a mousy voice behind him. *That's* what kind—the kind nicknamed Sammy.

Holding back a chuckle, I nearly choke on a piece of cantaloupe and try to give the girl my nicest smile.

"Lacey, honey," Sam says sweetly to the girl beside him.

"This is Adam Hoffmann. He's on my crew."

"Nice to meet you," she says, her nasally voice making me nauseous. Her hands are just as soft as his. What the hell?

"So how long have you been on?" I ask Sammy, trying to sound interested. Honestly, I couldn't care less, and I really hate talking to people.

"Six months," he says, a big smile on his face. He's still green, and it shows. But at least he has enthusiasm.

"How you liking it so far?" I ask.

"I've dreamed of being an officer my whole life, and so far, it definitely hasn't disappointed."

"Good deal," I say, hoping we can end the conversation there.

"Can I ask you something?" Sammy asks. I can feel his eyes burning a hole in the side of my head, and I know what he's going to say before he says it.

"Depends on what it is," I reply, my eyes fixed on my hamburger.

"Is it true?" he asks, his voice dropping to almost a whisper.

He doesn't need to say anything else. I know exactly what he's talking about. And for both our sakes, he'd better stop right there.

My hamburger drops from my hands, and I'm left staring at my palms.

"Yes," I say, my voice hardly audible over the hum of voices coming from the other end of the table.

"My older brother, Drake, was friends with Hawthorn," he says. "That was a hard day for us all."

I know he's trying to be empathetic, but what the hell does he think he's saying? It was a hard day for him? For *him*? What about me? I had a front-row seat to the accident. A flash of gray, the squeal of breaks, the smell of burnt rubber. *Where the hell is this coming from? Did someone just light a tire on fire? What the hell is going on?*

Nodding in agreement, I quickly stand and excuse myself, beelining it for the restroom, or at least what I hope is the restroom. I know I made a scene when I left, but I don't care. My chest is tight. It's happening all over again.

I've got this. You position yourself in front of the car, lights on.

Got it.

And with that, he was gone. Navy-blue uniform. Lights flashing. A man jumping out of the car. Stumbling. Puking. *What the hell is going on? Why can't I breathe?*

10-24. 10-24. All units respond immediately.

Hands shaking. Heart pounding. Pale as a ghost.

He's gone.

Sweat is dripping from my face. My shirt is sticking to my back. I'm hyperventilating. When did this happen?

Fast, shallow breaths. Light-headed. Room spinning.

I drop to the ground, clawing at the back of my neck. Please just let this stop. Just let this stop.

I barely hear the knock at the door and someone calling my name, but I'm frozen and my voice won't work. *Am I hyperventilating?*

Sliding down the wall, I feel my butt hit the floor, and I drop my head into my hands. Squeezing my eyes shut with all my might, I will my brain to stop. *What the hell do you want from me?*

The doorbell sounds dainty at the front of the house, but I remain slumped against the wall. It's not my house, so why should I care if someone is here?

Five minutes later, I'm still hunched over on the bathroom floor. Everyone outside is probably wondering what the hell is wrong with me, but I don't give a shit. I don't know why this keeps happening or what this even is. Am I going crazy?

Standing, I reach for the sink and turn the knob, splashing cold water on my face. My hands are shaking, but not enough anyone else should notice. What the hell time is it, and how long have I been in here?

Glancing at my watch, I realize I have no idea when I came in here, so knowing what time it is does nothing for me. It feels like it's been an eternity, but maybe it hasn't felt that long to anyone outside this room.

The doorknob is cold, a feeling I welcome as I grip it with my hand. There's no one in the hall, so whoever was knocking on the door is gone, as is the person who rang the doorbell. That's good. I'd rather not have an audience as I exit this bathroom. I don't dare check my reflection in the mirror because I already know I look like hell. *Good thing you don't have a date, eh?*

I nearly hit Hernandez with the back door as I open it and

step out onto the back porch.

"Hey, man," he says, trying a little too hard at being nonchalant. "You okay?"

Nodding my head, I say yes and give him a half-assed smile.

"I wasn't sure where you went. I was hoping you hadn't found something better to do with your Saturday evening," he says, nudging me with his elbow. *Liar.*

"Nope, nothing better than spending a romantic evening with you, Hernandez," I say, forcing a laugh as I slap him on the back. I can see Alicia talking to Erin and Chloe across the yard. She's giving me sideways glances every now and again. I know she's taking inventory and trying to figure out what's going on, but I'm not giving her anything.

Scanning the guests, I try to remember who was here before I went into the restroom to help me deduce who's just arrived. Until I spot him. He's hard to miss.

He's not really short, but he's not tall by any means. His hair is shaved, and the stubble on his head looks like a mix of salt and pepper. Even with the shaved head, he always looks a little unkempt. His shirt might be wrinkled, his shoe scuffed, his badge skiwampus, but even when nothing is out of place, something is off. Maybe it's the fact that he never smiles. Ever. Or that he talks too loud. Or that he always seems to be in some kind of trouble. If I had a dime for every time I heard a story about him being written up or reprimanded in some way, I'd be a very rich man.

Sergeant Carlson catches my stare and stares right back. Although I try to act cool as I turn away, I'm sure I look startled, and I know he's watching me. I try to fly just below the radar with Carlson. He's a little too gruff and old-school for me.

Glancing in his direction again, I can't see Sergeant Carlson standing by the food table anymore and wonder where he's gone. It's a good idea to always keep tabs on his whereabouts to avoid unnecessary contact with the man.

"Hey, bro," I say, turning toward Hernandez, "I think I'm going to take off."

"Okay, yeah," he says without breaking eye contact. I know he's attempting to peer into my soul and figure out what the hell just happened, but he's really better off not knowing. I just need to get out of here. I should never have come to this damn barbecue in the first place.

"I'm gonna go say bye to Sarge," I say, firmly grabbing Hernandez's arm. "I'll see you bright and early tomorrow morning."

"I'll be there," he says, giving me a little salute.

Running my eyes over the backyard, I spot Sarge standing with Smith, his arms folded, caught up in whatever Sammy is telling him. Sammy. I just can't get over that.

Making a beeline for Sarge, I try to catch his eye as I approach to avoid interrupting their conversation. Thankfully, he sees me just as I reach him.

"You out of here, son?" he asks, extending his hand toward

me.

"Yeah, I am, Sarge," I say, firmly shaking his hand. "Just feeling a little tired after today and want to make sure I'm well rested for tomorrow's shift."

"Well, thanks for coming, Hoffmann," he says, releasing my hand.

"Thanks for having me over, Sarge," I say.

Turning around, I give a little wave to Zamora and Franklin, who are both watching me. Zamora flips me off, and Franklin waves back. Alicia and the other wives stand in a close huddle, but she breaks free to give me a hug. "Let us know if you need anything," she says, her eyes full of concern.

"Thanks," I say, forcing a smile as I walk away.

Breathing a deep sigh of relief as the French doors close behind me, I blink hard and try to compose myself. When did normal life get so taxing?

Resuming my trek toward the front door, I exit the kitchen just in time to nearly hit square into Sergeant Carlson.

"Sorry, sir," I say, flustered, trying to figure out where the hell he's come from.

Carlson says nothing but just stares at me, long and hard. It's not an angry or disgusted look. It's the same look everyone else has been giving me tonight, like they're trying to figure out what is going on in my head. I'm not sure what to do, so I stand there until he finally speaks.

"Oftentimes life is just a shit storm we all have to get

through," he says. "Suck it up and you'll make it through."

With that, Sergeant Carlson disappears out the back door and into the night.

CHAPTER 7

MOLLY

It's only seven thirty and already I've received about a dozen texts from Todd. Seriously—what was I thinking when I told him I'd get together with him? Stupid panic attack. Sometimes I'd really like to punch myself.

Cara is in the bathroom getting ready to head out with some friends, but I've decided I need a night in. I plan to binge on popcorn and Diet Coke in front of a sappy romantic comedy. You know, the one where you can guess exactly how it will end from the moment the main characters are introduced. One where everything turns out perfect, life is rainbows and sunshine, and the ending is packaged up nicely with a little bow. This is what I imagine life looks like for normal people.

Within thirty minutes, Cara is out the door, but not before reminding me of the protocol to let her know I have a late-night visitor in the event I decide to invite a certain *someone* over. She's lucky my shoe hit the door *after* she closed it because I didn't hold back when I pitched that sucker in her direction.

There's my phone again, and I have only one guess who it might be.

Party at Shawn's. You down?

Hell, no, I'm not. Although this is exactly the type of response Todd deserves, I like to think I'm a little too classy to throw it at him.

Tonight is a no-go for me. I've got a hot date with some popcorn and a movie.

He must be waiting for my response because he texts back way faster than usual, which is so out of character for him.

You're breaking my heart, Mol!

Mol. I've always hated that nickname, and Todd knows it. He thinks of it as a term of endearment, but it really makes me want to just kick him in the nuts. Or punch him in the throat. Mol. It sounds so close to *mal*, the Spanish word for bad, or *mall*, as in the place people waste their money. For years, I told him to stop calling me this stupid name, but surprise, surprise—he's either forgotten or just flat-out doesn't care. He's just shot himself in the foot with that one.

Then we're even, I guess. As much as I'd like to send this, I can't. I'm afraid he'll take it to mean I'm still hurting over what happened. What he did to me. And even though it does still hurt like hell, there is no way on this earth I am letting him feel like he has any control over my emotions. Or anything else for that matter.

Sorry to hear that. But not tonight. Not in a going-out kind of mood.

Setting my phone down on the couch cushion beside me, I push myself up and walk into the bathroom. My face is makeup free, and the old ragged T-shirt I'm wearing has definitely seen better days. If Todd could see me now, he wouldn't be working so hard to win me over.

My phone buzzes in the living room, but I honestly don't care what Todd has to say. I am in dire need of a night to myself where I don't have to worry about keeping up the perfect facade, and a night with Todd would be more exhausting than a night with any other person I know.

* * *

So apparently I misunderstood the premise of this "romantic comedy" I rented because this is anything but funny—it's perhaps the single most depressing movie I've ever seen. This is not at all what I wanted my night to be.

Lacing up my running shoes, I am suddenly very aware that I'm still wearing this old T-shirt, and as much as I want to avoid contact with other people out on the street tonight, there is no way I'm leaving the apartment looking this way. Pulling a neon-pink sports bra from my top drawer, I retrieve a white tank top and pull it on, adjusting my yoga pants and slicking my hair back into a high ponytail.

Looping my house key onto my shoelace, I force myself to walk away from the door before I have a chance to even think about checking the doorknob again. My pills seem to be working well today, and I haven't felt the compulsion to give anything a second look.

Opening the gate to the apartment complex, I instantly regret my decision to go running. The sidewalks are so busy that if it weren't so dark I'd think it was the middle of the day. The only difference between now and then is the dress code; during the day, it's much more casual—miniskirts, tank tops, board shorts, T-shirts—while during the night it's like every person on the street is walking their own personal catwalk. While miniskirts and tank tops still abound, at night, girls are clad in much less fabric, which seems ironic considering how much the temperature drops when the sun goes down. No one cares, though. They're clearly not dressing for comfort, and they're not planning to be cold for long.

The wind always kicks up a little at night. I can hear waves crashing on the bluffs just a few blocks away. I am constantly in awe of this place. I mean, seriously—is this where I live?

Picking up speed, I set my pace at a very fast walk, hoping to break free from the hordes of people ambling through the streets until I have a little more space to really stretch out and run. Thankfully, just a few blocks later, the streets are relatively people-free and I'm able to let loose and kick my pace up to run. I am far from a skilled runner, and really anything but fast, but it sure does feel good to get out here and push myself until my legs and lungs ache. For safety's sake, I never listen to music while I run. I mean, come on—wearing headphones is basically like putting a target on your back and begging someone to attack you.

I know these streets like the back of my hand. I've been running them at least twice a week for the past three years. Although there is really never a time when the streets are completely empty (except maybe some unearthly hour like five or six in the morning—I mean, who in their right mind is up at that time?), I enjoy the solitude of running at night. Honestly, I really like the solitude of being anywhere that other people aren't. While I love dancing my little heart out in the middle of a cramped dance floor, I will take a run through the dark, empty streets over that any day.

My feet have found their rhythm and are pounding out a nice beat down the street. Who needs music when you can make your own? I can lay down a pretty sick beat with my running shoes.

A laugh escapes my lips as I realize how grateful I am that no one can read my thoughts. I quite constantly have some pretty dumb ones.

I'm still chuckling as I turn the corner and run smack into a pole—at least I think it's a pole. The next thing I know, I'm flat on my butt on the ground. What the hell?

* * *

ADAM

What the hell?

Did I just run into a pole or a person? I feel like I got hit by a truck or punched in the gut.

That's when I hear her. Muffled words. Heavy breathing.

"Oh, my gosh! I am so sorry!" I exclaim, leaning down to offer my hand.

"What the hell is your problem?" she shouts, refusing my hand and pushing herself up from the ground. Her elbow is bleeding, and she's surveying the rest of my body for injuries. I was able to stay on my feet, so I shouldn't be bleeding, but I'm starting to wonder if she's bruised a few ribs. Holy shit.

"I really am sorry," I say again. "Can I help you get back to your house?"

That's when she looks up. Her face is familiar. She's small, blonde, and has legs that go on for miles. Thin frame, slight build. She's not wearing any makeup—maybe that's why I can't place her. That look on her face, though. It's a look of recognition. Not a happy look of recognition. More like annoyed. *Shit, did I arrest this girl at some point?*

Her mouth opens like she's going to speak, then she clamps it shut again and stares at me.

Finally, she says something, and I know exactly who she is.

"It's okay," she says, and it's like déjà vu. It *is* déjà vu. It's the girl from the party, the one I slammed into in the breezeway. I'm a pretty tall guy—six foot two, to be exact—but right now I'm feeling about six inches high.

"Shit," I mutter. I'm not a man of many words, but at this moment I am a man of absolutely no words.

"Two nights in a row, huh?" she says with a smirk. "Are you following me?"

"No," I say, glancing around to see if there's anyone else on this street. This is definitely not one of my finest moments.

"Do you remember me?" she asks.

"Of course I do," I say. It's not every night I go plowing over girls. Until now. For some reason it's becoming a nightly event.

"I wasn't paying attention when I came around the corner, and I'm guessing you weren't either," she says, her smirk turning into something that slightly resembles a smile. She has nice teeth and a pretty face.

"Exactly," I say. All I've been able to think about since I left Sarge's house are the words Sergeant Carlson said to me. *Oftentimes life is just a shit storm we all have to get through. Suck it up and you'll make it through.* What the hell did Carlson mean? Why the hell did he say that to me?

"I'm Molly, by the way," she says, flashing me a smile as she extends her hand.

"Adam." I return the gesture. "You're Jill's friend, right?"

"Yep," she says. "And you are friends with Dawson."

I'd say "Small world," but that seems redundant. In this small town, it would be more surprising to find out we didn't have a friend in common.

"That's me," I say and instantly regret it. *That's me?* How big of a dumbass do I look like right now?

"Well, it's nice to formally meet you," she says, her lips turned up in a smile.

"You too," I say. And with that, she turns to run back the way she came.

My ribs ache, but I'm really tempted to smack myself in the face right now. Molly. I've made myself look like an absolute jackass in front of this girl twice now. And not just twice but two days in a row. In the exact same way. I was hoping to run into her again at some point, but literally plowing her over again was not exactly what I had in mind. Damn it all to hell.

CHAPTER 8

MOLLY

I run as gracefully as I possibly can until I'm certain I'm out of view, then lower my body onto the lawn of the house closest to me.

That did NOT just happen.

First off, how the crap did I end up crashing into him? Like, literally crashing into him. Not "Oops, sorry, I must not have seen you there," but plowing through the stop sign, full-steam-ahead, no-holds-barred crashing into him.

Second, of all the people in this tiny town, I have to bump into him in nearly the exact same manner two nights in a row.

Last night definitely wasn't my fault, but was tonight? I guess it was half my fault . . . No, with a body like that, that guy should be required to carry a freaking license to be barreling along the sidewalks.

Third, I'm pretty certain something is broken. Working slowly through every visible part of my body, I meticulously move from my shoes up to my elbows, checking everything for signs of bruising and bleeding, but aside from my scraped-up elbow, I appear to be okay. Other than my bruised ego, I suppose.

Pushing myself up from the damp grass, I timidly move down the street one step at a time. I must have twisted my ankle when I fell because it's difficult to put weight on my left side. And my hands—they don't appear scraped up, but they sure feel bruised. Based on the way I landed, I'm sure they're what broke my fall. Well, this freaking sucks. Seriously. How stupid and clumsy can I be?

Hobbling along the sidewalk, I turn left at the first street I come to, hoping to take the short way home. Big mistake.

About four houses down the block, there's a huge party. *Of course. Of freaking course.*

So we've all heard of the Six Degrees of Kevin Bacon, but I swear to everything holy there are only two or three degrees separating every person in this town. Glancing behind me, I contemplate turning around to avoid seeing anyone I know in this pathetic state—makeup free, covered in sweat, and visibly injured. I just don't know if my ankle can hold up the whole way home if I take another way.

Suck it up, Buttercup. We're doing this.

Head down, I make a break for it, limping as quickly as I can past this tiny white bungalow. Light and music spill out of every window. It's only a matter of time before police show up to shut this sucker down because it's obvious this party is getting out of control. At least fifty people stand around the fenced-in yard, talking loudly and laughing uncontrollably. A couple is making out up against some bushes on the far side of the yard. It's nice to see that romance isn't dead.

"Hey, babe!" comes a voice from near the fence. *What a tool. I can't believe some douche is actually planning to hit on me as I walk by looking like this.*

Turning my head slightly to the left, I resolve to pay no attention to anyone at the party and keep walking, trying to pretend like they don't exist. The last thing I need tonight is all eyes on me while some drunk idiot hits on me as I hobble down the street.

"Molly!" comes the voice again, this time a little louder. And I turn just in time to see him.

Mother of all that is holy. It's Todd. What the eff am I supposed to do now?

In a last-ditch attempt to avoid talking to him, I squeeze my eyes closed as tight as possible. This is all just a nightmare. This whole night. Maybe I hit my head when I fell. Yeah, maybe this really isn't happening. I'm actually still lying on the ground, knocked out from crashing into some street sign.

"Slow down, Mol!" he shouts, jogging out the front gate to catch up with me. There is no way I'm stopping or getting sweet-talked into staying at this party, so I pick up my pace as much as possible, which is maybe a half step faster than I was going—I am working with a potentially sprained ankle here.

"Hey," he says, grabbing my arm.

"Oh, uh, hey," I say, looking around, desperate for an out.

"Why didn't you stop?" he asks. His face is slightly flushed, and I know it's not from trying to catch me.

"Did Shawn move?" I ask, looking back at the house. Last time I went to his place, he was living a few blocks over from here. I shouldn't be surprised that he chose to move his last year. I'm sure his parents are paying for him to rent this whole place himself.

"Yeah, this place is pretty sweet, huh?" he says, motioning to the tiny house behind us.

"Uh, I guess," I say, shifting my weight.

"I thought you were home watching a movie tonight," he says, eyes narrowing as if he's putting the pieces of some great mystery novel together.

"I was," I say, slightly annoyed. "The movie sucked, so I decided to go for a run instead."

"Even in your running clothes, you look damn sexy," he says, leaning in so close I can almost taste the alcohol on his breath.

That is one good thing about Todd—he is typically pretty predictable. I could always count on him to get sloshed anytime he went to a party. Using both my hands and toes, I still don't have enough digits to count all the times he showed up at my dorm room or apartment inebriated as hell, looking to get lucky. *And this is only part of the reason I dumped your sorry ass, idiot.*

"Thanks," I say as sarcastically as possible. "I need to get going. Catch you later, Todd."

And with that, I force my legs to run even though I'm pretty sure in just a few steps my ankle is going to give out and I'm going to end up on the ground again. *Just carry me far enough to get away from him. Just enough that he can't catch up to me and won't see me when I fall.*

"What the hell, Molly?" I hear from several steps behind me. It doesn't sound like he's trying to follow me, but I don't dare turn around to look back. Putting weight on my ankle is absolute torture, but nothing could be quite as torturous as getting sucked back into something with Todd, so I'll happily deal with the pain. Well, maybe not happily, but I'll deal with it.

* * *

About a block after I start running, I have to stop, but thankfully Todd is nowhere to be found when I turn the corner. I'm sure he's gone back to drinking with his friends.

My apartment is dark and quiet when I step inside, which

means Cara is still out. Not surprising considering it's only about nine thirty at this point. Locking the door behind me, I lean against it and close my eyes. This is definitely not what I had in mind when I envisioned a night alone.

Slipping off my shoes, I start pulling off my tank top as I walk toward the bathroom. The water is cold when I first turn it on, but I don't care and shed the rest of my clothes, climbing into the icy stream. I wince as water hits my elbow, but the pain subsides within a few seconds. I step fully into the stream until water is covering my face and hair and enveloping me in a layer of silence.

What the heck, Universe? What was this night all about? And while I'm on it, what the hell has the last twenty-four hours been about?

The party, crashing into Adam, running into Todd at the beach, then literally crashing into Adam one more time before being spotted by Todd again. My life is usually a lot less dramatic. It's usually just Cara and me and maybe a few other friends. How on earth did I manage to run into these two guys so many times in the last day?

Warm water surrounds me now, and the room quickly fills with steam. Washing my body, I take extra care not to disturb the scab forming on my elbow, and rinse my hair. Ten minutes later, I'm dressed in pajamas, hair dripping down my back, sitting down to finish off the rest of the popcorn I popped earlier, which has gone stale already. Of course.

Dumping the popcorn in the trash, I drop the bowl in the sink and turn lights off as I head back into the bedroom. Cara and I have lived together since our sophomore year of college, sharing a room for the third time this year. Neither of us is particularly tidy, so our room is typically a mess of clothes, shoes, and textbooks. About once a month we coordinate laundry day—it's the only small window of time where we can actually see the carpet in our bedroom.

Kicking clothes out of the way to blaze a trail to my bed, I can't help but think how pathetic this is. We really need a roommate who cleans.

We keep our bedroom window cracked open at all times to allow the fresh ocean air easy access. I wonder how bad our room would stink if we closed the window. We're not slobs necessarily, and we're both very hygienic. I just can't imagine that week-old dirty laundry piled up all around our room would lend itself to a very pleasant smell if we didn't constantly have fresh air cycling through.

Folding down the comforter on my bed, I nestle deep into the sheets and lay my head on the pillow. What a night.

There's a constant stream of people walking past our apartment complex now, but over the next few hours, there will be fewer people on the streets as more of them head home to pass out.

Slipping three pills into my mouth, I take a big swig of water to chase down the sleep. Although I'm used to hearing people outside our window at nearly all hours of the night, it doesn't make it any easier to sleep through. Not to mention the nighttime is when my brain really goes to work. I used to think this was true of everyone since it was such a constant in my life, but it turns out it's not. Some people receive inspiration during these nighttime hours that drives them to stay up and work later than they should; unfortunately, my brain isn't nearly as productive, unless you count making me relive and analyze every stupid thing I've ever done in my life over and over productive.

My phone beeps just as I'm closing my eyes and focusing on clearing my head. It's either going to be Cara asking for a ride home, or Todd. Mother-effing Todd.

But I'm wrong.

CHAPTER 9

ADAM

I spent the entire run back to my house reliving two of the stupidest moments of my life, both in the last twenty-four hours with the same girl. Given that we have mutual friends (or at least friends who are currently mutual), I'd really rather not have this girl hating me. She wasn't flat out rude or hostile, but I can tell she's getting pretty annoyed with me.

After the collision, I headed straight back to my house to shower and go to bed. That girl is small, but holy crap, did she do a number on my ribs. I've had the shit kicked out of me before and walked away feeling better than this. I wonder if one of my ribs really is bruised.

Post-run showers are usually relaxing, but tonight all I can think about is where to go from here. My options are few, and I'm not sure what the best course of action will be. One, I accept the fact that I'm going to keep running into Molly every night until she absolutely hates me; two, see if I can get Dawson to get her number from Jill and text her an apology; or three, never leave my house again to avoid ever seeing her again. Option three is not even an option, so I'm not sure why I included it on this list. Option one pretty much sucks. I mean, don't get me wrong—I'm a cop. I get yelled at every day by people who tell me how much they hate me and what an asshole I am, or how they wish I would die. So yeah, I probably receive more than my fair share of hate on a daily basis, but the thought of Molly hating me doesn't sit quite right. Based on the process of elimination, I guess I have my answer.

Saturday night means Dawson is either drunk or hooking up with Jill. Come to think of it, this is probably true of any night of the week for Dawson. It must be the former because he texts me back pretty fast.

Molly: 805-682-4329. Jill says to be nice or she'll have to break your legs.

I knew this was a bad idea.

Don't read too much into this. I just want to apologize.

Whatever, dude. She's hot.

There's no doubt in my mind that Jill is watching Dawson

text me. What an ass.

Unsure of what to type, I stare at the blank new message, hoping the right words come to me. I don't want to come off as a jerk or like I'm trying to hit on her. I really just want to apologize.

Hey, Molly. This is Adam—you know, the guy who's knocked you off your feet the past two nights. I just wanted to apologize again. I really feel awful and hope you made it home okay tonight.

I hesitate before hitting send, but really, at this point, what do I have to lose?

Ten minutes later, I'm messing with my phone hoping she'll text me back, but still nothing, so I head to bed.

I must have fallen asleep at some point because a beeping shakes me awake. Groping in the dark for my phone, I knock it on the ground before realizing what I've done. My eyes are fighting against me as I struggle to get them open enough to read the message on the screen.

No problem. However, in the future, I'm going to start charging you a fee to knock me over. What's the going rate for bowling these days?

This message is drenched in sarcasm—definitely my kind of girl. At least I hope it's sarcasm and not a strange attempt at being rude.

I'll have to look into it. I haven't been bowling since about 1995. I'm sure the rates have changed since then.

Unsure if she'll respond, I shove the phone back on my nightstand and close my eyes, listening for the beep. And sure enough, it comes.

You do that so I know how much to expect the next time I see you. It feels like I got hit by a truck! I'm guessing you walked away unscathed.

Um, how do I respond to that? I don't want her thinking I'm weak shit for getting hurt, but I also don't want her to think I'm an arrogant prick. She seems pretty fun, and it would be nice to get to know her a little better—for the next time we end up at a party with mutual friends, of course.

I'm pretty sure you bruised one of my ribs, but I'll survive. I've definitely had worse.

I really should have read that before I sent it. Hopefully she won't think I'm some colossal douche.

Sorry! I'm guessing you moonlight as a boxer? And if that's the case, I guess you should be thanking me for exposing a potential weakness.

I'm definitely not ashamed of what I do for a living—I can't imagine a more rewarding job than police officer—but I'm always a little hesitant to tell people what I do for work when I first meet them. These days, it's rough being an officer, and especially in this little college town, there can be a lot of disgust and hostility toward us. Do I risk telling this girl and scaring her off, or do I just suck it up and hope for the best?

Kind of. I work for the local PD. Apparently I'm hoping for the best.

As the minutes drag on, I start losing hope that she's going to text me back. Oh, well. You win some and you lose some, right?

But then comes the beep.

Really? That's amazing. No wonder I bounced off you when we crashed tonight. You must be made of muscle!

How the hell do I respond to that? I work hard to keep my body fit, and I pride myself on my strength, but I can't think of any response that doesn't make me sound like a total prick.

Well, I try. Are you a student at the U?

Yes. This is my last year. So, I just have to ask you this—How the heck is an officer of the law like you friends with a jackass like Dawson?

Yep, she'd definitely my kind of girl.

CHAPTER 10

MOLLY

My phone goes off, and I reach for it, thinking it has to be the wee hours of the morning. It's still dark out. Who the heck is calling me at this unholy hour?

Squinting my eyes, I can just barely make out the glowing green numbers on my alarm clock: 4:14. What the eff?

Reaching for my phone, I knock everything off my headboard. And I mean everything. *Crap.* Phone finally in hand, I fumble with the buttons to try to unlock the screen. The extended-release melatonin makes it hard for me to focus right now, and I'm struggling to remember my password. Third time's the charm—my phone is unlocked. And there, shining bright as day, is a text from Todd.

I'm at your house. Open the door.

Am I reading that right? Looking at it again, I realize I must be. What in the name of all that is holy is Todd doing at my apartment at 4:14 in the morning?

Sitting straight up in bed, I'm suddenly very awake and very aware of my surroundings. Through the darkness of my room, I can't make out another figure in the bed across the room. Cara must have decided to stay at Veronica's tonight. Clicking my phone on again, I check for a text from her but find nothing. Shaking my head, I try to remind myself of the task at hand— figuring out what the hell Todd is doing at my apartment.

Staring through the peephole, sure enough, I see Todd standing on my doorstep, head drooping. *He's drunk. Wonderful.*

Flipping the dead bolt, I timidly open the door, unsure of what to expect. His head lifts slightly at the sound as he struggles to keep his eyes open enough to focus on my face.

"What are you doing here, Todd?" I ask, annoyed he's chosen me for his late-night afterparty.

"Hey, Mol," he slurs as he stumbles toward me. "Cara's with Shawn, so she sent me to keep you company tonight." Cara has officially earned a spot on my "People I'd Like to Kick in the Face" list.

"Um, I'm actually fine, but I appreciate the act of chivalry." It comes out rude and hostile, but I honestly don't even care.

What the hell was Cara thinking sending him over here?

Pushing past me, Todd walks through the front door and plops himself down on the couch.

"Todd, you need to leave," I say firmly.

"It's okay, Mol," he mumbles, a smirk forming on his lips. "You can stop acting like you don't want me anymore. No one's here to see."

"Todd, I need you to get the hell out of my house right now." I was irritated a few seconds ago, but now I'm just pissed.

"No, baby, it's okay," he insists. "I know you want me here." His eyes are closed, and it looks like he could pass out at any moment.

"Todd, open your eyes!" I shout.

His eyes flicker open enough to refocus on me for a second, but then they're closed again. Is he high?

"I came here for you, Mol," he slurs. "Stop fighting this. You know it's going to happen."

This idiot has definitely gone bat-shit crazy. But at this point, he's pushed me too far. Trying to keep my voice low to avoid attracting the attention of neighbors through these paper-thin walls, I open my mouth and finally let go of all the words I've kept pent up inside the past few months.

"How dare you come into my house and act like this! You have absolutely no ownership of me. You gave up any say in my life three months ago when you slept with that slut."

The last sentence must have really sunk in, because with that,

Todd is suddenly wide awake, his eyes darting wildly around the room. Then, just as suddenly as his face contorted in anger, it's back to calm. "You don't know what you're talking about," he growls.

"Yes, actually I do. You know I know exactly what happened that night. The girl, the party, the back bedroom. Stop treating me like I'm stupid. The only stupid thing I did was trust you." My heart is racing, and the room is spinning, but I'm not about to back down. Todd is standing now, his eyes focused on me, unblinking. The effects of the melatonin have completely disappeared, and I feel like I could run a rage-fueled marathon. *Make one move toward me, Todd, and I'll break your stupid nose.*

Maintaining his calm demeanor, Todd takes a step toward me.

"No," I say folding my arms across my body. My face is burning hot, and my hands are balled into fists.

"Come on, baby," he says, taking two more stumbling steps toward me.

"Don't you dare," I say, taking a few steps backward.

"Remember how good it was? I know you miss me."

"Well, apparently it wasn't good enough if you had to go cheat on me with some whore." I stand firm, giving him the dirtiest look I can muster at 4:00 a.m.

That must have really struck a chord with him because, in no time flat, it's like he's sobered up and turned into a completely different person.

"How dare you talk to me like that," he hisses. His face is red, his eyes are crazy, and his posture is threatening. If I was a guy, I would think he was gearing up to punch me. He moves quickly toward me and has his hand on my arm before I know what's happening. "I gave you everything, and how do you repay me? You dump me and completely blow me off. You owe me, Molly. You know you do."

I yank my arm back, trying to decide what to do next. Todd has never laid his hands on me before, and I'm at a loss. My brain struggles to focus, and everything around me goes fuzzy, moving in slow motion. *Is he going to hit me?*

Before I can react, I hear something. Was that a knock at the door?

* * *

ADAM

Sundays are my early days, which means they're pretty much the worst. I was up way too late last night texting with Molly and could barely drag myself out of bed when my alarm went off at 3:00 a.m. The only good thing about working Sundays is getting off early, and I know exactly how I'm spending this fine Sabbath afternoon: sleeping.

Tango 587, 415 on Pardall apartment 3D, appears to be one male and one female. Female is a primary resident at the unit.

"10-4," I say, "Tango 587 show me en route."

Pulling out of my hiding spot along State Street, I flip around and head north toward the address. Pardall is just beside the college, so it's likely this is a night of partying gone bad.

Activating my lights and siren, I race down the freeway toward the address, preparing myself for the worst.

Approaching apartment 3D, I can see why the neighbors called this in—there is clearly an argument going on between a male and female, and it sounds like it's escalating quickly.

I knock on the door, and the apartment goes silent. Knocking again, I announce myself and tell the occupants to open the door. It takes another few seconds for the door to open. Hand on my holster, I push the door the rest of the way open so I can see both people in the room, and I have to do a double take.

There stands Molly, gripping her arm, eyes wide with fear.

"We received a noise complaint from one of your neighbors," I state. "Can either of you tell me what's going on?"

The male speaks first, clearly drunk but trying his hardest to act sober. "Yes, Officer, my girlfriend and I had a disagreement, and things got a little heated."

Girlfriend?

Focusing my attention on Molly, I ask for her sequence of events.

Her face is flushed, and she's clearly upset. Her hand shakes as she pulls it from her arm, exposing a mark that looks like a handprint.

"I was sleeping when I received a text from my *ex*-boyfriend,

Todd." She motions to the guy in the doorway. Todd. What a stupid name. Might as well be Biff or Ace or Shit-for-Brains. "When I opened the door to see what he wanted, he pushed his way inside. We started arguing, and no matter how many times I ask, I can't get him to leave."

Shifting back to Todd, I catch the look of disgust he shoots Molly before turning to face me. "Clearly there's been some kind of misunderstanding," he says, offering me a smile he obviously thinks will get him out of anything.

"Did she ask you to leave?" I ask, narrowing my eyes at him.

"Well, um, yeah . . . uh, I guess she did," he stutters, his cheeks turning red. He looks at everything in the room except me. It's clear Molly's version of events is the true story.

"Do you want to press charges against him for trespassing?" I ask.

"No," Molly says quickly, shaking her head.

"In that case," I say, looking squarely at Todd, "I suggest you leave right now."

Todd's eyes shift to Molly, who gives him a dirty look, then back to me. "Yes, sir," he says, turning back one more time, pleading with his eyes for Molly to let him stay. Her head shakes ever so slightly, causing his shoulders to droop as he walks out the front door.

Turning back to Molly, I see tears running down her face.

"Are you okay?" I ask.

Wiping quickly at her cheeks, she tries to force a smile. "I'm fine," she says. "Thank you so much for coming."

She's clearly embarrassed, and I suddenly feel very self-conscious. I really don't even know Molly, but here she stands, crying, after what was obviously an upsetting confrontation with her ex-boyfriend. For professional reasons, I avoid physical contact on the job, but I'm not really sure what the protocol is when you're standing in front of a girl you've knocked over a few times and texted with for over an hour the night before.

Reaching for a blanket draped over the couch behind Molly, I take a step in her direction. Before my hand reaches the soft fleece fabric, Molly's thrown herself into my arms. Her shoulders rise and fall as she sobs on my shoulder. Unsure where to go from here, I wrap my arms around her and hold her as she cries.

CHAPTER 11

MOLLY

Adam stayed for a while after Todd left. I'm not sure if he felt obligated because I was crying or because he was genuinely concerned about me. He seems pretty devoid of emotion most of the time, which makes him hard to read. Wrapping myself tightly in my fleece blanket, I lay down on the couch until my body finally drifts into a restless sleep.

It's eleven o'clock by the time Cara gets home. Although she's clearly trying to be quiet, I wake up as she latches the door behind her. A look of concern crosses her face as she spots me watching her from the couch.

"What the heck are you doing out here?" she asks, discarding her heels beside the doormat. Her makeup is smudged, but somehow she still looks flawless, like she intentionally applied it this way.

I prop myself up on a pillow and close my eyes, trying to erase the memories of just a few hours earlier, which will be forever burned into my mind.

"Todd," I whisper.

"Oh, Todd is here?" she asks glancing toward the bedroom.

"No, Todd *was* here," I say.

"So he wised up and took my advice, eh?" she asks with a smile.

"Yeah, he said you told him to come over here," I say. "But I would say he was far from wise."

"What do you mean?" she asks as she drops down on the other side of the couch.

"He showed up here at four in the morning looking for something he was never going to find," I say with disgust.

Cara's smile begins to fade as she tries to understand what I'm saying.

"He forced his way into the apartment and wouldn't leave," I say, picturing his face. "We got into an argument, and I guess a neighbor called the cops. An officer came over and got rid of him, and then I fell asleep."

"I can't believe he did that," she says, her eyes glazed over as she shakes her head.

"Yeah, he came over here all high and mighty like I should be begging him to come back to me. How dare he do that after what he put me through."

"Honestly, Molly, I thought you were overreacting when he kissed that other girl, but—"

"*Kissed* that other girl?" I say incredulously. I feel my face turning beet red and think I might actually implode. "Cara, he didn't just kiss that girl, he slept with her. Kissing would be reason enough for me to break up with the douche, but sleeping with someone? That's pushing it past the point of no return."

My hands are shaking, and I feel my head start to spin. I can see Cara's mouth moving and know she's saying something to me, but I can't hear her. I can't hear anything. There's a *whooshing* sound pulsing through my ears as my breaths become increasingly shallow. Everything is blurring into one big mishmash of color and light. Spinning and spinning.

My whole body is shaking now, then everything goes dark.

* * *

There is a shooting pain in my skull as my eyes flutter open. Where am I, and what just happened?

Cara stands over me, cell phone in hand, frantically dialing a number. She must see me open my eyes because she ends the call and drops her phone on the floor.

"Are you okay?" she asks, her eyes filled with panic.

Shaking my head, I try to sit up, but my body is just too weak.

"What just happened?" she half shouts.

Should I tell her? "I'm not sure," I lie. "I think last night just caught up with me."

"You passed out!" she exclaims, rising to her feet. "I didn't know what the hell was going on and was trying to call 911!"

"I'm okay," I say, forcing a smile. As much as I know right now would be the perfect time to tell Cara everything, I can't bring myself to do it. I can't let her know that side of me, no matter how close we are. Telling her means being branded a freak and never being looked at the same again. I just can't afford that.

Swinging my legs over the side of the couch, I slowly rise until I'm standing. "See," I say, motioning to myself. "Totally fine."

Cara breathes a sigh of relief. "You scared me half to death, you jerk!" she yells, whacking my arm.

I mumble some excuse about exhaustion again as I slowly make my way toward the bathroom, praying that a nice hot shower will do the trick and I'll be able to salvage the rest of the day before it's a total bust.

Closing the door behind me, I hear Cara start talking. Her voice is muffled, but from her tone and the few words I can make out, she's on the phone with Shawn, giving him an earful about what happened with Todd this morning. At least now maybe everyone will drop the whole Molly-and-Todd thing. That ship has definitely sailed.

CHAPTER 12

ADAM

I'm off at noon today and head straight home, crossing my
fingers that no calls come out before I sign off. 12:01. I'm in the
clear.

"Tango 587 10-42," I say, listening for the response from
dispatch.

10-4.

This is usually the point in the week where exhaustion takes
over and I'm ready to sleep off the effects of continuous
adrenaline rushes and crashes, but unfortunately, that's not the
case today. All I can think about is Molly. I keep picturing her

wrapped in my arms, sobbing until she couldn't cry anymore.

I haven't dated anyone the past two years. I've been too busy with the other things on my mind. And honestly, I haven't found anyone worth dating. But there's something about Molly that's drawing me in. Maybe it's the fact that our lives keep colliding.

Pulling into my driveway, I log out of my computer, shut my car down, and retrieve my gear. The sun is high in the sky, with no clouds in sight. Perfect day for the beach. Too bad I won't be headed that way.

The front door closes behind me, and I flip the lock, taking a deep breath as I'm finally home. Dropping my bag and laptop on the bench in the entryway, I kick my boots off and proceed into the bedroom. Twenty minutes later, I'm in gym shorts and a T-shirt, debating whether I should go running or take a nap. I close my eyes as I sit down on the soft fabric of the couch and don't move again until I wake up around three o'clock.

My mind plays back through the morning's events: receiving the call, showing up at the apartment, finding an obviously shaken Molly inside with her ex-boyfriend. I feel a strong urge to keep her safe, which is ironic considering two of the three times I've seen her, I've personally caused her some kind of injury.

Sliding on my running shoes, I grab my phone and my keys and head out the door.

Running has always been a release for me, ever since my days on my high school track team. I was a skinny kid, not much to look at, and, on a whim, I decided to go out for the track team.

Not being one to scare easily or give up without a fight, I knew I could become a great runner if I put my heart and mind into it. The first day on the track, I knew I was home. I went to state every year of my high school career and even ran in college. That is until I realized college wasn't for me and I joined the police force. My parents were so disappointed when I dropped out. It was as if all their hopes and dreams were resting on me. Which, in reality, they were. Who else could they rest them on? I was the only one left.

My feet hit the pavement in rhythmic thuds, a sound that has always offered me some comfort. Most days, I can shut off my brain when I run and just be. Unfortunately, I can tell that today will not be one of those days.

Thoughts of Molly flow through my mind like sand through an hourglass. Her eyes as she looked up at me that first night. The shock as she registered what had just happened the second. And this morning—the pain and embarrassment.

Pushing myself harder, I try to shake Molly from my head and focus on hands-on tactics for work. Grab here, hit here, twist here, kick there, and on the ground they go.

Did Todd try any of those moves on Molly this morning? The thought makes me sick to my stomach. My breaths are deep but fast, my heart rate through the roof, but still I press forward.

Before I realize it, I'm at the beach, running along the boardwalk, overlooking the waves crashing in the distance. *Thud, thud, thud, thud, whoosh.* The ocean joins in with my footfalls, trying to distract me with its song. But it's not working.

Do I call her and see if she's okay? Do I just let her be? Where the hell do I go from here?

My eyes focus on the path ahead of me as my mind runs on overdrive. Sweat drips from my forehead and runs down my face, reaching my neck, then continuing its journey down my back. My shirt is soaked, and even my legs feel wet. I'm not sure how it's even possible, but I swear my shoes are filling with sweat.

A woman with short black hair and a golden retriever passes me, running in the opposite direction. She smiles, and I nod as we pass each other. Two bikers pass me on the left, calling out their position before making their move to ensure I won't step into their path. I see two girls up ahead of me walking at a rather fast pace but not enough to maintain the distance between us. The tall one wears only short black spandex shorts and a purple sports bra, while her friend sports gray yoga pants and a bright-pink tank top. They must hear me because without even turning, they fall into single file, hugging the right side of the path, offering me plenty of room. They're both silent as I approach, and I'm suddenly very aware of how loud I'm breathing.

I glance at both women as I pass. The tall one in the back looks familiar, but I can't place her. The one in the front, though—I don't even need to give a second look. At this point, I would recognize her face anywhere.

"Molly," I say, slowing to a brisk walk just a few steps ahead of her. And, of course, I run into her while I'm dripping sweat and no doubt smelling like a gym sock.

Her eyes register recognition immediately but then shift to the side in obvious embarrassment. *Should I keep going and leave her be?*

"Hey, Adam," she says, a smile crossing her lips. "Out for a run, I see."

"Always," I say. Always? What the hell does that even mean? "And you?"

"Cara and I—you remember Cara, right?" she asks, motioning to her tall friend behind her.

It's obvious Cara doesn't remember me, but now that I can place her, I definitely remember my run-in with her the other night. "Nice to see you again," I say, nodding at her.

"Um, yeah, you too," she says, looking to Molly for clarification as to who I am.

Molly seems to pick up on this and says, "Adam is Dawson's friend. Remember, the guy from the party the other night that about broke my shoe?"

Her eyes widen slightly. "Oh yes," she says, suddenly narrowing them. "You almost made me spill a drink on my new shirt."

"Yeah, sorry about that," I say, running my hand along the back of my neck. Is it possible I'm sweating more now than I was while running?

"Cara and I are out for our Sunday evening stroll," says Molly, refocusing the conversation. I see Cara glaring at me from the corner of my eye, and I try to keep my eyes on Molly.

"Well, I'll leave you ladies to finish up your walk, then," I say, slightly increasing my pace.

"Okay," says Molly, a smile spreading across her face. "I have a feeling we'll be running into each other again soon."

CHAPTER 13

MOLLY

Since we ran into Adam on the path Sunday evening, I've run into him every night since. Honestly, if I didn't know any better, I'd think the guy was stalking me. This should be so romantic, right? Fate throwing me into the same guy time and time again. If my life was a movie, this would be the perfect storyline. So why doesn't it feel so perfect when it's happening to me in real life?

To his credit, though, Adam hasn't been anything but kind and has kept his distance during each awkward encounter. And he still hasn't asked me about Todd. That is one story I'd rather not get into with a guy who comes close to breaking my shoes or my tailbone almost every time I see him.

Me and Todd. Todd and me. What can I say? There was an instant attraction, probably more because he was the cool guy in the dorms, and definitely the best looking. His screen-worthy smile, those obvious good looks—I mean, he was a combination of every male lead in the movies: that perfect guy everyone wants but only one lucky girl gets to keep. And for some reason, that lucky girl was me. Of course, I use the term lucky very loosely.

Todd always wanted more from me than I was willing to give. Looking back, I'm honestly surprised we lasted as long as we did. And I guess what he did to me should have come as no surprise—if you're not getting milk from your own cow, might as well find one giving it away for free. I still can't believe he chose *her*, though. Of all of the girls on campus—the women on the planet—he chose Stacey. He knew she made me feel inferior. He knew how she'd targeted me for her mean-girl games. Todd sleeping with Stacey was the icing on the cake of her terrorizing plan. He threw it all away so easily.

The beeping of my phone pulls me from my thoughts, and I realize I'm standing in the middle of an incredibly humid room, the pot of water I was boiling now half empty. Flipping the burner off, I retrieve my phone from the countertop beside me.

Since it seems inevitable we'll crash into each other at some point anyway, would you like to go for a run together this evening?

Adam. I'm not really sure how to respond. While I wouldn't

mind having a running partner who actually runs (Cara prefers not to sweat during physical activity), I'm just not sure I want to go with Adam. For one, I know next to nothing about him aside from the fact that he seems to be everywhere I am and he's a cop. We have mutual friends, but it's not like we've ever seen each other at any social gatherings up until the party Friday night.

Remembering the way my arm tingled when Adam touched it that first night has me leaning toward accompanying him on the run. Part of me is curious to learn more about him. But another part is scared to death of letting anyone get that close again.

Holding my breath, I text back. *Where should I meet you?*

It's only a few seconds until my screen lights up with his reply. *Staircase on the bluffs at the end of the Embarcadero. 8:00 p.m.*

The bright-blue numbers above the stove read 6:47. That gives me an hour to eat and change.

Rather than gorging myself on a pot of Top Ramen as planned, I grab a granola bar and head to the bedroom to try to find workout clothes that look remotely cute. Since I typically run alone late at night, my main concern isn't how I look, which I'm now seeing is a problem. Digging through my drawer, I realize that on top of not having anything cute to begin with, I'm even more limited in my options given that I haven't done laundry in over a week.

My gray yoga pants and navy-blue tank top will have to do.

Stepping into the bathroom, I take inventory of my reflection in the mirror. My hair is pulled back in a ponytail, tiny wispy ringlets framing my face, where my makeup is still perfectly applied. *Do I leave it like I'm trying to impress him, or do I wash it off?*

He doesn't seem like the kind of guy who will expect me to be dressed to the nines and covered in makeup for a run. In fact, he seems like the kind of guy who might consider that a total turnoff.

Removing everything but my mascara, I reinspect my face in the mirror. *That's more like it.*

Before I know it, it's ten minutes to eight, and I'm locking my front door behind me as I head out into the evening. Autumn is thick in the air tonight. The breeze blows colder than usual, but not enough to make me turn back for my jacket. Goosebumps cover my bare arms as I exit my apartment complex, letting the gate swing shut a few steps behind me.

It may be Thursday evening, but around here, Thursday is as good as Friday. Since it's still pretty early, rather than people filling the sidewalks in all directions, anyone who is out is gathered in the area near where the restaurants and coffee shops are. The streetlights haven't come on yet, leaving the streets bathed in dusky darkness. Inky indigo fills the sky as the sun dips below the horizon, the darkness and nighttime imminent. Although I know I live in a beautiful place, I don't take enough time to appreciate it. The sound of the waves crashing on the bluffs as the tide comes in, the constant saltiness of the air, the perpetual feeling of being at the beach. Because, let's face it, we live in paradise.

I arrive a few minutes before eight at the designated meeting place to find Adam waiting for me.

"I'm guessing you're the kind of guy who's always on time," I say, a smile on my face. He's wearing gym shorts and a loose-fitting T-shirt, but the way the sleeves hug his arms, it's clear his shirt is covering up a whole lot of muscle.

Shrugging, he says, "Ready to get going?"

Ready as I'll ever be. "Yep."

And with that, Adam motions south, and we start off at a steady jog up the street.

It's a little awkward running with Adam—he's obviously faster than I am, but he's trying to keep pace with me. I'm not sure if I should start a conversation or if it's best to stay quiet and focus on the run. Should I even be out here? I know next to nothing about this guy. His last name was pinned to his chest Sunday morning, but I was too shaken up to read it, and now I feel stupid for not taking notice of that detail.

There's an awkward silence for a few minutes before Adam speaks.

"So, did you grow up near here?" he asks.

"No," I say, slightly out of breath already. *This is embarrassing.* "I grew up about five hours north. You?"

"I'm a local," he says. "Born and raised." His eyes remain focused on the sidewalk ahead.

"How long have you been a cop?" Might as well take this opportunity to learn a little bit about this guy.

"Three and a half years," he says, eyes still forward.

"What made you want to be a cop?"

He pauses before speaking, and I can tell he's trying to formulate a response. "I don't really know, actually. I guess every little boy dreams of becoming a policeman, and I never lost sight of that dream."

Good enough answer. It takes a mentally and physically strong person to be in law enforcement, especially in this climate of turmoil across the country. He has to have some pretty strong convictions to stick with it.

"What about you?" he asks, glancing sideways at me as we follow the sidewalk in a left-hand turn. "What made you decide to come to college here?"

A smile crosses my lips, and I can feel him watching me. "Well, basically, it was come here to the beach or go to college in the mountains. I chose the beach."

His lips twitch upward for a moment in a slight smile. *Was that a dumb thing to say?*

"So you're a beach lover?" he asks.

"I think you kind of have to be to live here. I'm pretty sure it's some kind of prerequisite to get in."

He chuckles a bit, and I think it might be the first time I've ever heard him laugh. Come to think of it, have I ever seen this guy smile?

I watch him for a minute until he catches my eyes on him. My face flushes red as I look back at the path in front of us. His expression remains unchanged as he turns his eyes ahead.

"Do you want to cut through campus or take the path over the bluffs along the beach?" he asks after a considerable silence.

"Either is fine with me," I say, wondering if the campus route might be best.

"Let's cut through campus," he says.

We cross two large parking lots in silence. The waves crash loud in the darkness to our right as we turn left and head toward the pathway that cuts straight through campus.

The bike path is like a ghost town, completely empty, with no sign of bikers anywhere. Lights flicker on along the path as we near it, much like the lights in the freezer section of the grocery store, anticipating our presence.

By now I've hit my stride and can feel a continuous stream of sweat dripping from my brow. My legs ache, but it's the good kind of ache that gives you a rush and makes you feel alive.

It takes me a moment to realize Adam is looking over at me. The steely-blue eyes from our previous encounters seem to have softened a bit. He's watching me so closely I wonder if he's trying to read my thoughts.

That is, of course, until I hit the pavement with a thud. *What the heck?*

Before I realize what's happened, I'm nearly flat on my face. *What the heck just happened?*

"Holy shit," his voice comes from my right. "Are you okay?"

I can hear the alarm in his voice, but I haven't registered any pain. *After a spill like that, I have to be hurt, right?*

Pressing my hands firmly on the pavement, I slowly push myself up until I can sit back on my butt.

"Be careful," Adam says, squatting down beside me to assess my injuries. It's obvious I'm not getting off as lucky tonight as I did Saturday night. From the look on his face, I can tell I'm in pretty bad shape.

My knees are both skinned and bleeding, and a quick glance at my palms shows much of the same. My neck and head are starting to ache. *Whiplash. Awesome.*

Adam's eyes remain on me, analyzing every limb for injuries, applying pressure to my arms and legs to check for broken bones. He is so focused it's obvious he's clicked into first-responder mode. His hands are calloused and beat up, unlike most of the guys I meet here on campus, but even as he touches me, they feel gentle—not at all what I would have imagined. The tiniest hint of stubble dots his face, and small droplets of sweat drip down his temples. His face remains hard and jagged, but his eyes—his eyes have returned to that steely-blue color.

"You okay?" he asks.

"Um, yeah, sure, I think," I stutter, struggling to refocus on the task at hand: making sure I'm not seriously injured.

"Hold on," Adam says, brushing back some hairs that have escaped my ponytail. I can't help it—he's so close I can't take my eyes off him. *What is it about this guy that's pulling me in?*

Leaning in close, Adam's eyes remain focused on my forehead. Before I know what's happening, he's pulling off his shirt and pressing it against my hairline.

Wincing in pain, I realize I must have hit my head on the pavement when I fell. "Am I bleeding?" I ask? *Dumb question.*

"Yeah, you have a pretty good-sized cut across your forehead," he says, eyes never leaving my forehead. "I'm going to clean it up a bit and make sure you don't need stitches."

Stitches? Just the thought of needing stitches makes my stomach turn in knots. Adam must sense it, as his eyes drop down to focus on mine.

"You feeling okay?" he asks.

"Yeah, just I'm not a big fan of needles," I say, praying I don't throw up right here in front of him.

"Don't worry," he says, eyes lightening a little. "I think you're okay. It doesn't look deep enough to need stitches, but I just want to be sure." *Thank everything holy!*

"Do you want to sit here for another minute, or do you want to try to stand?"

"I'd like to try to get up," I say, feeling my face flush with embarrassment for the first time since I hit the ground. *What the heck did I trip over?*

"Okay, give me your hands," he says, gently taking both of them into his and easing me up.

Putting weight on my feet, I don't feel like anything is

sprained or broken. I swing my arms around and turn them over, inspecting my skin. There aren't any scuffs or scrapes on the backs of my legs or arms, but like my knees, palms, and head, it looks like my forearms and shins took a bit of a beating too. Lifting my tank top ever so slightly, I see my hip bones are bruised. "Ouch," I wince as I gingerly touch them.

"Let's get back to your place and get you cleaned up," says Adam, shoving his bloody T-shirt into one of his back pockets. I'm suddenly very aware that he's half naked and standing so close to me I can feel the heat from his skin.

"Sounds good," I say, turning myself toward the way we came.

It takes us twenty minutes to get back to my apartment. I try to convince Adam I'm fine and can at least speed walk home, but he refuses to leave me. "We're not in a hurry," he reassures. "Let's take it easy."

Finally, I relent, but I'm feeling more humiliated by the second. Blood is dripping down my legs from the cuts on my knees, and my head is pounding. The silver lining? At least I won't have to make a trip to urgent care tonight.

Adam walks close to me, his arm at the ready to catch me in case I trip again. It's sweet, but again, completely embarrassing. I'm sure by now he realizes what a total mess I am and is ready to take me home and get rid of me.

The apartment is dark and silent when we step over the threshold. Cara must be running late at the coffee shop.

Flipping on lights as I make my way to the bathroom, I feel Adam right behind me.

"I'm pretty sure we have a first-aid kit in the bathroom," I say.

Adam nods his head and stops, waiting for me at the edge of the living room. I can see him looking around the room as I dig through drawers trying to remember where the heck we put the dang kit. He steps close to a framed picture on the wall, and maybe it's just this angle, but it looks like he smirks a bit. Making his way around the room, he stops at one picture after another and gives each a good, hard look.

Focus on the task at hand. I continue rummaging through every drawer, then turn my attention to the cupboards under the sink, and, sure enough, there it is.

"Found it!" I shout a little too enthusiastically. My outburst doesn't seem to affect Adam at all. He calmly turns toward me and nods, his hands outstretched to retrieve the first-aid kit.

"Come sit down at the table, and let's get you patched up," he says, pulling out a chair for me to sit in. He pulls out the chair beside it and sits down, snapping back into first-responder mode as he scans the first-aid kit, pulling out the items he'll need to treat my wounds. Lots of Band-Aids, some gauze, some ointment, and hydrogen peroxide. Soaking a gauze pad with the bubbly liquid, Adam gently applies it to my forehead, working his way down, making sure to address every injury. I watch him intently as he works so efficiently; it's obvious he does this for a living.

Fifteen minutes later, bandages have been applied, and I feel like a mummy. *Of course, this would happen to me tonight of all nights.*

Adam returns the unused first-aid supplies. Assuming he's getting ready to leave, I stand up too. He hands the first-aid kit back to me, and I stand there watching him, waiting for him to say the usual parting words and be on his way. But he doesn't.

"Hey, have you had dinner yet?" he asks, turning so his eyes are on mine. They're back to the beautiful deep-blue color they were earlier.

"Um, not really," I say, remembering the granola bar I downed before meeting him for the run.

"Are you hungry?" he asks.

"Yeah, I could go for some food," I say, trying to play it cool as my stomach growls out of control.

"Let's go grab something, then," he says. "But first I need to go back to my place and get a new shirt. I can't quite wear this one anymore," he motions to his back pocket, "and I'm not sure of any establishment that will appreciate me coming in shirtless."

Anyone who doesn't is seriously crazy. I'm once again very much aware of his body and mine as I look down at his solid, muscular chest. His abs are defined as what can only be described as an eight pack. The skin beneath his shirt is smooth and pale, much unlike the skin on his arms. Most guys around here have evenly tanned skin, but not Adam. I never thought I'd find a farmer's tan so sexy, but I just can't help it—he wears it so well.

"Shall we?" he asks, making me realize I'm probably gawking at him with my mouth open.

"Yeah, let's go," I say, turning toward the door so he can't see the blush on my cheeks.

CHAPTER 14

ADAM

The walk back to my place takes twice as long as usual since it's clear Molly is in pain and I don't want to push her. She stays quiet most of the walk, never once complaining. It's her eyes that give her away.

Walking through the front door of my house, I instantly regret the condition I've left the living room in. Kicking my boots out of the entryway, I eye my duty belt lying on the kitchen table, my taser, knives, and everything else sprawled out across the countertop. Walking quickly into the room, I retrieve my discarded uniform hung over the back of the couch and toss it into the laundry room. *I wish I would have thought about the mess before I invited her over.*

"I'm just going to grab a T-shirt, and we'll head out and get some food," I say, looking back at Molly before heading down the hallway to my bedroom. Nodding in agreement, she stops near the cluster of picture frames on the bookshelf, picking them up one by one, studying each intently.

Discarding my bloody T-shirt in a nearby laundry hamper, I pull on a clean T-shirt and head back down the hall toward Molly. She's still standing close to the bookshelf, holding one particular photo in her hands. Before she even holds it out to me, I know which picture it is.

"Is this your family?" she asks.

"Yeah," I say, hoping she won't press for more information. Talking about my family means spilling secrets—secrets I've kept inside since I was young, and secrets I have no intention of sharing with anyone else.

"How old were you here?" she asks.

"Eight."

"Is this your little brother?"

"Yes." My stomach is turning, and my palms feel damp. *Please drop it here. Please don't ask about him.*

"You were a cute little boy," she says, smiling as she turns back toward the bookshelf. Running her fingers along the dusty books, she stops on one and pulls it out.

"*The Yellow Wallpaper?*" she asks, her lips upturned in a smirk.

"Have you read this?"

"Yeah," I say, taking the book from her hands and flipping through the pages. It was required reading in high school, and for some reason, lame as it sounds, the story scared the hell out of me and has stuck with me ever since. "Have you?"

"In high school," she says, smiling again. "That is hands down one of the creepiest things I've ever read. I keep my copy handy so I can pick it up anytime I want to feel inspired."

"Inspired?" I ask. That's definitely not the word I'd use to describe the short story.

"Yeah, inspired," she says, retrieving the book. Her eyes sparkle as she lovingly runs her hands through its pages. I've never seen anyone treat a book this way. "It's such a simple story, but it takes you on this journey through the main character's mind that makes you feel like you're unraveling along with her. It inspires me to add more depth and feeling into my writing."

Gingerly, she hands the book back to me, staring longingly at the cover. Then, as if she's snapped out of a trance, she looks up at me again. Gauze covers the left side of her forehead, and her blonde hair is disheveled. Her green eyes sparkle even though the smile has left her lips. Those lips, pink and kissable.

A grumble breaks my concentration, and Molly grabs her stomach in embarrassment.

"Ready to go get some food?" I ask.

Molly nods, and with that, I grab my keys and we're out the

door.

"Let's take my car," I say, opening the door for her.

Molly slides into the passenger seat and pulls the seat belt across her body in one solid motion. Closing the door, I walk around the car and climb into the driver's seat. Molly has her legs crossed, her hands in her lap, and it's obvious she's trying to keep herself from bumping or touching anything. "Is this your first time in a patrol car?" I ask. I forget that not everyone drives around in one of these on a daily basis.

"It is," she says, looking up at me.

Pulling out of the driveway, I turn right and head toward town.

"Where are we headed?" Molly asks, looking out the window as we drive slowly down the street.

"Do you like Chinese food?" I ask, realizing I maybe should have consulted with her before making a decision.

"I love Chinese food," she says. "There's a little hole-in-the-wall in town called The Lotus that is my absolute favorite."

"Mine too," I say. "My crew has lunch there at least once a week. Their orange chicken is so good."

"Oh, my gosh, yes. That and the dumplings!"

"Dumplings." We say in unison and laugh. "Where else do you like to eat here in town?"

"The Eatery has the best burgers, hands down," she says, using her fingers to count down. "Definitely Osaka for sushi. Oh, and Margarita's for burritos."

"What about you?" she asks, watching me from the passenger seat.

"I've never met anyone outside the department who's been to Margarita's," I say, smiling. *This girl is full of surprises.*

"Seriously?" she asks incredulously. "It was our favorite place to eat off campus our freshman year. It's the reason I started running—Margarita's was the true reason for my freshman fifteen!" She jokingly pats her stomach, and I can't help but smile. There is something about Molly that continues to draw me to her. She's definitely attractive, which is what initially caught my attention—slender, toned arms and legs, full hips—but the more I'm around her, I'm starting to realize her personality is by far her best feature.

"Add Ike's for sandwiches, and Woodstock's for pizza, and our lists are identical," I say.

"Oh, yes to both of those. I cannot believe I left them off my list."

By the time we pull into the parking lot of The Lotus a few minutes later, Molly has listed off her favorite items on each of the restaurant menus. "Well, now that we've talked about food and I'm officially starving, shall we eat?" she says, sliding out of the passenger seat and closing the door behind her.

The Lotus is the most eclectic restaurant I've ever been in. While it's a Chinese place, it's decor is that of a seafood restaurant. And the music—most Chinese food places maintain a soundtrack of soothing Chinese-inspired instrumental tunes. At least most of the Chinese food places I've been to. The Lotus is definitely not most Chinese food places. You never know what kind of music will be playing from one day to the next. It could be rock, country, eighties, or classical. It's like a whole new restaurant every time you visit—you never know what to expect. Tonight seems to be eighties night.

"Oh, my gosh," says Molly, eyes wide. "I love eighties music!"

I can't help but chuckle as she starts bobbing her head to the beat of whatever horribly amazing hair band is currently blaring from the speakers.

A pretty, young girl with long dark hair greets us and seats us at a table near the back of the restaurant. Three other tables are occupied throughout the room, but other than that, the place is empty.

"Usually, it's a lot busier in here on a Thursday night," I say, looking around.

"Yeah, I don't think I've ever seen it so quiet," says Molly. "Apparently not everyone is such a fan of classic eighties music." Using her hands, she motions around the room, a smile on her face.

"Apparently," I say, grabbing a menu even though I already know what I want.

When the waitress returns a few minutes later, we place our orders. Molly mouths the words to every new song that comes on the sound system while we wait. *This girl really does love eighties music.*

Our food is out within minutes, and once the smell of orange chicken hits my nostrils, I realize just how hungry I am, and from the looks of it, the same is true for Molly.

"Delicious as always," says Molly, savoring each bite of her orange chicken. Plopping a dumpling down on her plate, she reaches for the soy sauce. She's not stuffing her face by any means, but she's definitely not afraid to eat in front of me. I like that.

Molly asks more questions about my job and tells me about her classes. She's majoring in English and looking to secure a spot in the program to earn a distinction in Professional Writing. Her love of books is clear, and thankfully, she's quite talkative, which means I don't have to do much more than ask questions and give a few one-word answers every now and again. It's strange to think that just over an hour ago I was helping Molly hobble back to her apartment.

"Have you given any thought to what you want to do when you graduate?" I ask.

Nodding her head as she swallows a mouthful of dumpling, Molly smiles and holds up her finger. "Oh yes," she says. "I've been dreaming about what I want to do when I graduate since I was in high school. I have a contingent offer from a magazine down in LA—I've got to secure this Professional Writing distinction and I'm set."

"That's awesome," I say. Hopefully she doesn't pick up on the insincerity in my tone.

"Yeah, a couple girls who lived in my hall my freshman year are also planning to head down to LA, so we figure we'll all get a house together . . ." Out of nowhere, Molly stops talking. Her face turns almost pale, her eyes looking instantly dull, the sparkle that made them emerald green just moments before gone. She shrinks a little in her chair, looking like a deflated balloon.

I'm slightly thrown and not really sure where to go from here, so I just watch Molly stare off in the distance, a dazed, almost horrified look on her face. After about thirty seconds, Molly's eyes refocus, and the color begins returning to her face. *What the hell just happened?*

* * *

MOLLY

Adam is an interesting guy. He doesn't smile often, but when he does, you know it's genuine. I've caught him smiling twice tonight—I wonder if he's even realized it himself. I never had the chance to notice before, but he has perfect teeth and a great smile.

Everything is going well until I hear it. I haven't heard it in years, but apparently, no amount of time will take away this feeling.

It's just another manic Monday . . . I wish it was Sunday. . .

The words swirl around my brain like an image I can't shake. As a young girl, I would dance around the house to this song, a wooden spoon as my microphone, my stuffed animal collection my enthusiastic audience. I was a star. This was my jam. But now? Now everything is different. This song makes me feel nauseated.

My mind shoots back to high school and the day I chose to start hating this song.

I'm suddenly very aware of my racing heart and sweaty palms. And Adam. I know he's watching me, but I can't bring myself to make eye contact. I can't believe this has happened here. Eating dinner at The Lotus. Sitting across from Adam. How humiliating.

Pushing some vegetables across my plate, I finally spear a piece of onion and some chicken and force it into my mouth. My appetite is gone, but I can't let Adam see that.

With everything I have, I muster a smile and force my eyes to meet Adam's.

"So yeah, if all goes well, I'll be moving to Santa Monica after graduation and living the dream," I say, hoping we can continue the conversation like nothing happened.

Adam nods his head but doesn't take his eyes off me. Looking back at my plate, I struggle to come up with something else to talk about. Anything. *Why the heck can't I think of anything to talk about?*

I can still feel Adam's eyes on me, and unsure of what to do, I look up to meet his stare and hold it. We sit in silence staring at each other for what feels like an eternity.

"Can I get you anything else?" comes a voice from above us, breaking my focus. The waitress tops off our cups of water as Adam glances back at me, looking for a response. "I'm good, thanks," I say. Adam nods in agreement.

"All right, I'll be back with your check," she says, turning to walk through the doors to the kitchen.

"How are you feeling?" Adam asks, concern filling his deep-blue eyes.

"I'm fine," I say, looking away. "My head just hurts." Without thinking, my hand is on my forehead, leaving me wincing in pain.

"Let's finish up here and get you home, then," he says, retrieving the bill from the waitress and shoving a twenty-dollar bill inside before handing it back.

"I'll be back with your change," she says.

"Don't worry about it," he says, looking back at me.

"You ready?" he asks.

Nodding, I smile and rise from my chair. Stepping past Adam toward the door, I feel his hand brush against my lower back as he turns to follow me. Once again, his touch sends electricity surging through my body and leaves me wishing he'd let his hand linger longer. He doesn't, though, pulling back abruptly as though he's realized he's made a mistake.

The night air has turned cold, much too cold for the tank top and yoga pants I put on a few hours ago for our run. *Why didn't I bring a jacket?*

We sit in silence most of the drive back to my house. Adam parks, then meets me halfway around the car, returning his hand to the small of my back. *There's that electricity again.*

"Thanks for dinner," I say. "And for helping patch me up."

"No problem," says Adam, stopping as we reach the apartment gate.

There's an electricity in the air tonight. Maybe it's just Adam's hand on my back, but I can feel it all around me. Like something is going to happen.

"Well," I say awkwardly. Why can't I be smooth like the girls in the movies, always saying the right thing at the right moment?

"Well," echoes Adam. He tucks a piece of hair behind my ear, and I think I might explode. Thankfully, I don't have to wait long, because the next thing I know, he's leaning toward me, his lips gently pressing against mine.

And man, if I thought his touch was electric, his kiss is off the charts. There's an energy pulsing through my body, making me feel more alive than I've ever felt. My first kiss with Todd was intense, but it was nowhere close to this. This is one of those kisses you read about in books or watch played out on the big screen. *Is this real life?*

CHAPTER 15

ADAM

Throwing myself into my work today, I'm trying hard to focus on anything but Molly, which, of course, means she's pretty well all I've been thinking about. Something happened at dinner last night, and I can't quite figure out what the hell it was.

Heading back to the office, I struggle to push thoughts of her from my mind as I run through a mental checklist of the reports that need to be completed before I go home today. The parking lot is empty, so there's a chance I'll actually be able to get these damn things done.

An hour later, I'm sitting in the office, fully immersed in these reports, with just one left to complete, when I hear the door open behind me. Sure I'll find Hernandez ambling in, I turn, ready to hurl a smart-ass comment at him the second he enters the room. Only it's not Hernandez.

Sergeant Carlson doesn't say a word as he walks in, just glances over at me before grabbing a cup of coffee and sitting down at the opposite end of the conference-room table. He remains silent, staring at his hands between gulps of coffee. *If I can just get this last report done, I can get out of here.*

"It's almost been a year," he says, eyes fixed on his Styrofoam cup.

"Yeah, it has," I say, keeping my eyes on my computer screen.

"How you holding up?" I can tell he's watching me, but I refuse to make eye contact. Rather than answering him, I type more vigorously on my keyboard, hoping he'll get the clue. But, of course, he doesn't.

"Have you gone to talk to anyone about it?" he asks, unfazed by my silence.

Why the hell does he care if I've talked to anyone? How is this any of his damn business?

We sit in silence for another few minutes, me refusing to speak and him refusing to back down.

"You know they don't blame you, right?" he says. "No one does. But it's obvious you still blame yourself."

I can't take it anymore. I can't sit here and listen to this man

119

trying to have a heart-to-heart with me over something he doesn't know shit about. He wasn't there. He wasn't on the scene. He was only called out hours later to help with the investigation.

Squeezing my eyes closed as tight as I can, I bang my forehead down on my balled fists. "Forgive me if I don't want to talk about this with you," I say, venom filling each word. It takes everything I have not to explode.

"It's normal to feel angry," he says. "If you weren't angry, you wouldn't be human."

Slamming my fists down on the table, I finally look up at him. "What the hell do you mean by that?" I ask, instantly regretting my choice of words as soon as they've left my mouth. Carlson is my superior. The last thing I need to do is go and get myself fired for insubordination.

"You have every right to be angry," he says calmly.

"While I appreciate your justification of my feelings, sir, really, I'm fine," I say, trying to control my voice.

"Do you have the list of counselors the department covers?" His eyes remain fixed on me. I don't think he's blinked even once since this conversation started.

"Yes, sir," I say through gritted teeth.

"I've been to about everyone on that list and can give you my recommendation if you'd like," he says.

"Thanks, but I don't need to talk to anyone," I say, closing my laptop. I stand a little too fast, leaving my chair toppling over backward but somehow catching it before it clatters to the ground. "I'm fine. I really should finish these reports and get back out on the streets."

Before he can say another word, I'm out the door and in my car, throwing my laptop on the passenger seat and slamming the door behind me. Slumping into my seat, I rest my forehead on the steering wheel. I'm very aware of an aching thud in my head as my mind races and realize I'm repeatedly slamming my head down hard onto the steering wheel. *What the hell is wrong with me? Everyone else involved is fine. Why am I so weak I can't move past this?*

Sergeant Carlson's words echo in my head. My eyes are burning, and so is my throat. Why am I breathing so fast? Why does it smell like flares in here? I'm burning alive. This is what it feels like to die.

Before I know it, the sky is dark, the only light coming from the soft glow of flares scattered along the shoulder of the freeway. Red and blue lights flash closer as a patrol car arrives on the scene. It's Hawthorne. He's heard me call for backup on the radio and came to help.

"Do you want me to close a lane?" he asks.

"No, pull ahead and set up a new traffic pattern. Fire is on its way. I'll have them pull here to block the car."

A white Camry sits upside down a few yards away, passengers huddled together along the side of the highway with various non-life-threatening injuries. Broken arm, possible cracked ribs, bruised back, facial lacerations. Excessive speed, blown tire, three and a half rolls into the ditch.

Red and blue lights disappear as Hawthorne pulls several yards in front of the vehicle, and it's dark again.

"Tango 587. Can I get the status of Fire 1?"

"10-4 Tango 587. Fire 1 about two minutes out."

"10-4."

A vehicle approaches behind me, getting louder by the second. It's all happening in slow motion. I turn, expecting to see the ladder truck but instead see a semi barreling down. Time is nearly at a standstill as the semi passes me. Despite throwing myself backward to avoid getting smashed, something on the semi catches my boot, flipping me over in the air before throwing me straight down onto the pavement. My body slams down with a thud, knocking the breath completely out of my lungs.

Metal crunches nearby. Did he just hit my car?

No, my car is behind me. Did he hit the Camry?

No, the Camry is still upside down behind me.

No!

The word leaves my mouth before I know what I'm saying. Scrambling to my feet, I stumble up the road to realize my worst fear.

His car is a heap of metal pushed about fifty yards down into the ditch. I know before I see him.

"Officer down! Officer down!"

I don't recognize the voice, but I know it came from my mouth. The earth is spinning, and I'm on the pavement heaving over and over until there's nothing left in my body. He's gone. Dead.

Flashing lights. Burning flares. Bright camera flashes. I'm sitting in someone's car. Where the hell am I? Is this really happening? This can't be happening. This didn't happen.

The air in my car is thick with the smell of smoking flares. My eyes burn, my lungs burn, and I know I'm hyperventilating.

Slowly, the smoke evaporates and the smell of flares disappears, leaving my nostrils burning from the fumes. My heart is still racing, but my breath seems to be slowing.

I was responsible for him, and I stood by and watched him die.

CHAPTER 16

MOLLY

Friday morning. Again. Last Friday's party feels like a decade ago.

Cara is still sleeping, her breathing heavy, on the verge of snoring. She had a late night at the coffee shop and probably won't be up until this afternoon. I was relieved when I went to bed and she still wasn't home yet. I didn't really want to have to explain the scrapes and bandages all over my body.

Makeup on. Hair done. Clothes on. All that's left to do is take my pills.

Humming to myself, I fill a bowl with cereal and milk and sit down to quickly eat it before heading out the door. My mind is flipping between the information I've been studying for the test I have this morning in my English Literature class and Adam. I really hope I didn't scare him off last night. What a cluster that whole night was. But wonderful at the same time.

". . . kissing Valentino in a crystal blue Italian stream . . ."

The words come out of my mouth before I realize what I'm singing. And it all comes back.

Manic Molly.

The kids at my high school were real idiots. They clearly didn't understand the meaning of the word *manic*. Unfortunately, that didn't make it hurt any less. They'd follow me through the halls, singing to me. "Just another Manic Molly."

They teased me relentlessly. I couldn't wait to get out of that godforsaken town and into the real world where no one knew me as Manic Molly.

Tears well up in my eyes. I haven't allowed myself to think about high school in over a year, but the emotions hit me like a ton of bricks. One by one, the tears begin to fall, forming tiny rivers over my cheeks and dropping to the ground like salty raindrops. All of this because I was different. Was. Was?

Am I really different? I take two white pills each morning to keep the symptoms at bay, but am I really normal now? What would my friends think if they knew about my secret prescription? What would Cara think knowing she lives with a crazy person? Or Adam? What would he do if he learned my secret?

Sheets rustle in the bedroom, and it sounds like Cara might be getting up. Wiping my eyes, I hold my breath and pray she's just rolling over. When thirty seconds pass and I haven't seen her stumble into the bathroom, I know I'm in the clear. Dumping my mostly uneaten cereal and bowl into the sink, I quietly tiptoe toward the bedroom. Toward my pills—the only thing that keeps me sane.

As quiet as I possibly can, I slowly lift the jewelry box lid and feel around for the tiny cylinder of pills.

"Hey," comes Cara's voice from the other side of the room.

The jewelry box lid closes with a loud snap as I pull my hand away in surprise. I'm sure I look guilty, but at least Cara won't have any idea why.

"Hey," I stammer. "Did I wake you?"

"No," she says, yawning and stretching her arms. "I got home late and really didn't sleep well last night. How was your night?"

Her eyes go wide as soon as they focus on my face. "What the hell happened to you?" she exclaims, sitting up quickly. "Todd?"

Feeling for the bandage on my forehead, I shake my head. "No, definitely not Todd. I fell on a run last night and scraped myself up pretty bad."

"Oh, my gosh. Are you okay?"

"No, but I'll be fine," I say, forcing a smile. "Hey, I've got to get to class, but what are the plans for tonight?"

"Rumor has it Jill is having another party. Or knows of

another party. I swear that girl is drunk every time I talk to her. Anyway, plan on going out tonight. We'll find a way to wear your hair so that bandage isn't so noticeable." She squints her eyes to take inventory of the monstrosity on my face, and I can see the wheels turning in her head as she tries to figure out how on earth to work with it.

"All right, text me later and let me know when and where and I'll make sure I'm ready to go." With that, I sling my book bag over my shoulder and step out into the bright morning sun.

No marine layer this morning. That has to be a good sign.

* * *

ADAM

I struggle to force myself out of my patrol car on every stop today. Each time I step out of my car, the smell of flares is fresh in the air. Am I going crazy?

Dawson hit me up about a party, but I really just feel like being by myself tonight. Even the thought of going running with Molly is unappealing. I just need to be alone.

Each time I hear Sergeant Carlson key up on the radio, a knot forms in my stomach. Why the hell has this guy taken a sudden interest in how I'm feeling? Does he see me as a threat? Is he trying to get some dirt on me so he can badmouth me to the brass?

The end of the day can't come soon enough, so when I pull

up into my driveway and see Mrs. Mitchell from down the street out watering her lawn, once again, my stomach drops.

Forcing a smile, I wave and say, "Hello, Mrs. Mitchell. How are you today?"

Her mousy brown hair is pulled back into a loose bun at the nape of her neck, and her glasses sit low on her long, crooked nose. Adjusting her frames, she glances up at me, and a look of disgust crosses her face. I still have no idea what I did to this lady, but she has made at least three different complaints against me with the department. One for running code out of the neighborhood one evening on my way to a rollover involving a family with three young children. She thinks I drive too fast. She doesn't like when I test my equipment in my driveway. And every time an officer-involved shooting occurs anywhere in the country, she is the first to stop me on the street and give me an earful about what the officers did wrong. Some days I think she stands out in her yard for hours, waiting for me to come home so she can give me the what for.

"Fine," she says, her voice terse through her tight lips.

"Good. Well, have a nice evening," I say in the friendliest voice I can muster. I'm sure she'll find a way to turn this into some kind of complaint I'll hear about from LT tomorrow.

Although the neighborhood is quiet, taking that first step into my house feels like walking into a soundproof room every time I come home. Closing the door behind me, I stop for a second to take it all in. Silence hangs thick in the air, surrounding me immediately, welcoming me home.

And, of course, my phone has to be the one to break the silence. It's a text from Dawson.

Dude, party at my house tonight. You have to come.

Staring at my phone, I debate whether I should push myself to go or just stay home.

Not tonight, man. Maybe next time.

You have to come.

I had a long day today, and tomorrow is another early morning. I'll catch you next time.

If you change your mind, you know where to find me.

Setting my phone on the countertop, I walk down the hall into my room and begin the process of peeling off my uniform and equipment. Normally, I'd spend a night like this navigating the streets on a long, exhausting run, but I just don't have it in me tonight. There is something about the adrenaline rush and crash that comes with these rough days that drains every ounce of energy from my body.

* * *

MOLLY

As much as I've tried all day, I just can't shake the feeling that something is wrong. It's not until the middle of the afternoon I realize I didn't take my pills this morning. I was so startled by Cara waking up I completely forgot to take them. Walking back to my apartment, I try to decide if taking them when I get home is a good idea or if I should wait until tomorrow morning to keep on track with the dosage.

The funny thing is, I haven't had a single panic attack today. Not one. Not even the hint of one. And today was a pretty stressful day with tests and classes. It's been hours since I should have taken my pills, and I'm not noticing any adverse side effects. I thought missing a dose would leave me backsliding into the usual compulsions, but somehow it's not. Do I really need to be taking these pills?

Cara is sitting on the couch, flipping through a magazine when I walk in. Looking up from her reading, she smiles as I close the door behind me.

"How are you feeling?" she asks.

"Amazingly well," I say, trying to hide the enthusiasm in my voice. I haven't felt this good in years—maybe ever. Perhaps it's time to consider going off of my pills completely.

"Are you up to going out tonight?" she asks.

"Yes." I feel strangely confident, and for the first time in a very long time cannot wait to go to a party and be surrounded by a room full of people.

"Excellent!" she exclaims, tossing her magazine aside. "I've given it some thought, and I know just what we're going to do with your face tonight."

Normally, the idea of Cara styling me for the night leaves me nervous, but not today. "Bring it," I say, smiling as I walk to the kitchen table to unload my book bag. I'm feeling good, and I'm going to enjoy myself tonight.

"Jill texted me and told me Dawson is having a party at his house tonight," Cara says from the couch.

Grabbing a glass, I fill it with water and take a sip, savoring the cool liquid in my mouth. "Sounds good," I say, swallowing and closing my eyes. Tonight will be a very good night.

CHAPTER 17

ADAM

Tonight is not a good night. I've spent the evening sitting on my couch, staring at something on the television screen, but I can't even tell you what it was. My mind is elsewhere. I had pushed all thoughts of the anniversary of Hawthorne's death to the deepest parts of my brain and left them there. Being reminded of the upcoming milestone is not something I needed today.

My mind is racing. There's a memorial planned at a local park next Thursday to mark one year since he's been gone. Floating lanterns will be released to honor him and his sacrifice in the line of duty. I can still hear the bagpipes playing. "Amazing Grace" was always a favorite hymn of mine, but now I can't stand it. It reminds me too much of what was lost that night.

So here I lie, praying for sleep. A doctor offered me prescription sleeping pills a few months ago, and refusing them seemed like a good idea at the time, but now I'm wondering what the hell I was thinking. I could definitely use sleeping pills tonight.

The room is pitch-black and silent around me; all but the thoughts racing through my brain. If I lie here with my eyes closed long enough, sleep is sure to come.

Does counting sheep really work? Because that whole concept has always seemed like absolute bullshit to me. I'm getting desperate enough to give it a try tonight. What do I have to lose?

This has been my worst idea yet. Each number brings with it a memory and a ten code. I'm not even to fifty before I give up. I just keep seeing his face, the car. Smelling the flares.

Why are my eyes burning so badly? Why the hell are they still open? Didn't I close my eyes when I started counting? Have I even blinked in the last few minutes?

Clamping my eyes shut, I can still feel the burning. *Please, please just let me sleep.*

* * *

I have no idea how long I laid in bed praying for sleep, but the incessant beeping of my alarm tells me I must have fallen asleep at some point.

One more day. I just have to make it through one more day. Just a few years ago I had no fear, but here I am sitting in my bed, full of fear at the mere thought of going to work. It's Saturday, so aside from people visiting the beach and downtown area, the city should be quiet.

Splashing cold water on my face, I take in my reflection as I wait for the shower to heat up. *Who is that staring back at me?*

My eyes are bloodshot, and my face is pale, droopy black circles punctuating my eyes. I definitely didn't get enough sleep last night.

Life is a series of moments all tied together, most of which we just have to survive. The joy of life is realizing it's worth living before it's too late. Before time has run out. But how the hell do I live when all I can think about is death?

* * *

MOLLY

My head is pounding, but somehow the aching in my feet is even worse. I'm wide awake but not ready to pull my body out of bed yet, so I keep my eyes closed and try to will myself back to sleep.

A rustling in the bed across the room tells me Cara is awake.

She groans as her feet hit the floor, and she shuffles toward the bathroom, closing the door moments before the shower turns on.

Keeping my eyes closed, I focus on relaxing every muscle in my body. Why am I so tense?

It wasn't a particularly crazy night. Dawson's house party was going off by the time we arrived. I hadn't talked to Adam all day, but I assumed he'd be there and had a hard time hiding my disappointment when he wasn't. Although I know him showing up to Jill's party was a fluke, I held out hope I'd find him out last night, but no luck.

Cara and I danced the night away until the party was shut down around two thirty in the morning. She made me borrow a pair of her shoes that, while really sexy, hurt like the dickens. There was one point during the walk home where I contemplated chewing my feet off at the ankles. It was the kind of evening Cara and I needed to reconnect. She's been working so much lately and classes have been so busy we haven't seen each other much the last week. Thank goodness for Saturdays and our weekly trip to lay out at the beach.

Grabbing my phone, I pry my eyes open and force them to focus. Eleven o'clock. And it looks like I have an unread text message from Adam.

Hey, Molly, sorry I missed you last night. Hope the party was fun. Strange not seeing you. How about brunch tomorrow?

That's right! I completely forgot that I texted him last night. I forced Cara to make the rounds with me through the party, and

Kelli Thalman

when the search for Adam came up fruitless, I went so far as to ask (in a completely casual way, of course) Dawson if he expected Adam to grace us with his presence that fine evening. Texting Adam was the logical next step in trying to (casually) determine his whereabouts, but I never received a reply.

So Adam wants to have brunch tomorrow? Is this him asking me out on a date?

Brunch sounds great. And I agree—I half expected you to ram into me out of nowhere at any moment!

It's almost like we went on a date the other night to The Lotus, except workout clothes aren't typically what I wear on these types of occasions. It'll be nice to get together when we're not working out and I'm not in my pajamas or dressed like a streetwalker headed to a party.

Great. Pick you up at 11?

I'll be ready. See you then.

My phone buzzes again almost immediately, which I assume is a quick reply back from Adam. But it's not.

Mol, I think we need to talk.

It's Todd. I haven't seen him since last Sunday morning and have no desire to ever lay eyes on him again. If Cara put him up to this again, I am seriously going to have to throat punch that girl. Or burn all her beautiful shoes. Burning her shoes would probably cause significantly more pain.

Hearing the water turn off in the bathroom, I exit Todd's text and set my phone on the headboard, closing my eyes once

136

again.

Cara walks in the room moments later, wrapped in a towel, her hair pulled up.

"Wake up, sleepyhead," she says in an uncharacteristically cheery voice.

"Mmmmm," I grumble, still not ready to start the day.

Throwing open the curtains on the window above her bed, she turns to look at me, either hoping to get a reaction or maybe thinking I might turn to dust, like a vampire.

"It's beautiful out today," she says in a singsong voice.

"Why are you in such a good mood so early?" I ask, squinting as I pull myself into a sitting position.

Cara stops and ponders the question for a moment. "You know, I've recently come to realize `we only have a few more months left of this before we have to strike out into the real world." She uses her hands to motion around the room. "I don't want to waste my time being jaded and taking this all for granted. Let's drive downtown and do breakfast at one of those fancy cafés on the beach."

I can't argue with that. While we do try to take advantage of the beach every Saturday, living in such beautiful surroundings really has left me taking it all for granted. We have eight months left until graduation. Eight months. I still remember very vividly my first day of classes my freshman year, wondering if time would ever go by—if I'd ever actually reach this part of the journey. Three years have flown by much faster than I ever could have imagined. And here I am, standing on the edge of the cliff, ready to make the leap. More like ready to be pushed. I'm not super excited about taking on all of the adult responsibilities that will be laid on my shoulders in just a few months.

"I will do breakfast at a fancy café if you promise I can read you my cover letter later today," I say. In the past week, I've gathered up nearly every element of the portfolio that will be used to judge whether or not I am awarded a distinction of Professional Writing in my degree. With the deadline hovering just a few weeks away, I want to make sure this is absolutely perfect, then get it turned in so I don't have to worry about it for another minute.

"Deal!" she exclaims, turning toward the closet. "And a fancy breakfast deserves a fancy outfit." Before I know it, cocktail dresses are flying out of her side of the closet until I'm pretty sure every single one she owns is lying on her bed before about a dozen wide-brimmed hats come flying out. Has Cara lost it? Last time I checked, we live nowhere near the Kentucky Derby.

"Pick a hat," she says, motioning to the pile on her bed. "And if you need a dress, take one of those too. We're going big this morning."

* * *

An hour later, we're on our way south toward the fancy cafés that line the beachfront. I can't believe I let Cara talk me into dressing this way, but after hearing what she had to say this morning, I think I need to start letting go a little more and try harder to live in the moment.

All eyes are on us as we step through the front doors of our favorite little café. I'm pretty sure I even see a few mouths gape open. Cara struts in, her tight black cocktail dress clinging to every movement she makes. I'm not sure how she does it, but even with a hat the size of a flying saucer, she's looking graceful and pulled together.

I, on the other hand, am a different story. Opting for a short blue number, I can barely move my legs enough to project forward as I step, and this monstrosity on my head is only punctuating the point. Hoping my smile does more talking than the rest of my ensemble, I can't help but laugh as we make our way to a table, which, ironically, or perhaps not, is dead center of the room. I'm sure half the people in this place think we're drunk and the other half are questioning whether or not they can purchase our services for the night. Normally, the thought of doing something crazy like this would send me into a panic attack, but not today. Today, I find it funny and am actually enjoying every moment of the spectacle we have created. I should have tried going off of these pills a long time ago.

We order nearly half the menu between us and spend the next two hours eating between giggles and snorts. This. This is what college is about. What life is about. Living in the moment and taking hold of it with all you've got.

"Oh, my gosh—I almost forgot to tell you," I say, leaning in closer to Cara as I lower my voice. "Guess who texted me this morning."

"Adam?" she asks, her eyes growing almost as wide as her smile.

"Well, yeah, actually he did. We have a date tomorrow for brunch. But that's not who I'm talking about."

"Hold up—you have a DATE?" she asks.

"Yes, but that's beside the point," I say, trying to get the conversation back on track. "Guess who else texted me?"

"I'm almost afraid to say it. Todd?"

"Bingo."

"What the hell does that jackass want?" Ever since last Sunday, Cara has completely written Todd off, finally seeing him for the douchebag he is.

"He thinks we need to talk."

"You need to talk?" she asks, her voice getting louder. "That ass wipe owes you an apology." Shoving a bite of pastry into her mouth, she looks back up at me. "You're not considering talking to him, are you?"

"No way," I say. "Do I text him back and tell him to eff off, or do I not reply at all?"

"Give me your phone," she says, reaching across the table. What do I have to lose?

Placing my phone into her hand, she lifts it to her face, concentrating hard on what she's typing, smirking a few times before handing the phone back.

"Well?" I ask.

"He won't be bothering you anymore," she says.

CHAPTER 18

ADAM

Even with no sleep, I'm having a surprisingly okay day. I'm pouring myself into my work and have continuously been making stops throughout the day. Expired insurance. Expired plates. Speeding. Texting and driving. No seat belt. I even got my first nonalcohol DUI in a while. Normally I'm happy that I caught the dirtbag driving under the influence and got them off the street before they hurt themselves or an innocent driver on the road. Today, though, I'm just grateful I was there.

An ATL comes out for a black 2010 Ford Mustang, female driver. Failure to maintain her lane and following too closely, nearly hitting several cars as she swerves across the road. Before I can even start searching for her, she passes me going the opposite direction on the street. She's slumped low in her seat, eyes barely above the steering wheel, so far into my lane I have to swerve to avoid a head-on collision.

Flipping on my lights and siren, I make a quick U-turn and pull up behind her, but it still takes her a whole minute to pull over. When she does, I'm immediately out of my car and at her window, hand on my gun just in case, a sense of urgency that I need to get to her.

Approaching her car, all I can see is long red hair. Her forehead rests on the steering wheel in a way that makes her look passed out. Knocking on the window, I receive no response. Another knock yields nothing. I announce myself as police and try her door. Unlocked. Opening it, I catch a whiff of a tropical car deodorizer, not the telltale smell of alcohol or marijuana. Jostling her shoulder, I try to wake her, but she's unresponsive.

"Tango 587, I've got a 10-55, unresponsive. 10-52 immediately," I say into my radio. "I'm about ten yards south of the intersection of Spruce and Main."

10-4 Tango 587, medical en route.

"I need backup. Send me two more."

10-4.

"Miss," I say, shaking her. "Miss, can you hear me?"

Her head sways in my direction, and her deep red hair falls away from her face, revealing a pale complexion and eyes only half-open.

"Miss, did you take any pills?"

Her mouth droops open, and something that sounds close to yes comes out. I can't tell if her inability to talk is due to overdose or a severely dry mouth. She appears to have no muscle control, but aside from that, her face just looks tired and defeated.

"Can you tell me what you took and how many?"

Her hand loosely motions toward the center console of her car, and there I can see an orange, cylindrical pill container. It's empty, and the lid is missing. Retrieving the container, I find the name Angela Sorensen along with the name of the drug: Prozac. Sixty milligrams.

"Angela," I say, trying to hold her attention and keep her awake. "Angela, are these pills what you took? Did you mix these with any other drugs or alcohol?"

Her mouth moves, but no words come out, although a slight nod tells me that's an affirmative.

"Alcohol?"

Another nod.

Sirens blare in the distance as they draw closer. We need them here now.

"Did you do this on purpose?" I ask. "Angela, stay with me, please. Angela!"

Lights flashing. Sirens wailing. Paramedics pull her from the car and immediately begin assessing her.

"She took these." I hand them the prescription bottle. "And it sounds like she chased them with alcohol."

The paramedic closest to me grabs the bottle as he says thanks, and with that, they've loaded Angela onto a stretcher and are lifting her into the back of the ambulance, and it's gone, lights flashing, siren blaring, horn honking, heading toward the hospital as fast as possible, where Angela will likely have her stomach pumped in an attempt to save her life.

* * *

Three hours later, I'm sitting in the hospital talking to Angela's parents.

"How old is Angela?" I ask.

"She just turned seventeen," her mother says through tears.

"Does she have a history of drug overdose?" I ask as softly as possible. Her parents are clearly devastated, and I don't want to add to their grief.

"No!" exclaims her mother in anger. "Never! And this isn't a drug overdose. She didn't shoot something up. She just took too many pills!"

Angela's dad touches her arm, softly saying, "Calm down, Suzette. He's only trying to help. If he hadn't stopped her, God only knows what could have happened."

"I'm sorry," Suzette sobs, resting her head on her husband's shoulder.

"It's okay," I say. "I'm sorry to have to ask these questions. I just need the information for my report so we have a clear picture of what happened."

"We understand," says Angela's dad. "She's never done anything like this before. She's seventeen, for goodness' sake. She has her whole life ahead of her. She struggles with depression but was doing so well on her new medication. I just can't believe this happened. She has her whole life ahead of her."

The doctors say Angela will make a full recovery, but once she's out of the woods medically, they'll keep her for psychiatric observation for a few days to make sure she's okay. She'll have a long road ahead of her, but she still has the option to live.

What sadness has she seen in her short life that would make her feel life isn't worth living?

* * *

Even after I'm home for the night, I can't shake Angela and her parents from my mind. When she finally came to, she told me she took the pills in hopes that she'd slowly lose consciousness and crash badly enough that she wouldn't survive. She had a fight with her best friend and felt like the world was caving in on her. The darkness was just too strong. She saw death as the only way out. Damn it all to hell. She's seventeen years old.

I've been sitting in silence for at least two hours now. The day has become night. Streetlights are turning on, illuminating the sidewalk out front, but every light in my house is off. I've slowly watched the sun fade to darkness. Darkness. While I don't understand Angela's darkness, I've had my own darkness to keep me company for the last year. I'm just grateful I could be there in Angela's darkest hour and give her back the option to live.

CHAPTER 19

MOLLY

After brunch, Cara and I decide to head home and change into our swimsuits before going to the beach. Not ready to give up our classy looks entirely, we both don our oversized derby hats, a style choice that earns us a whole lot of attention on the walk to the bluffs. It's not very often you see two bikini-clad twenty-somethings walking down the sidewalk in hats that would put the queen of England to shame.

Speaking of shame, our walk back from the beach to our apartment looked more like a walk of shame. Oversized floppy hats, bikinis, and sunburned skin are not a very pretty combination.

In an attempt to avoid eye contact with people, I focus on the houses we pass. I've lived here three years but never really paid much attention to the homes. They're all small, mostly one-story, with oversized driveways crammed full of cars parked mere inches apart. Based on the number of cars in each driveway, you'd think the streets would be completely car-free, but that is definitely not the case. Cars line the streets, packed together nearly as tight as the ones in each driveway—the closer to campus, the less space between cars.

Some yards are manicured, while others are really nothing more than dirt. The majority are overgrown with flowering plants and bushes. Even the most neglected yards are beautiful in their own right. It's clear that the streets are used more for parking than actual driving, given how many people are riding their bikes or strolling along through them. Driving around here is a real pain. The pedestrian and cyclist are most definitely king.

Everything in this run-down town is ridiculously overpriced, but we'll all line up to pay for it just to live in this prime location. Where these homes probably run $50,000 elsewhere in the country, these outdated places will set you back at least a million, maybe even more, depending on the size and location.

The sun is high in the sky, making my burned skin ache as we pass house after house on the way back to our apartment. It's strange that nearly every house we walk by holds some sort of memory for me. Cara and I lived with four other girls in that small white house, I've been to countless parties at that big brown one, and that little blue one there is where Todd lived two years ago with six other guys. It was essentially a frat house.

A light breeze blows across my skin, carrying the scent of salt and seaweed along with the sweet smells of hibiscus and honeysuckle. Surfboards and wetsuits clutter balconies all along our way, towels hanging over nearly every railing. Someone must be cooking steaks on a charcoal grill in this neighborhood, maybe at that house with dozens of bikes littering the front yard. Loud voices, happy laughter. I can't imagine any other place in the world that's even close to this one.

A few guys call out to us from a second-story window as we pass a tall beige house on the corner before turning up our street. Looking at each other, Cara and I shake our heads. I'm pretty sure if they saw our crispy skin up close, they would save their offer for someone else.

"Molly," comes a voice from my right. I would know that voice anywhere.

"Todd," Cara grumbles under her breath.

Keeping my eyes forward, I do my best to pretend I don't hear him.

"Molly, hey, wait up," he says, his voice getting closer. Is this where he lives? Mental note: take another way home next time.

Without saying a word, Cara and I pick up our pace.

"Molly!" his footfalls are fast, so I can only guess that he's running to catch us.

A hand grabs my arm as I hear him say, "Hey!"

Do I yank my arm away and keep walking, or do I yank it away and punch him?

Pulling my arm quickly from his grasp, I turn to face him. "What do you want, Todd?" I growl. Apparently I'm choosing option three.

Cara turns around lightning fast and looks like she might pick option two and punch Todd square in the nose. We make eye contact for a moment, no words are needed..

Todd retrieves his hand from my arm, a look of shock registering on his face as he steps back defensively, holding his hands up as a sign of surrender.

"Sorry," he apologizes, taking another step backward. "I just wanted to talk to you. Did you get my text this morning?"

"Yeah, I got it," I say between gritted teeth. "And no, I don't want to talk."

"Molly, please let me explain," he pleads. If I didn't know him better, I would think he was being sincere. But he's not. He doesn't have a sincere bone in his perfectly sculpted body.

"I have nothing to say, and I sure as heck don't want to hear anything from you," I say, giving him my most defiant look.

"Molly, please," he says, and I almost feel bad for him. Almost.

"You said everything I needed to know last Sunday morning. And actions speak louder than words. Didn't your mother teach you that?" With that, I grab Cara's hand, and turn to continue up the street at the fastest pace we can manage shy of running.

"I just wanted to tell you that I'm sorry," he says quietly behind us.

"It's a little too late for that," I mumble, beelining for the open gate of our apartment complex.

CHAPTER 20

ADAM

I receive a call around ten thirty that night confirming that Angela will survive her overdose. *Please let her get the help she needs.*

I've been lying in bed with my eyes open for at least an hour now, trying desperately to get to sleep. My body and mind are exhausted, but sleep won't come. After what little sleep I got last night and the events of today, I am in desperate need of some kind of rest if I want to be fully functioning tomorrow morning on that date with Molly. I can't let her see this side of me. What would she think?

My phone buzzes again and I grab it, half expecting to find a message from Dawson bugging me about missing his party last night and trying to talk me into attending whatever one he's at tonight.

I was just thinking about you and wanted to say hi.

It's from Molly.

Hey. How was your day?

That might have been the wrong thing to ask because I sure as shit don't want her to ask me about my day.

Well, I managed to successfully burn myself to a crisp, so I've had better. How are you? Anything exciting happen at work?

I don't know Molly well enough to feel comfortable talking about the incident with Angela and how it's shaken me to the core. I hope eventually I will because it sure would be nice to have someone to talk to about this stuff, to help me sort through it and get it off my chest, but for now, I definitely don't want to burden her with it or scare her off.

Same old, same old. Are we still on for tomorrow?

You bet. I'm looking forward to it. By the way, where are you taking me?

You'll have to wait until tomorrow. See you at eleven.

See you then!

* * *

Sleep evades me for the second night in a row. Who am I kidding? It's probably more like the three hundred and sixty-first night in a row.

I keep thinking about Hawthorne. I can't believe it's almost been a year. How has it almost been a year? Some days it feels like it was a lifetime ago, and others like it's that horrible night all over again.

My mind jumps around, and suddenly I'm thinking about Jake. He was so young and had everything ahead of him. What if it had been me? What if I'd died instead of him that day? Would that somehow change Hawthorne's fate?

Being responsible for the deaths of two people I cared about is almost more than I can bear. My hands are shaking, and my heart is racing. Sweat beads drip slowly from my forehead. *Wait, are those tears?*

I haven't cried in over a year. Not since that night. I just can't muster the emotion. To be honest, I haven't felt too much of any emotion since then. No matter how good the highs or how bad the lows, everything just flows even keel through me. I used to think that one day things would feel normal again. But then everything happened last year, and I realized life as I know it will never be normal.

Mom and Dad took me to a therapist when I was eight—they thought talking to a professional would help me, but if anything, it just reaffirmed to me that the accident was my fault. The department wanted me to go see someone after what happened to Hawthorne, but I really don't see the point. I mean, a professional couldn't help me all those years ago, so who the hell is to say talking to one is going to help me now? Probably just help me come to terms with what I already know and confirm that my guilt is rightfully placed.

I turn from one side to the other. Flat on my back. Nothing helps. I'm trapped here in the endless hell of night. Is it possible to escape when hell is holding you hostage within your own mind?

CHAPTER 21

MOLLY

It's Sunday morning. Ten o'clock. Adam will be here to pick me up in an hour, but I'm so nervous I've been up for hours and now sit restlessly on the couch, waiting. Is it possible the second hand on the clock has actually slowed down? It usually moves faster than this, right?

My leg shakes up and down as I drum my fingers on the arm of the couch. Nervous habit.

Cara is still asleep in the room. I've tried to be as quiet as possible to let her rest. She was up puking half the night, thanks to all that sun we got yesterday. Maybe we aren't drinking enough water. Whatever the case, she's sick, and I'm trying not to bug her.

My phone begins to buzz, and I retrieve it, hoping it's Adam checking to see if he can pick me up early. No luck. It's my mom and dad.

"Hello?" I ask as if anyone else could be calling me from the number popping up as Mom and Dad Home.

"Hey, Mo," my dad says. I really hate that nickname. Note to self: remember to kill Ryan the next time I see him.

"Hey, Daddy-O, what's up?" Although I'm disappointed it's not Adam on the line, there's probably no one else I'd rather talk to more than my mom and dad. We've been through a lot together, and I know how lucky I am to have them. My early life was full of nightly family dinners, at least one parent at every sporting event, and nonstop support. If things had turned out differently, I would say my family was perfect. Unfortunately, we're not. And no matter how hard mom tries to make our lives feel normal, it's an impossible feat.

"Haven't talked to you in a few days and wanted to see how things are going," he says, his tone hopeful.

"Things are good," I say so they can hear my smile.

"What are you and Cara up to today?" he asks. I can hear the relief in his voice. I'm pretty sure he doesn't breathe for the first minute of our conversation in fear of hearing the words he dreads: "It's happening again."

"Well, actually, I have a date," I say, somewhat hesitant since things with Adam are so new. I don't like to talk about a guy until I know where things are going. Adam may have asked me on a date, but he is so hard to read.

"Oh, a date, huh?" he asks, his tone light. "Have I ever met the young man taking my one and only daughter on a date?"

"No, Dad, but I promise he's a nice guy," I say. Just thinking about Adam makes me smile. "He's actually a cop, so you don't have to worry about him being some crazy hooligan."

"A cop, huh?" Dad says, the interest evident in his voice.

"Yep, he works here in town."

"And how did you meet this upstanding cop who's taking you out today?"

"Funny thing. We ran into each other at a party. And then every night after that. We went running together the other night. There's something about him I can't figure out, but he's really sweet and considerate. You don't have anything to worry about."

I really shouldn't have said that last part. My dad always has something to worry about when it comes to me.

"I just want to make sure my little Mo is safe and taken care of. You make damn well sure this guy is worthy of you. I'd hate to see you go through the same thing you did with Crap Wad Todd." Oh, Dad, you always were one for the nicknames.

"Believe me, Dad, Adam is the absolute opposite of Todd." Just saying Todd's name makes me want to vomit, and if I listen close enough, I'm pretty sure I can hear my dad gag anytime that name leaves his mouth too. I don't dare tell him about my recent encounters with Todd. He will be in the car and on his way down here to put the fear of God into that idiot before I can even say bye.

"Good. You deserve nothing but good things, Mo."

"Thanks, Dad," I say. And he doesn't even have to say it. I already know.

"Have fun on your date. And you make sure this Adam treats you right."

"I will, Dad." I smile. With all of the crappy things I deal with in life, I am beyond grateful that I have the parents I do. I don't know where I'd be without them. And not in that cliché way where people just say that. I mean I honestly have no idea where I would be without their patience and understanding.

"Love you, Mo," he says.

"Love you too, Dad."

And with that, the line goes dead.

* * *

I've cleaned the kitchen and bathroom and decluttered the living room by the time eleven o'clock finally rolls around. I'm too anxious to sit still. Nervous flutters fill my stomach, and I'm pretty sure my heart rate is significantly higher than it should be. My legs bounce out of control every time I sit down. But no panic attacks, so I must be okay. Day three without the pills and I'd say I'm doing amazingly well.

Eleven o'clock on the dot and there's a knock at the door. Cara's still in bed asleep, so I tiptoe to the door as quietly as possible and open it. Of course it creaks loudly. I can't hear anything coming from the bedroom, so Cara must not have heard it.

Grabbing my purse, I slip my sandals on and am out the door. And boy, does Adam clean up nice. Not that he doesn't always look good, but he is looking especially good this morning. It looks like he's had a haircut since I last saw him, and instead of the workout clothes I've become so accustomed to seeing him in, he's dressed in a nice pair of jeans and a snap-up shirt rolled to his elbows. I still can't believe he grew up here. He is nothing like any of the other guys in this town.

"You look nice today," I say as I step past him and head toward the stairs.

"So do you," says Adam, motioning for me to lead the way. "You look amazing, actually."

I'm glad I'm walking ahead of him because I know my cheeks have turned the brightest shade of red. "Thanks," I say, starting my descent down the stairs. Then suddenly I stop. Did I lock the door? I'm sure I did. I always lock the door. But I don't specifically remember locking it this time. Would it be stupid of me to go back and check?

"You know what," I say, "I think I left something in my apartment. Let me just run back and get it really quickly."

"Okay," says Adam, stepping aside so I can hurry past him.

Turning the knob, I expect to find resistance but don't. The door opens. *The door opens.* How did I forget to lock it?

Turning back toward Adam, I smile and hold my finger up to show him I'll just be a second, then disappear into the apartment, leaving the door cracked open behind me. The apartment is still dark, so I step to the side and press my back up against the wall, closing my eyes. *It's totally fine. You caught it. Now you'll lock it, and you won't forget again. You've got this.*

Breathing out a deep sigh, I put on the best smile I can muster and step out the door, turning to lock it immediately, double-checking the knob just to be sure.

"Sorry about that," I say, breezing past Adam who's still waiting for me at the top of the stairs.

"No problem," he says with the hint of a smile. "Ready?"

"Definitely."

CHAPTER 22

ADAM

It's been over a year since I went on a date. And before I stopped altogether, I had never really been one for dating. Sure I've had the occasional girlfriend here and there, but it all seems so pointless. I guess I just haven't met the right one yet.

Attempting to be as discreet as possible, I've been watching Molly out of the corner of my eye through the drive. She seemed nervous and maybe a little hesitant when I picked her up. I hope she's not having second thoughts about this.

Fifteen minutes later, we pull up to the front of a tiny whitewashed beachside café. It's one of the few places that holds any good childhood memories for me. I haven't been here in years, but the place looks just as I remember it.

"We're here," I say, turning off the car and pulling the key from the ignition.

Molly looks around like she's just realized we aren't still in her neighborhood. "Where exactly are we?" she asks.

"Neighborhood Café," I say, suddenly doubting my decision to bring her here. "It's the best breakfast place in the area. I used to come here all the time." Looking up at Molly, I see her eyes have softened and she's smiling. "I hope you'll like it."

"I'm sure I will," she says, opening her door and stepping out into the sunshine.

Shit. I'm starting to think this was probably a bad place to bring her. I really hope she does like it.

Holding the front door for Molly, I let her step inside ahead of me. She stops and turns toward me, signaling me to go first. Putting my hand on the small of her back, I guide her toward the greeter. Her back tenses at my touch, and I quickly remove my hand, hoping I'm not making her uncomfortable.

"Hello, and welcome to Neighborhood Café," says the young guy behind the desk. Red hair, confident smile—definitely a high school student. "Table for two?"

"Yes, please," I say, stepping forward. "Are there any tables available in the back?"

"There sure are," says the young man whose name is Caleb according to his name tag. "Right this way."

We follow Caleb to an open table near the back windows. Molly gasps as she sees the view, and I hope she can see why I brought her here.

"Oh, my gosh," she says. "This is beautiful."

I pull out a chair and she sits, her eyes never leaving the seascape just beyond our table. My dad always asked for a table in the back, and we would sit and watch the waves break while we ate. I think the view took the pressure off of us actually having to talk to each other, and that was what we both preferred after Jake. We just didn't know what to say anymore. Hell, it's been fifteen years and we still don't know what to say to each other.

Sitting down, I watch Molly as she stares at the view. I've never seen eyes as green as hers. They're like two oversized emeralds, bright and sparkling.

"Do you still come here often with your dad?" she asks, picking up her glass for a sip of water.

"No." I avoid eye contact. "We haven't been here together in years."

"Oh," she says, picking up on the obvious cues that I don't want to talk about it. "Well, I'm really glad you brought me here."

"Me too."

After what feels like forever, Molly smiles and looks out the window again, then down at her menu.

"So what's good here?" she asks, looking very interested in the words on the page in front of her.

"Well, as a child I always got the chocolate chip pancakes, so I can definitely vouch for those," I say, watching a smile cross her lips. "I haven't been here since my palate matured, so I can't really speak for anything else. My dad always got the Eggs Benedict and seemed to really enjoy them, so I am pretty confident those are good."

"Hmmm," says Molly, surveying the menu. "I'm a sucker for chocolate chip pancakes. I might have to try those."

I can't help but smile a little.

When our waitress arrives with a basket full of blueberry and chocolate chip mini muffins, we place our order and sit in silence, savoring the sweet goodness of what are basically tiny cupcakes.

While I'd prefer to sit here and enjoy a quiet meal with Molly, I'm not sure she's as into the silence as I am.

"So where did you grow up?" I ask.

Molly chews her muffin a little quicker and swallows before answering. "I grew up in a tiny town in the valley," she says. "My parents still live up there, and both my brothers stayed close for college, so I'm the only one who's not in the area anymore."

"Two brothers?" I ask.

"Yes. Sam is a year and a half older than me, and Ryan is two years older than Sam. They both received academic scholarships to Cal State near where we grew up, so it was a no-brainer for them when the time came to go to college. After graduation, they both got jobs in the area, and I honestly doubt they'll ever leave."

"Interesting," I say, shoving a tiny muffin into my mouth. Mmmm . . . chocolate chip.

"I saw in the picture at your house that you have one brother. He's younger, right?"

"Yeah," I say, looking out at the ocean. *Please don't ask about Jake.*

"Did he follow suit and stay local like you?"

I hold my breath. How do you tell someone you just met about one of the most horrific events of your life?

"Actually, he died when I was eight." My eyes fix on the crashing waves.

"Oh, my gosh, I'm so sorry," she says, her cheeks flushing. She's clearly flustered. "I never would have—"

"Hey, don't worry about it," I say, trying to force a smile. From the look on her face, I'm afraid it's come out looking more like a grimace.

We sit in awkward silence for a moment. I can tell Molly is struggling to find a new topic to bring up, and I'm afraid if I try I'll say something stupid.

"Jake was six and I was eight. We were out playing in front of our house one Saturday afternoon when Jake ran out into the street and was hit by a car."

I can see the hurt and pity in Molly's eyes as she keeps them fixed on me. Staring at my water, I'm not really sure how to change the topic now either. When I look up, Molly is still. She hesitates before reaching across the table to place her hand on mine. As cold as her tiny hadn't is, it somehow sends a surge of heat up my arm.

"I can't imagine what you've gone through," she says, her eyes watery. Is she going to start crying? *Please don't start crying.* I'm afraid if she starts, I might start, and that is yet another surefire way to never get a second date.

Shrugging my shoulders, I take a deep breath and let it out slowly. "So, other than running, what do you like to do when you're not in class?"

The smile returns to Molly's face, and she pulls her hand back to her side of the table. "Well," she says, "Cara and I go to the beach every Saturday to lay out. I'm not sure I'd call that a hobby, but it's something I enjoy. I like to write and read in my spare time, but recently I've been really focused on gathering writing samples, letters of recommendation, and other fun stuff for a portfolio I'm putting together in hopes of earning the distinction of Professional Writing in my major."

"Really?" I ask. Pretty impressive. "So I'm guessing that's why you seemed so passionate about *The Yellow Wallpaper* the other night."

Molly laughs. "Yeah, I do have a tendency to get a little overzealous when I talk about literature, particularly that short story. I have always felt a connection to it. I don't know if it's the main character, the writing, or the author, but it just really inspires me."

"I think that's great. I wish I was that passionate about something. Well, other than my job."

"What made you decide to be a cop?" Molly asks, picking at the blueberry muffin on her plate.

"Well, I actually got through two years of college working toward a degree in accounting before realizing it just wasn't for me. The city was hiring officers, so I thought I'd apply and see if I could get hired. I've always had a passion for helping people, and public safety seemed like a good fit."

"I'm impressed," says Molly smiling. "What do your parents think about your career choice?"

"Well," I clear my throat and wipe the crumbs off my fingers, "I think they're okay with it. Honestly, I don't talk to them much, and I really never ask their opinion on my life choices."

Molly's eyes go a little wide as she smiles and says, "All right."

Our waitress appears with Molly's chocolate chip pancakes piled high with whipped cream, and my mushroom-and-cheese omelet.

"These look delicious," says Molly, smiling as she unrolls the silverware from her napkin.

"Yeah, they look just how I remember."

We both fall silent as we eat, savoring the delicious food and perfect view in front of us.

* * *

MOLLY

After brunch, Adam and I walk down the beach as far as we can before mist completely fills the space between us and the restaurant, making it almost impossible to see.

"So, how long have you worked for the police department?" I ask. The more I learn about Adam, the more fascinated I am.

"Four years now," he says, looking down at the sand in front of us.

"What has been your favorite thing about the job?" I ask, hoping it doesn't come out as dumb as it sounds in my head.

"There have been lots of highlights, but I think my favorite thing is running into someone I arrested months or years after the fact and having them thank me. Rather than hating me for arresting them, they take the arrest as a turning point in their lives and either get clean or get the help they need to fix things."

"People actually thank you for arresting them?" I ask. I know there is no way I'd ever thank the cop who gave me that speeding ticket two years ago. Dad was so mad he threatened to drive down and personally take my car away from me.

"Yeah, the first time it happened, I was really confused," he says. "It's not something you'd think happens, but it does, actually, and way more often than you would imagine. Sure, there are the people who see you at the gas station and try to heckle or harass you because they recognize your face and the DUI you gave them is the reason they lost their job, but knowing I've somehow affected a change in someone for the better and set them on a good path is everything." His gaze wanders out to the crashing waves. He's clearly deep in thought. I wish he would just open up and let it all spill out.

"So, tell me," he says, looking at me. "What do your older brothers do for a living? Are your parents fine with you pursuing your dreams of becoming a famous magazine writer?"

It's hard not to laugh when he puts it that way. "Well, Ryan just finished law school and was hired by a corporate law firm. Sam has one more year in his graduate program to earn his master's in molecular engineering before he starts working toward his PhD. Let's just say that of everyone, I'm the free-spirited wild card." I laugh as I remember the looks on my parents' faces when I broke the news about my career aspirations. "My dad owns a few businesses near our house, and my mom has always been a stay-at-home mom, but not before earning her master's in psychology. Let's just say this apple fell pretty far from the tree."

From the corner of my eye, I see Adam watching me, and all I can do is laugh. My parents had high hopes for me. But with my diagnosis, everything changed, and they're trying to just be happy that I'm graduating from college.

"But enough about me. Tell me more about you." I attempt to shift the focus back to him. "Did most of your buddies stay local after graduation? Or are you the only one?"

"I'm pretty well the only one," he says, shifting uncomfortably. "I really don't keep in touch with many people I grew up with."

"Oh, well, that's too bad," I say, biting my lip.

"It's fine," he says reassuringly. "I didn't have many close friends after Jake died, and I've learned to kind of keep my distance from everyone over the years."

Everyone but me? "Are you close to anyone you work with? Spending so much time together in such stressful situations, I imagine you're pretty close to at least a few people on your crew."

Adam looks away again and stays quiet. Clearly, he's trying to formulate a response, but I'm not sure why he's having such a hard time. Oh, my gosh—is the love of his life on his crew? Did he experience some horrible breakup that's left him distant from everyone else?

We walk in silence for a minute before he finally speaks. "I have a really good buddy on my crew. Hernandez. He's probably the closest thing I have to a best friend. I lost a buddy to a car accident almost a year ago. Ever since then, I've had a hard time connecting with other people."

"I am so sorry to hear that," I say, looking down at my hands and feeling like an idiot that I thought his silence had something to do with a girl. I'd like to press for more information, but I don't dare. It's clear from Adam's body language that he'd rather not proceed with this topic.

As we continue down the beach, Adam is obviously lost in thought. His brows are furrowed, his mouth slightly downturned.

I hope I haven't just completely sabotaged our entire date with my stupid questions.

Walking in silence, I try to focus on the waves hitting the shore beside us—the roar as they come in, the fizzle as they lick at our feet and then slowly retreat. As a child, the beach was always my happy place. It was one of the only places I felt safe. The ocean is so big, and I'm so small I always imagined that if I focused hard enough, I could will the sea to swallow me whole. Gobble me up. Make me disappear. For some that might be a scary thought, but for me it was comforting. What could be more beautiful than becoming part of the ocean?

I'm suddenly very aware of myself and my thoughts as I feel Adam's fingers brush against mine. Were we always walking this close to each other? Oh, my gosh. Did I zone out and completely miss something?

Looking to my left, I see Adam's face turned toward me as his fingers brush against mine again. Should I say something? Or will saying something screw up the moment again?

Deciding to go the silent route, I smile at him, sure that my face is the color of a cherry. He stops walking and turns his whole body to face me.

"Hey, I'm really sorry I asked about—" I start, but before I can finish my sentence, Adam's lips are brushing against mine. I can feel his hot breath on my mouth and can't believe how badly I want those lips on my lips.

In a bold move, I close the space between us and let my lips find his. Soft, strong, and gentle. His hand is in my hair, holding the back of my head firmly as our mouths part. I can't believe this is happening. Is this really happening? Even after all the stupid things I said at brunch? Is this some kind of pity kiss?

But there's no denying it. This is definitely not a pity kiss. I can feel the yearning in his lips and his hand that's found its way to the small of my back, pulling me tightly to him.

What feels like a blissful eternity later, he steps back and looks at me. "I'm sorry. I hope that was okay," he says, his hand traveling to the back of his neck.

"Mmmm . . . it was *okay*," I say, but can't even get the words out before a huge smile spreads across my face, calling my bluff.

Adam smiles at me. A real, genuine smile. And I think my heart may stop beating. How did I not think he was gorgeous that first night I met him?

He leans toward me again, and our lips meet, this kiss even more tender and longing than the last. If we were in a movie, we'd have fallen over in the sand by now, the waves washing over us as we kissed. Unfortunately, my life is anything but movie worthy, so I'll forgo the romp in the sand and just enjoy this amazing moment.

As we pull apart from this kiss, Adam kisses my forehead, sending an electric surge through my body that's so powerful I wonder if he's just staked some kind of claim on me. If so, I'm totally fine with that.

I smile at him as he retrieves my hand from my side and

wraps it in his, intertwining his fingers with mine. His hands are rough and calloused, but they're also strong and warm, and my hand seems to fit just perfectly together with his, like they were made for each other.

Hand in hand, we walk back toward the café. When we reach his car, he holds the door open for me as I slip inside. It takes all I have not to squeal and dance around while I sit alone in the car, waiting for him to walk around to the driver's side. Two weeks ago, I didn't even know he existed. And now here he is. Here we are.

Two weeks ago I was still taking two pills every morning. Two white pills. Small oval pills the likes of which I thought controlled my brain and my sanity. But here I am now, pill free and feeling more alive than ever.

But still, with all of the perfection in this date, I can't help but feel like the good can't last forever. Deep inside, I know that something not so good is probably waiting for us, but right now, I feel invincible.

CHAPTER 23

ADAM

I usually don't mind working overtime, but today's mandatory overtime shift is kicking my ass. Thinking about the date with Molly kept me up most of the night. Her soft, sweet lips on mine. I need to be with her again and get my lips on hers.

By the time five o'clock rolls around, I am happy to be backing into my driveway. There is nothing sweeter than the sound of the Velcro when I rip this vest off. This must be what it feels like for a girl to take off her bra at the end of the day. There is seriously nothing more satisfying. Except kissing Molly.

Pulling on my gym clothes and running shoes, I grab my keys

and am out the door, feet pounding the pavement as I head down my quiet street toward the wharf. Cars are lined up down the block, waiting for each light to turn green during the after-work rush hour. I wonder if Molly would ever consider staying here after graduation and being one of these people lined up in five-o'clock traffic in our little city.

Shaking my head hard, I try to kick myself back to reality and stop thinking about Molly. I need to focus. Our annual physical test is coming up next month, and I need to make sure my mind is clear and I'm in the best condition possible. It's not the thought of failure that's driving me. I am hoping to claim the fastest finish time in the mile and a half for the fourth year in a row.

Turning west, I run down Palm Street and head for the pathway that parallels the beach. With most people stuck in traffic, the walkway is virtually empty.

The sky is particularly clear today—bright blue with just a few puffy clouds scattered about. A lonely seagull swings low through the air, dropping down to rest in the water just a few yards beyond the break. A handful of surfers dots the lineup, waiting for the next set of waves to blow in while the seagull sits watching them, rocking back and forth.

Even during the busiest traffic here, it's pretty quiet out, the only sounds coming from the breaking waves and the rustling palm fronds overhead. That and my heartbeat and rhythmic footsteps on the pavement.

Running past one of the little coffee shops that lines this main street, I see it. First I just see his face, then I see the writing around it.

Memorial for Jared Hawthorne
Thursday October 24 @ 7:00 p.m.
Come help us celebrate the life of a hometown hero
with a candlelight vigil, followed by the release of
floating lanterns.
Gone but never forgotten.

It takes me a few seconds to realize I'm no longer moving. When did my feet stop? And just a few more seconds to realize I'm not breathing. When did I stop breathing? And why the hell won't I start again?

My face is burning hot, but my throat won't open. I'm sure my eyes are nearly bulging out of my head, but I don't care at this point. Why am I not breathing?

It's then that it hits me like a ton of bricks. The scent of smoke floating through the air. Flares. What the hell is going on?

I'm choking, gasping for air. This must be what it feels like to drown. But how am I drowning outside of the water?

Dropping to my knees, I realize I'm on the verge of passing out. *Breathe! Breathe!*

My throat finally opens as cool ocean air fills my lungs. I'm still coughing and choking. I know the flares are gone, but for some reason I can still smell the smoke burning in my nostrils. Gagging and breathing shallow, I attempt to regain my composure as I realize I'm probably not going to suffocate. I'm okay. But am I really okay? What is happening to me?

Shifting to sit on the rough, solid pavement beneath me, I drop my head into my hands. Suddenly I'm sobbing. Hysterically. And I can't stop. Hawthorne is gone. It's all my fault. Jake is gone. That's my fault too. Where will it end? How can I ever expect anyone to care about me when all I leave is destruction in my wake?

Crawling onto my knees, I do my best to rise on wobbly legs. I need to get home now. I can't be out like this in public. I used to be able to run for hours without any issues, covering miles of this city, never thinking of anything except the burning in my chest. Now I can barely get through a run without having some kind of psychological meltdown.

With unsteady steps, I start the trek back to my house, walking slowly to avoid falling down again. My knees are cut up, and warm blood is trickling down toward my socks, but I can't bring myself to care enough to wipe it off.

The closer I get to the one-year anniversary, the more in pieces I feel. Will this ever stop? Will I ever feel normal again?

CHAPTER 24

MOLLY

I've spent the entire day in bed. I'm starting to think that maybe Cara didn't have heat exhaustion the other day. She must have had the flu. The pounding in my head, not to mention the nausea, is enough to make me wish I could sleep the day away. I was hoping to see Adam today after his overtime shift, but I really don't think that's a possibility at this point. I don't need him seeing me pathetically lying in bed like this.

Between classes and the coffee shop, Cara has been gone all day, leaving me here alone to wallow in self-pity and be swallowed up by my thoughts. The fact that I haven't heard from

Adam all day is only making it worse. Yes, I know he's working and I can't expect an officer to have time to sit around and text me all day, not to mention he never told me he'd call me. I had such a great time yesterday I was hoping he'd want to talk to me today. I mean, if he liked me, he'd call, right?

I bet I said something stupid. Did I laugh at something I shouldn't have? I knew I should have picked a different outfit. I should never have asked about his job. He has it all together, and I am such a frazzled mess. There is no way he could ever really want to be with me.

The thoughts are coming fast and hard, and I'm having trouble distracting myself. I almost wish I was puking at this point to give me something else to focus on.

So it's a good thing I haven't heard from Adam. Crap, what if I have the flu and gave it to him when he kissed me yesterday? I'll feel horrible. Then he'll really have a reason to think I'm gross and never call me back. I wonder what he's doing right now.

Oh, my gosh. I remember the time during my freshman year when I tripped over the threshold of the doorway at that party and nearly fell flat on my face. And the time I snorted during a conversation with that really cute guy in my algebra class. And high school. All of high school.

The floodgates have opened, and there's no stopping the deluge.

The compulsions. The obsessions. The constant facial

twitches. One eye always blinking more than the other. Walking the same path to each class every day. Sitting alone in the quad during lunch. The constant chorus of "Manic Molly" bouncing off the concrete walkways. The staring. The doubting. The constant worry I'd do something wrong. The humiliation.

The Prozac helped. At least for a while. Because look at me now—no pills in four days and my panic attacks are gone, and none of the compulsions have returned. My psychiatrist told me OCD isn't something you just stop having, but it looks like she was wrong. Ha, if only she could see me now.

Retrieving my phone for the second time in the last ten minutes, I refresh my text messages. Nothing. Refresh. Nothing again.

I set my phone down on the headboard above me, then grab it again. Should I just text him? Yeah, maybe I should just text him. Show him I'm bold and fearless. Or at least that I do a good job pretending to be.

Hey, Adam, I just wanted to thank you again for yesterday. I had a great time.

Delete.

Hey, Adam, how was work today?

Definitely delete.

Hey, Adam, I hadn't heard from you yet and wanted to make sure I didn't do something to offend you yesterday.

There's no way in hell I'd ever send that. What is wrong with me?

Setting the phone back down, I let my mind drift back to kissing Adam. Oh, my gosh—I know what went wrong! I bet I had bad breath! I'm absolutely mortified.

My heart beats fast as my face flushes red. Apparently I don't need to be in the presence of anyone to embarrass myself. I'm all the audience I need. Why am I such an idiot?

There's a jingling at the door as the lock flips. Thank everything holy.

Cara steps into the entry a moment later carrying a bag in one hand and a to-go cup in the other. Closing the door behind her, she looks up and sees me through the open bedroom door.

"Hey there, sleepyhead," she says, smiling as she sets down the cup and carries the bag into our room. "I brought you back something from work. How are you feeling?"

Taking the brown paper sack from her, I open it to find my favorite—a chocolate chip scone. My stomach rumbles in response, reminding me that I haven't eaten anything all day. Reaching into the bag, I break off a piece of the buttery, flakey goodness and shove it into my mouth. Heaven.

"I'm feeling okay, I guess." I adjust myself in bed. "I'm actually just really glad you're home."

"Me too." She sighs as she slides out of her jacket and tosses it toward the clothes hamper. Dropping down onto her bed, she kicks off her shoes and lies back on her pillow, her hair forming a perfect crown around her head.

"I need to get up and shower so I can deliver my portfolio to the English department before the office closes tonight," I say, trying to muster the energy to drag my sorry butt out of bed.

"That's right," Cara says, propping herself up on her elbow. "Did you make those changes we talked about? Are you feeling good about the finished project?"

"Yeah, I did. And I am. Mostly, I'll just be happy to have this part over and the whole thing out of my hands."

"I know what you mean," says Cara, twirling a perfectly spiraled ringlet. "Are you feeling up to doing anything tonight?"

"Other than eating dinner, not really." I'm still trying to will myself out of bed. "Let's go out and get something tonight. I need something light, but nothing in the house sounds good."

"Fine with me," she says, rolling onto her back and closing her eyes. "Wake me up when you get back from the English Department, and I'll change and we can decide where we want to go."

With everything I have, I throw my legs over the side of the bed and force my feet to touch the ground. *One, two, three, go.* And I'm up.

"Will do," I say, tiptoeing to the bathroom door.

By the time I'm out of the shower, Cara is lightly snoring and most definitely passed out. Pulling on a gray T-shirt and jeans, I grab the binder and purse off of my desk and head toward the door, taking a mental inventory of what I've grabbed. *Portfolio— check. Purse—check. Phone—check. Keys—check. Perfect.*

I lock the door behind me, then turn toward the stairs,

hesitating ever so slightly. I know I just locked the door, but I really should double-check the knob, just in case. Cara is asleep, and I would hate to have someone sneak in undetected.

The doorknob jiggles securely, as I knew it would. Nodding my head in confirmation, I turn toward the stairs again and begin the long walk to the English Department. One hour from now, this will be out of my hands and we'll be on our way to dinner. *Just get this there and you're set.*

CHAPTER 25

ADAM

I'm trying everything I can think of, but nothing is working. My eyes are wide open, and my brain is racing. The flashbacks keep coming no matter how hard I try to think of something else. Anything else. I even tried some over-the-counter sleeping pills, but still no luck.

After a hot post-run shower, I sat at my table staring at a plate of eggs and toast, willing myself to eat. I can usually put away at least eight eggs and a few pieces of toast, but not tonight. I couldn't even take one bite. We sat there, the eggs and I, until they were cold and I was sick of sitting in that damn chair at the kitchen table.

I spent the next two hours sitting on the couch, staring at the television screen, but can't even remember what was on. After taking this party on the road, I am now here, lying flat on my back, staring at the ceiling in my bedroom. Every now and again a car passes the house, sending light from its headlamps washing over the bumps and grooves in its texture, and it's almost like watching the clouds in the sky—every shape looks like something different and changes every time the light shifts.

Maybe I should call Molly. I feel bad I didn't call her today, but I honestly couldn't. I still can't. My brain is filled with doubt and the most painful scenes of my life. I'm in no position to talk to anyone I want to consider me sane.

So here I lie. In my bed. Staring at the ceiling. Praying for sleep. Praying for a miracle.

* * *

MOLLY

It's ten o'clock, and Adam still hasn't called or texted. I was really hoping this would turn into something, but the longer I go without hearing from him, the less hope I have. Normally I don't sweat it if I don't hear back from a guy the day after a date—I mean, I'm not crazy . . .

Cara fell asleep on the couch around nine o'clock, leaving me once again trapped with my own thoughts. At least I got my portfolio turned in so I don't have to worry about that anymore. I hope it's good enough. I'm sure it is. I worked so hard on it, and I know I'm a good writer. It'll be good enough. What if it's not good enough?

My eyes spring open, and I'm here again, lying in bed, staring at the ceiling. Sitting up, I lightly pad to my desk and fish out the melatonin I keep tucked out of sight in the back of my top drawer. In the past, thirty milligrams has been enough to knock me out for the night, but tonight, that amount hasn't even made me yawn. My heart is beating, my mind is racing, and the fact that sleep isn't coming is really starting to stress me out.

Popping two more tablets into my mouth, I return to my bed and lie back down, focusing on my breathing in an attempt to slow down my heart and my thoughts. If I can just get some sleep, everything will be better. Everything will be better tomorrow.

But really, why hasn't Adam called me back yet? I mean, he could have texted me. Everyone has time to send a quick text to say hi. Or "I'll call you tomorrow." Anything.

Seriously, Molly, shut up and go to sleep!

I've tried counting sheep in the past, to no avail. I'm so desperate tonight, though, I roll my eyes, take a deep breath, and start counting.

One, two, three, four, five . . .

Five past ten o'clock. Dammit. Why is this night taking an eternity?

Fifty-three, fifty-four, fifty-five, fifty-six . . .

Positive affirmations. Think positive. Okay, what is it I used to say to myself? *You are calm. You are relaxed. People like to be around you. People want to be around you. You are smart. You are successful. You've got this.*

Hmmm, those sure worked a lot better when I was younger.

A group of people from a few doors down walk past our apartment on their way to the elevator, shattering the silence surrounding me like glass.

What did dad always have me do when I was younger? Closing my eyes, I relax every muscle in my body, then, starting at my toes, tense my muscles, one by one, for fifteen seconds, then allow that part of my body to relax and focus on letting it sink into my mattress. By the time I reach my head, I'm feeling amazingly relaxed. As a child, my dad was always the one to come in and talk to me when I was having a rough time. He'd tickle my face or talk me through tensing and relaxing my muscles. I sure wish I had someone here to tickle my face tonight.

And back to counting sheep.

One, two, three, four, five . . .

The melatonin is finally starting to kick in.

Twenty, twenty-one, twenty-two, twenty-three . . .

A car alarm goes off somewhere down the street, but I can barely hear it. My mind is finally tuning everything out, even my own thoughts.

Sixty-seven, sixty-eight, sixty-nine . . .

Tomorrow will be a better day. It has to be. Right?

CHAPTER 26

ADAM

I'm out of bed at five o'clock in the morning after yet another sleepless night. Aside from a few errands, I have nothing planned for today, so I should be able to take a nap when the exhaustion finally catches up with me.

Slipping on my running shoes, I shove a granola bar into my mouth and grab my keys as I head toward the door. The streets will be silent and empty at this time of day, so I shouldn't have any outside distractions to break my focus.

To avoid repeating the events of yesterday's run, I head the opposite direction down my street, running through neighborhoods rather than heading to the beach.

Dewdrops cover grass and plants, shimmering in the headlights of passing cars. The world is silent. Dark and silent. The only sounds I hear are my feet hitting the pavement and my steady breaths as I move through the darkness.

I'm here, and I'm alive, and I should be grateful for that. I am grateful for that. But sometimes I wonder what it would be like to run into oblivion. To just keep going and going and never stop. Maybe if I run fast enough or long enough I'll somehow cross over into a place where I can run forever.

The sun is beginning to peek out from behind the mountains, and it dawns on me that I've been running for over an hour if it's already sunrise. Slowing my pace, I glance at my surroundings to figure out where I am. Without even thinking, my legs have carried me to the exterior gate of Molly's apartment. It's almost six thirty now, and I'm pretty sure I stink. I know I'm drenched in sweat. But I came here for a reason.

Retrieving my phone from my back pocket, I pull up Molly's name.

Are you awake?

It's so early there's no way she's up already. No person in their right mind is awake at this hour in this college town.

I wait two full minutes before I give up hope and turn to resume my run toward campus when the phone vibrates in my pocket.

Kind of. Are you?

The thought of waking her up doesn't even make me feel guilty. I really want to see her.

So, I'm kind of right outside your apartment. Come down?

Not thirty seconds later, her reply comes through.

Seriously? I'll be down in two minutes.

Don't forget your running shoes.

Just as promised, two minutes later, Molly appears at the gate. She's like a breath of fresh air, her face free of makeup, her hair pulled back in a slightly disheveled ponytail, her gray leggings and blue sweatshirt emphasizing her figure. Her expression is shy and a little embarrassed, but that smile makes everything else fade away.

"Hey," she says, stepping out onto the sidewalk. "Can I ask why you're at my house at this unholy hour before the sun's come up?"

My cheeks feel a bit hot, something that rarely happens, and I'm not sure how to explain why I'm here in a way that doesn't make me sound like some crazy stalker.

"I couldn't sleep, so I decided to go for a run, and I just ended up here." I hope she won't dig too deep about my insomnia.

"Well, I'm glad you did." She smiles as she takes another step toward me.

There is no way I look or smell good right now, but Molly doesn't seem to notice. The smile hasn't left her face since she's walked through the gate, and I can tell she's genuinely happy I'm here. Thank goodness.

"The sun is going to be up soon. Care to join me to watch it rise?"

"There's nothing I'd like more right now," she says, rocking back and forth on the balls of her feet.

"All right, shall we?" I ask, motioning for her to proceed. She falls in step beside me, and we silently walk toward the bluffs.

The sky is lightening more and more by the second, meaning the sun will rise in no time. From the bluffs, we'll have a perfect view of the mountain with the waves crashing in the background on the beach below. I can't think of a more peaceful place to spend this moment.

When we're nearly at our destination, Molly finally breaks the silence.

"I was wondering if I would hear from you again," she says, her eyes focused on something in the distance.

"What makes you think you wouldn't?" I ask, confused. We had a great time Sunday. I assumed she knew it wouldn't be the end of things with us.

"Uh, I just know you're busy," she says, cheeks flushed, eyes still focused ahead.

"I was thinking about you all yesterday and wanted to call, but work was busy, and then something came up." Or, rather, down. Crashing down.

Her posture relaxes, and she looks at me. "I was thinking about you too." Her eyes are fiery in the rising light of day, but her facial expression is relieved. "I must say, though, I was quite shocked to receive a text from you so early in the morning."

"Yeah, sorry about that." I'm suddenly very aware of how early it is. I figured she wouldn't text back if she wasn't already awake. My sleep is so messed up at this point it didn't even cross my mind how early six thirty is for most other people. "I hope I didn't wake you."

"It's okay," she says, smiling again. "I haven't been sleeping well the past few nights anyway, so I was really just lying in bed, thinking."

"Has anything been going on the past few days that's keeping you up?" I ask, realizing how personal that question really is.

"There's just so much to think about and plan for this year," she says, looking at the seagulls bobbing up and down in the waves below. "I feel like I don't have enough time to think during the day with everything else going on. Plus, I tend to do my best thinking at night."

She smiles again and looks sideways at me. "What about you? What's your excuse for the predawn wake up?"

"Pretty much the same," I say, which is partially true. My brain goes into overdrive once the sun sets and remains that way until dawn, replaying every moment of my life I'd rather forget.

I try to be slick in the way I slide my hand into hers. The heavens are smiling on me this morning because the move goes off without a hitch and she grips my hand tightly.

"Do you have anything going on Thursday evening?" I ask. I've debated over whether or not to attend the vigil for

Hawthorne that night but have finally come to the conclusion that it might be a good idea. Maybe I can gain some kind of closure and get these damn flashbacks to stop.

"Thursday evening," she says, her voice trailing off. "You know what, I'm actually free that night."

"I was wondering if you might go to a candlelight vigil with me."

"A candlelight vigil?" she asks. "Did something happen? I'm horrible at keeping up on the news."

"No, not recently," I say. "It's for Hawthorne, my buddy who was hit and killed last year. Thursday marks one year since he passed away."

Without hesitation, she's nodding. "Of course I'll go with you. I'd be honored to attend."

"I know it's not exactly the ideal date night, but I need to be there and really don't want to go alone."

Molly stops walking, gripping my hand in hers. "You don't have to do it alone. Thank you for asking me."

Leaning in, I press my lips to hers, gently at first, then with more passion as the kiss goes on. Her arms are wrapped around my neck, and I'm pretty sure she's on her toes since she seems to have grown a few inches. Her body melts into mine as we stand in the rising sunlight. I feel like we're in one of those romantic movies girls seem to love, but for some reason this moment doesn't feel as perfect as it does for the people in those dumb movies.

Pulling away, Molly looks up at me, her eyes searching mine. Can she hear my thoughts?

From the look on her face, I can tell there's something more she wants to say. She hesitates for a moment, then leans into me, resting her head against my chest. I hate that I feel so much for this girl already. But I just can't help it. There's something special about her. I just wish I could give her what she deserves. Because my life seems to be crumbling before me—or maybe it's my brain—and I'm not sure how long I can hold this all together before everything falls apart and I shatter into a million pieces.

CHAPTER 27

MOLLY

It's afternoon already, and I'm still reeling from this morning. I can't believe Adam showed up outside my apartment building. As he kissed me goodbye, he told me he'd pick me up tonight to go get some dinner. Ever since my strange bout with the flu yesterday, food really doesn't sound good, but there's no way I'm turning down that invitation.

Cara should be home soon, and she and I are headed downtown to go shopping. I'm flattered Adam asked me to accompany him to the memorial for his friend Thursday night, but I'm not really sure what to wear. Everything I own feels wrong, so Cara's promised to help me pick something out.

Ten minutes later, we've got our purses and are out the door. The drive downtown is quick, and the shopping is always amazing. For such a small town, we are privy to some really great stores. Although it's less busy on this Tuesday afternoon, there are still more people shopping than normal for this time of day. I guess it comes with the territory when you live in a highly sought-after vacation spot.

It takes awhile to find something, but when it rains, it pours, and I've even found something perfect to wear tonight.

"You're going to knock him dead tonight," says Cara, a look of satisfaction on her face. "Seriously, though, Molly—I don't know what's changed, but you seem happier and more relaxed than I've ever seen you. Adam is working some magic or something!"

Swatting at her, I feign disgust with her comment but know just what she's saying. This is the best I've felt. Probably ever. Maybe it's no more pills, maybe it's Adam, maybe it's a combination of the two. Whatever it is, I'm really happy with the new me, and every day that passes makes me feel more and more confident that OCD doesn't rule my life anymore.

* * *

Adam picks me up that night looking so handsome, his short hair combed just right, his gray button-up shirt rolled up to his elbows. I can't get over how strong this guy's arms are, and having seen him shirtless just a few nights ago makes the shirt even more irresistible.

His smile makes a rare appearance as I open the door. "You look amazing," he says, his eyes wide. He maintains eye contact with me, but I can tell he's struggling to not look me up and down and take it all in.

"Thanks," I say. I can hardly contain my smile, but I'm trying to keep cool. Grabbing my clutch from the table beside the door, I turn back toward him. "Shall we?"

"We shall," he says, extending his arm for me to hold on to in a classic gentlemanly gesture. Taking it, I nod, close the door behind us, and we're headed to the elevator. There's no way I'm clunking down the stairs wearing these patent-leather stilettos.

My head spins just thinking about him. In such a short time, I've fallen pretty hard for this guy, and he is absolutely nothing like the douchebags I've dated before. Maybe I'm maturing and finally choosing the right kind of guy. Aw, little Molly is growing up.

I feel like a million bucks for the first time in forever and I can feel the confidence radiating around me. It's going to be a great night.

* * *

ADAM

I'm having a really hard time keeping my eyes focused on the road ahead of me when I'm sitting next to Molly in that dress. Holy shit, this girl is beautiful. I mean, I knew it the first night I met her, but holy hell. I can't believe this girl is sitting next to me right now. Her dress is snug in all the right places, showing off her perfectly slim figure and accentuating her long, lean legs with those bright-red shoes. It's going to take everything I have to keep myself in check tonight.

Pulling off the freeway, I take us straight toward one of my favorite restaurants in town. I don't often have an excuse to go somewhere fancy, but I sure am glad I chose this place for tonight. Molly deserves to be seen, and I'm not gonna lie—I'm pretty anxious to see all the nasty looks I'll get from any other guys in the place who wonder how the hell a guy like me got a girl like her.

Finding a lucky spot in front of the restaurant, I park the car.

Molly looks out and then back at me. "Sushi Ono?" she asks, pointing at the sign.

"Yeah, this is the best sushi place in the area."

"I have been dying to eat here," she says happily. "How did you get reservations on such short notice?"

"I grew up with the owner's son." I'm pleased she's so impressed by this.

She shakes her head, smiling, as I open her door and extend my hand. Taking it without hesitation, Molly steps from the car.

How is it possible she got even sexier on the drive over?

Her hand in mine, I guide Molly toward the front door, holding it open as she thanks me and steps inside. Placing my hand at the small of her back, we step toward the smiling greeter.

"Hi, we have a reservation for two under Hoffmann," I say.

Glancing at her list, she locates our name quickly and looks up at me curiously. "Yep, I've got you down here," she says. "And your reservation has been marked VIP, so let me escort you to our finest table."

She leads us to a table toward the back of the jam-packed restaurant. Every head in the place turns as we pass, and I'm feeling pretty good. Pulling out a chair, I motion for Molly to sit down, then seat myself, before taking the menus from the greeter. "Enjoy," she says, smiling as she walks back to her spot at the front of the restaurant.

"Well, I must say I'm pretty impressed," says Molly, opening her menu. "I had no idea I was dining with a VIP tonight."

"Quite the opposite," I say. "It's *me* who's dining with the VIP tonight." I hope she knows what I mean by that because it sure came out sounding stupid as hell.

Molly's cheeks flush as she smiles. She is just glowing tonight. Damn, I'm glad I crashed into her at that party two weeks ago.

"So, what's good here?" she asks, turning her attention to the menu.

"You really can't go wrong with anything on the menu," I say, which is definitely the truth. Everything here is delicious.

The first time I came here was the last I ever went anywhere else for sushi—every other roll in the area pales in comparison to the ones you find here.

"Why don't you just order for us both," she says, folding her menu and setting it on the table. "I trust your judgment."

"I'm suddenly feeling a lot of pressure," I say, perusing the menu. "Is there anything you don't like?"

She's watching me, smiling. I've noticed her doing this a lot the past few days.

"Nope. I'm feeling adventurous tonight. Your choice." She gives me a wink. How the hell does this girl not have a boyfriend? On second thought, I've seen what her ex looks like. I'm sure glad she's here with me and not still with him.

When our waiter arrives at the table, I order my five favorite rolls while Molly tries to discreetly check the menu to see what I'm ordering. Handing her menu to the waiter as he leaves, she looks over at me again. "Those all sound delicious," she says.

Thank goodness.

"So, how was your day?" I ask. "And, hey, thanks for coming with me to watch the sunrise this morning."

Smiling, Molly says, "My day was pretty great, actually. I give most of the credit for that to the early-morning wake-up call."

"Yeah, sorry about that. I wasn't even thinking you might not be up yet."

"Well, this is your official invitation to wake me up to watch the sunrise any day you want," she says, her eyes flirty and sweet.

I haven't let myself relax and be happy this entire last year, and here Molly walks into my life and I'm the happiest I've been in a long time. She radiates this energy that's just fun to be around. She makes me forget. Almost.

"Noted," I say. "Does Thursday still work for you?"

"Definitely. You don't have to worry about anything changing. I'll be there."

"Great." I'd like to say I'm looking forward to it, but I'm not. In fact, I'm dreading the idea of being surrounded by a large group of people and having to relive one of the worst nights of my life. I am, however, looking forward to being with Molly.

"Will your family be there that night?" she asks, taking a sip from her water glass.

"I don't think so." I look down at my hands resting on the table. I'd rather not discuss my family, especially when being with Molly is helping me move past some of the things that have been holding me down for so long.

The silence between us is thick, and if we weren't in a restaurant, I'd pull her to me and kiss her. Long and hard. But alas, we are in the middle of a crowded restaurant, even if we are tucked back in a corner, and I'm not sure that would be very appropriate.

Molly opens her mouth to say something when her eyes go wide and her mouth drops. She inhales sharply, and I can tell she's not looking at me. She's looking past me. Turning around to see what she's looking at, I have to bite my tongue to prevent a long stream of expletives from falling out of my mouth.

It's Todd.

CHAPTER 28

MOLLY

My mouth hangs open for what feels like an eternity but is probably less than five seconds. There's an instant tightening in my chest. I'm trapped. Adam turns to follow my gaze, and his body goes rigid as he sees what I see.

I know I should say something to take the focus off the fact that my ex-boyfriend is walking through the restaurant, but I can't think of anything, my mind completely blank. Unfortunately, my heart doesn't respond similarly but starts drumming out a beat even the most skilled drummer could never keep up with.

Todd doesn't see me at first. He's too busy grabbing the butt of the girl beside him, who I can only assume is his date. Unlucky bitch.

The closer Todd and his date draw to us, the lower I sink into my chair. Glancing from side to side, I locate the only empty table in this part of the restaurant. It's right next to ours.

This can't be happening. How on earth is this really happening?

My water glass is suddenly the most interesting thing in the room, and I keep my eyes fixated on it, hoping that if I don't look directly at him, he won't look at us and we can avoid whatever confrontation is inevitable.

But because life is just that fair, as Todd sits down about three feet away from us, right next to Adam, he looks up and spots me. Even without looking at him, I feel the tension in the air shift and am just waiting to burst into flames, courtesy of the hellfire burning in his eyes.

Looking back to Adam, I give him the most natural smile I can and can tell he's doing his best to pretend he doesn't see what neither of us can deny.

I don't know the girl with Todd, but she looks familiar. I'm pretty sure she's a sophomore, so for her, this is probably the night of her life: out with a senior at the most popular restaurant in the area. She has no clue what her date is really made of or she'd run the other direction. Fast.

"So, do you work Thursday?" I ask in a vain attempt to shift the attention at our table back to something else.

Adam's jaw is tight, and I could be wrong, but it looks like his fists are clenching and unclenching. If I didn't know better, I'd say it looks like Adam is going to reach over and punch Todd right in his perfect douchebag face.

Adam releases the breath he must have been holding, his face returns to its normal color, and he relaxes ever so slightly. "Yeah, I work normal hours Thursday, so I'll come pick you up when I'm off."

"Sounds perfect," I say, smiling.

I see Todd rise from his seat out of the corner of my eye, and before I know it, he's taken the five steps to reach our table. Closing my eyes, I wish with all my might that he would just disappear.

"Hey, Mol," he says. "Fancy seeing you here." He keeps his back toward Adam, all of his focus on me.

"Yeah." I refuse to make eye contact, hoping he gets the message and walks away.

"So I'm not sure I've met your date before," he says, disdain in his voice. "Are you going to introduce us?"

"Todd, this is Adam," I say quickly. "Adam, this is Todd."

"Hey, Adam," Todd says, flashing his prize-winning smile and extending his hand toward Adam. I see Adam stiffen for just a second and doubt Todd even caught sight of it. He takes Todd's hand in his and nods.

Glancing back to Todd's table, I can see the death glare his date is shooting at me and almost burst out laughing. She really has no idea what's going on or what she's getting herself into.

"Well, Mol, I'm going to get back to my date," says Todd, motioning to the girl at his table. Her face changes on a dime when she sees him look over. With a smile that could give you a toothache, she waves happily at us.

"Enjoy," I say, rolling my eyes as I look back at Adam. I owe Adam an apology the second Todd walks away. But apparently, once again, life won't be that fair tonight. Before I realize what's happening, Todd leans in and wraps his arms around me, pulling me into a tight hug. Completely caught off guard, I just sit there, eyes wide, looking to Adam trying to figure out what the heck is going on. And that's when I hear it.

"You look amazing, Mol," he whispers directly into my ear. "I sure wish you were coming home with me tonight."

My face flushes red, and I want to die. What the hell is wrong with this guy, and what kind of stunt does he think he's pulling?

Stepping back, Todd flashes me his signature smile and winks, then turns to head back to his table.

Just then, our waiter returns with our sushi rolls and sets them on our table. "Let me know if you need anything more," he says as he turns to leave.

Staring at the food in front of me, I contemplate jamming a piece into my mouth just to give myself a few extra moments to compose my thoughts before I say anything. Thankfully, I don't have to speak first. Adam does.

"Well, that guy sure is a piece of work, isn't he?"

I can't help but laugh out loud. And once I start, I can't stop. Adam joins in. It's taking everything I have not to project myself across the table toward him and kiss him.

And with that, things are back to normal. There's not much conversation between us over the course of the meal. These sushi rolls are by far the best I've ever had, and I can't stop shoveling them into my mouth. In the most ladylike way possible, of course. Thankfully, the sushi is having the same effect on Adam, and he's jamming pieces into his mouth one after the other too.

Stopping for a moment, he leans toward me. "You've got a little sauce right here," he says, smiling that smile that makes me want to melt and reaching across the table to wipe something from my cheek.

"Thanks," I say, shrugging my shoulders. I should be embarrassed, but I'm not. In fact, I'm half tempted to wipe a whole roll across my face so he leans over and touches me again.

We're both slowing down at this point. With three pieces left on the platters in front of us, I sit back and breathe deep. Adam looks up at me and motions to the last pieces.

"They're all yours," I say.

"I'm too full to eat anymore," he says, resting his back against his chair.

We sit staring at each other for a few seconds before Adam leans forward. "Hey—" But before he can finish, the waiter is at our table removing platters and asking if he can bring us anything else.

Adam looks up at me. Shaking my head, I put my hand up to accentuate my point. "No thank you. These rolls were amazing."

"I think we'll just take the check," Adam says. The waiter hands it to Adam, who pulls out his credit card and gives it to the waiter.

"I'll be right back," the waiter says and steps away from the table.

For the first time since he came over, I'm very aware that Todd is sitting just a few feet away from me. My initial reaction is to adjust my posture and hold my breath, but then it hits me. Why do I care? I mean, why should I let him being anywhere near me bother me? Adam won't hesitate to protect me if he tries anything, and I have nothing to prove to him.

It's like a weight is lifted from my shoulders and I'm at least ten pounds lighter. I can feel Todd watching me, but it doesn't faze me. I keep my eyes fixed on Adam. Todd's date is exactly what I would expect. She looks like a Barbie doll. I shudder at the thought that anyone has ever said the same about me. I know it's killing Todd that I'm here with Adam. I have no doubt that Todd is sizing him up, trying to figure out what Adam has that he doesn't. The short answer? Me.

Adam signs the receipt and looks up at me. "Shall we?" he asks.

"Definitely," I say, rising from my chair. Shoulders back, perfect posture, smile on my face, I slide my chair in and take

Adam's outstretched hand. Reaching his side, I take hold of his arm and hold on tight. Being so close to him makes me feel safe. His arms are so strong.

Brushing past Todd, I feel his eyes burning a hole into my back and sense the knife his date no doubt wants to throw at me, but what would normally make me uneasy now makes me want to laugh. Squeezing Adam's hand, I look up at him. He's unlike anyone I've ever dated or even been interested in before. He's something special. And I feel lucky to be on his arm right now.

CHAPTER 29

ADAM

As soon as we're out the door, I can't help it. I lean down and kiss Molly on the top of her head. Opening the door for her, I watch her slide effortlessly into the passenger seat, and then I walk around to my side of the car. Aside from Todd showing up, that was hands down the best date I've ever been on.

I smile as I slide behind the wheel of the car. Molly is watching me again. I usually don't like being watched, but there's something about her that makes this okay.

She holds my stare, and a smile crosses her lips. No words need to be spoken. Gravity pulls our lips together and we're kissing. I feel so much urgency, like these moments are fleeting and I need to kiss her while I can. Molly seems to be feeling the same burning, because the next thing I know, her hands are behind my head, pulling me closer, the kiss intensifying by the second. Moving my hands down her back, I pull her toward me. That's when she stops things.

"I'm sorry," she says, sitting back in her seat.

"It's fine," I say and am only half lying.

Her face is flushed, her breathing fast, and it's clear she's nervous.

"Hey, Molly," I say softly, reaching over to touch her arm. "It's really fine."

Mouth slightly downturned, she glances at me and shakes her head.

"I've just never . . ." Her voice trails off as she turns to look out the car window.

She's a virgin. Given her relationship with that douchebag Todd, I assumed she wasn't. It's obvious she's afraid this is a deal breaker. Maybe that was the problem with Todd.

Taking her hand, I wait until she turns to meet my eyes. "I'm serious, Molly, it's not a problem. If anything, it makes me respect you even more."

She sits a little taller in her seat. "Really?" she asks, obviously surprised by my response.

"Really," I say.

A smile spreads across her face as she nods. I bring her hand to my mouth and gently kiss it. She sighs in relief. Nothing more needs to be said.

"So, do you want to go see a movie? Maybe go for ice cream? I can take you home if you're ready. It's your call."

"I have an idea." Molly smiles at me. It takes everything I have to keep myself in check and start the car.

After fifteen minutes and two wrong turns, we finally enter a nearly empty parking lot and pull up beside a building I thought the city tore down years ago. A neon sign on the top of the building flashes the words "Batting Cages" while another flashes "OPEN."

I look at Molly. "The batting cages?" I ask.

Smiling, she nods, throwing her door open and stepping out into the bright neon lights. I shake my head and chuckle. This girl is full of surprises.

Walking around the car, I meet Molly at her door, where she grabs my hand and pulls me toward the front door. A bell sounds as she pushes the door open, and I hold it for her to walk through.

The place is empty, and if I didn't know any better, I'd think it was closed. Approaching the old dirty desk at the back of the room, I look around to see we're in what's essentially an empty, dingy room, with a door behind the desk leading out to the rundown batting cages. Not long ago, this place was filled with people almost every afternoon and evening and covered in bright wallpaper, with large benches and lockers lining the walls. In its heyday, the batting cages were the place to go and see or be seen, but now this place is nothing more than a ghost town.

A bell sits on the desk with a sign that says "Ring for service." I touch the cold metal top, and the bell rings out much louder than I anticipate, and apparently louder than Molly thinks since she nearly tips over as she jumps back.

Moments later, a young man with blond curly hair comes out from a back room. He's clearly a high school student and very likely the son of whoever owns this place now.

"What can I do for you?" he asks. I wonder how long it's been since the last customer walked through the door.

Looking at Molly, I wait for her to answer. She glances up at me, smiles, and then turns back toward the young man behind the desk. "Enough for one hundred pitches, please," she says, winking at me. "That is if you can handle it."

"Yeah, I'm pretty sure I can," I say, wrapping my arm around her waist and pulling her close.

"Good." She turns back to the kid behind the counter. "We need helmets and bats too, please."

"No problem," he says.

Five minutes later, I'm standing outside a batting cage watching Molly wind up before the pitching machine starts firing balls at her. There's a popping noise from the darkness where the pitching machine stands, and a streak of white flashes through the air before it cracks hard against the aluminum bat in Molly's hands, then flies back in the direction it came from. Not bad.

Pitch after pitch flies toward Molly. Her hair's pulled back in a fancy twist, she's wearing a form-fitting black dress and red stilettos, and ball after ball goes flying back into the darkness. This has got to be every man's fantasy—a beautiful girl all dressed up smacking the hell out of a few dozen baseballs.

She finishes hitting her fifty balls and turns around to look at me outside of the chain-link fencing. "You ready?" she taunts.

"Damn right, I am," I say, opening the gate and retrieving the bat from her.

"Batter up," she says, pulling the helmet off her head and tucking a few stray hairs behind her ears.

Holding tight to the bat, I wind up, preparing for the first pitch. It has been forever since I've hit a baseball. I sure hope I don't make a fool of myself.

Hearing the *thwap* of the pitching machine, I prepare for the ball flying toward me. Swinging, I feel the bat connect with the ball with a loud crack and watch it sail off into what would be left field. With little break, the second pitch is whizzing toward me, and I wind up and swing again, smacking it in the direction of center field this time. I forgot how good it feels to hit a ball.

Pitch after pitch, I feel the bat connect with the ball and watch it speed away into the darkness. Why has it been so long since I've played baseball?

Without warning, I get my answer. Palms sweating, I try to maintain a grip on the bat but am finding it nearly impossible given that it's just gained about a thousand pounds. A ball whizzes by me as I struggle to keep my composure. *Whoosh* comes another ball. Then another, then another. Stepping back from the plate, my heart pounds out of control. Am I having a heart attack?

I feel Molly's eyes on me but can't bring myself to turn around and face her. Not like this.

Flashes of memory and I'm back. Eight years old, tossing the baseball back and forth with Jake. Dad lobbing us balls as we swing and miss, hitting a few here and there. Jake laughing. Dad smiling. Happiness. I feel the happiness. Then it's gone. Shattered. Splintered into a million pieces.

Jake, no! It's my voice, but it's not. There's so much panic. I'm reaching toward him, but he's gone. It's happening again. A flash of white. Red. His little red Converse standing alone in the middle of the road.

Balls continue to whiz past me. I hear the crack of the bat. Feel the impact. The crack of the bat. The crack of Jake's tiny body connecting with the car. The tears. Hot, salty tears streaming down my cheeks.

I'm dizzy. The world is spinning. Or is it me? I'm on my knees. Molly is beside me. She's shouting something, but I can't make it out. My head is in my hands. Am I crying?

Someone's pulling on my arm. Jake? Red shoes. Baseballs.

Black dress. Focusing my eyes, all I see is Molly. Everything else is fuzzy, but her face is clear. Her green eyes. I see the panic, but she's strangely calm. She's saying something. I can't make out her words. I can't hear her voice. The ringing in my ears is so loud I can't hear anything anymore. Anything but the screeching brakes. My screams.

I'm suffocating. Am I sitting on the sun?

I can't breathe. My chest is tight.

Molly's mouth is moving. Numbers. Numbers? Is she counting?

"One, two, three, four, in," she says, her voice calm and steady. "One, two, three, four, out. Come on, Adam, you need to slow your breathing. Breathe with me."

Everything else fades away, and all I see is her lips moving, counting out my breaths. The ringing is still loud, but it's fading. Molly's voice is louder and clearer.

"Hey," she says quietly, touching my cheek.

Turning my eyes up to meet hers, I expect to see a look of terror on her face. What kind of guy has a panic attack on a date? I'm mortified. And should probably consider this the last time I'll ever see this beautiful girl.

But what I see when I look into her eyes is the complete opposite. There's worry, but also concern. Genuine concern.

She's helping me stand, supporting my weight as best she can as my knees wobble a little. I'm sure what's happening now is a sight to behold. A cute, thin, blonde in a dress and heels helping a grown man to his feet. Thank everything holy there's no one else here.

"Are you okay?" Molly asks, helping me to a bench.

"Yeah," I nod. "I just got a little light-headed there."

"Oh, okay," she says. I can see there's more behind her eyes, but she doesn't want to push the issue. Did she recognize the signs of a panic attack? Is that even what the hell just happened to me? How did she know that breathing technique would work?

"I should probably get home and get to bed." I change the subject. "I think I might be coming down with something." I remember Molly saying she thought she had the flu Monday. Hopefully she buys that as a plausible explanation.

"Definitely," she nods. "Let's get you home."

Molly holds on to my arm all the way to the car, acting as though she just wants to be close to me, but I can see right through her. She's worried about me. I can't tell her the truth, though. I can't let her know how messed up my head is right now. How I can't stop thinking about the accident. Hawthorne. Jake. I can't let her in.

Gently pulling my arm away, I pretend to fish through my pocket for my keys. Wrapping her arms around herself, Molly reaches the passenger door and waits for me to "find my keys." Unlocking the door, I hold it open for her. She hesitates before sliding in. "Do you want me to drive?" she asks.

Forcing a smile, I shake my head. "I'm really fine. I'm sure I'm just coming down with something. I'll get you home and go get some rest."

"Okay." She's clearly debating whether or not to push the issue but finally gives in and drops down into the passenger seat.

Closing her door, I make my way to the driver's-side door, running my fingers along the cool, smooth bumper as I walk around it just in case my legs give out. I can't let her see my weakness. I'm so mad at myself that she even saw what she did. What the hell is wrong with me?

We're both silent on the drive back to Molly's apartment. She undoes her seat belt as I pull my car to the curb beside the front gate. Hesitating for a moment, she looks at me, and I can feel her searching my face for answers. There's so much I wish I could say, but I just can't. I can't let anyone know what's been happening in my head. There's not a person I know who wouldn't think I was crazy.

"Well, thanks so much for dinner," she says, obviously forcing a smile. She waits for me to respond, but I keep quiet, merely nodding my head. "I hope you feel better."

"Thanks," I say, looking down at the steering wheel.

"Okay, well, I'll see you Thursday night?"

Thursday night. Thursday night? Oh, shit. I've completely forgotten about Thursday night. Going to that memorial is the absolute last thing I want to do right now. What if the same thing happens while I'm there? It's bad enough that it happened in front of one person, but to happen in front of hundreds? And the people I work with? Residents of the city I've sworn to protect? Hell, no. I cannot let that happen.

"I'll talk to you Thursday and let you know if I'm feeling better." I avoid eye contact.

221

Her hand touches my arm, her eyes burning a hole in the side of my face. "Call me," she says in a way that sounds like a question, statement, and plea all at once.

Once I've nodded, she closes the door, pausing briefly to wave as she reaches the gate.

What the hell do I do now? Where the hell do I go from here? How do I ever expect to have a normal relationship with someone when nothing in my head is normal? Nothing about my life is normal. My head is bombarded with these guilty thoughts and images so often, how can I expect a girl to ever see me as anything but broken? Broken. I am broken.

Pulling away from the curb, I snake through the streets until I reach my driveway. I stop the car and soak up the silence of the night. The darkness is consuming me. Why can't I just man up and deal with this? What the hell is so wrong with me that I can't make these thoughts stop? No one else I know struggles the way I do. Why is this so hard for me?

CHAPTER 30

MOLLY

Lying on my back, I stare at the dark ceiling, watching the fan spin around and around. Cara must have stayed late to help close up the coffee shop tonight because there was no sign of her when I got home. So here I am, in the dark, alone, trapped with my thoughts.

Something happened to Adam tonight. I'm not sure what, but it was significant. If I didn't know any better, I'd say he had a panic attack. He says he's sick. I really don't think he is, though.

I wonder if this has something to do with me. Did I do something wrong? Say something stupid? Was I not pretty enough tonight? Maybe the whole encounter with Todd threw him off?

Wracking my brain, I replay the entire night, searching for something. Something I did wrong. Something I said wrong. Something embarrassing I did that I didn't realize at the time I should be embarrassed about. I can feel my anxiety levels peaking, but I'm sure it's just because I'm tired and worried about Adam. Yeah, that's all it is. My anxiety levels have felt slightly higher than normal the past few days, but I've also been under a lot of stress.

A new relationship. Important school deadlines. Todd. The flu. Just one of those items is enough to make a normal person feel anxious, so it's totally expected for me to feel a little off with all four happening at the same time.

My heart beats faster just thinking about my anxiety level. If I focus hard enough, I should be able to slow it down. I mean, I'm sure everything is fine, right? Everything is going to work out. It's all okay. There is nothing that's happened today that I can't undo. Is there?

Who am I kidding? If Adam is done with me, that is completely out of my control. You can't make someone love you, no matter how hard you try. Love. What a stupid concept. What if no one ever loves me?

What if no one ever loves me? What if I'm alone my entire life because I can't find anyone who can put up with me? I mean, I get sick of myself sometimes. Of course, a guy is going to get sick of me too. I'm not that pretty, I'm not that smart, and I can count on both hands the number of girls I know who are better than I am. Smarter than I am. Who are so flawless and always pulled together. No amount of makeup will ever be enough to cover my imperfections. No dress will ever be fitted enough to make me look perfect. There will always be flyaways in my hair, scuffs on my shoes, and blemishes on my face. Imperfections. I'm comprised of a never-ending list of imperfections. Why on earth would anyone ever want me? Who would be so pathetic and desperate to want me forever?

My stomach drops, and a pit forms deep within me. There is no hope for me, is there? I need to face the fact that Adam doesn't want me. I'm sure there are countless other girls out there who could actually make him happy. Gorgeous girls who really have it all together. Flawless. Perfect. The complete opposite of me. Of course he doesn't want to take me Thursday. It would be too embarrassing, especially when he must have so many other options.

There's something in my eye. There has to be. Why the heck is my eye blinking uncontrollably? It just doesn't feel right. One eye keeps blinking harder than the other. I've got to remedy that by blinking extra hard with the other eye. Why does my eye feel so weird? This blinking is giving me a headache.

Okay, close your eyes, and then you won't have to blink. How is it possible I'm blinking when my eyes are closed? My face is twitching.

Oh, my gosh. Oh, my gosh. Oh, my gosh. This can't be happening. This most definitely is not happening.

And just like that, I'm back. Back in high school, walking the halls alone.

"Hey, you winking at me, Manic?"

Turning around, I see that I've just passed Blake, the quarterback of the football team. I've had a crush on him since my freshman year. I can't believe he knows who I am! But wait, did he just call me Manic?

"Is that your idea of flirting?" he pushes.

My mouth is open, and I'm not sure what to say. "Um, no, no. I'm not winking at you," I stutter, looking down at my feet.

"Sure you are," he proceeds. "I've known for years you had the hots for me. Is this your way of making a move?"

My face is burning hot, and I know I must be the color of a hot pepper. "No, no, of course not," I mumble.

There's a small group forming around him now, consisting of just about every popular kid in our class. A handful of cheerleaders stand to his left, shaking their heads and whispering to one another. Blake's best friend, Tony, stands to his right, flanked by his minions, who follow him around everywhere. They're all looking at me. Judging me.

"Well, Manic," Blake says, taking a step toward me. "Do you really think I would go for a freak like you?"

The crowd behind him giggles, egging him on. "There is no way I would ever go out with you. Nothing on God's green earth could make me do that. You are disgusting. You should really be embarrassed."

If it's possible for a face to turn purple in embarrassment, I'm pretty sure mine has. Tears are welling up behind my eyes. I have to get out of here before they start dumping down my cheeks.

"I'm sorry," I say, dropping my head low and turning to continue on to my next class. Unfortunately, I hit an uneven spot in the pavement and catch my toe, which sends me falling forward. Reaching out, I stop myself before hitting my head on the locker in front of me. Laughter erupts all around as a chorus of "Manic Molly" begins to rise above the roar. I have to get out of here.

Pushing myself back from the locker, I start walking toward the front office. Before I know it, I'm in an all-out sprint, running past the office and to my car. I jam my key into the ignition.

Just another Manic Monday . . .

Of all of the songs to be on the radio, why? Why this one? Why right now?

Throwing the car into reverse, I back out of my spot and jet out of the parking lot as quickly as possible, praying the bump I feel is just a pothole and not a fellow student I've just mowed down.

I have to get out of here. Once I graduate, I am leaving this town and never coming back. Ever. I'll find a way to move on to bigger and better things, and the horrible kids at school will just stay here. I'll make my life better one day, I'm sure of it. Things will work out, and I will be happy. And everyone here will regret being so mean.

Adam doesn't want me. I'm sure of it. I need to get out of here. I need to run.

Jumping out of bed, I pull on a T-shirt and leggings, then retrieve my running shoes from the closet. I'm going to get out of here and run until I can't feel anything. Until these thoughts stop and my head is clear. I'm going to run until I can't run anymore. I'm going to run until I can't remember him. Any of them.

CHAPTER 31

ADAM

It's Thursday morning. I haven't spoken to Molly since Tuesday night. The memorial is tonight, but I don't know if I can make it. I called in sick to work and have spent the morning lying in bed with the blinds closed. My head hurts. So do my eyes. I'm starting to wonder if maybe I really do have the flu.

Staring at a spot on the ceiling, I struggle to force my mind to go blank. I just want to stop thinking. And feeling. I wish this would all just go away. The memories. The pain. Everything.

Closing my eyes, I focus on the silence around me, but even the silence makes my head pound.

Molly is supposed to attend the memorial with me tonight, and I just can't bear the thought of talking to her right now. I'm really starting to care for her, and that scares me. I just can't let her know these horrible things I've done. The horrible events that haunt me daily. Should I text her and back out? If I do that, I know it will be over. I'll never see her again.

Unsure of what to do, I lie still, holding my breath, eyes closed, praying for this headache to go away. Why does everything have to hurt so damn bad?

* * *

Four hours later, I'm still lying in bed. I haven't eaten anything but don't feel any hunger pangs, so I guess I'm okay. Well, okay as far as my stomach is concerned.

It's three o'clock in the afternoon, and I need to make a decision. If I'm going to back out, I need to let Molly know, but I just can't bring myself to do it. As much as I want to pull away, I can't make things final. I'm not ready for this to be the end.

Reaching for my phone, I squint at the screen. The light is enough to send my head pounding again. Pulling up her name, I open a text message for Molly.

Had the flu the past few days. Can't make it tonight. I'm sorry.

My thumb hovers over send, but I just can't do it. Deleting the message, I start again.

Sick. Can't make it. Sorry.

That's even worse.

We still on for tonight?

I click send before I can change my mind.

The stillness and solitude of my room surround me. It's comforting but threatening all at the same time. I want to yell and scream, but I also want to let it consume me and drift away silently into the darkness.

My phone vibrates, and I know it's her. Opening the screen, I see the response I knew I'd receive.

Yes.

She definitely has some character to give me another chance after our last date. The flashback, the pain, the panic.

I'll pick you up at seven.

Great. I'll be ready.

Setting my phone aside, I close my eyes again. I know I have to be there. I have no choice. Even if I did, I don't. And I can't bear to face this night alone. Molly will stand beside me and be what I need. The problem is, I know deep down I can never be what she needs.

* * *

MOLLY

After not hearing from him for a day and a half, I had given up on going to the memorial with Adam until he texted me to ask if we were still on. Am I completely overreacting? Am I going crazy? I thought for sure his silence meant he was through with me, especially after whatever happened that night.

Standing in front of my mirror, I give myself a good once-over. My hair is down and perfectly straight. My makeup is on point and completely flawless. These gray jeans hug my curves like they were made for me, and the navy coat is the perfect finishing touch. I'm glad I thought ahead—the temperature has dropped significantly over the past few days, and there's no way I'd make it without a coat tonight.

I turn to head into the bathroom to brush my teeth when something catches my eye and I have to turn back. When did I start gaining weight? I love this outfit, but it really just doesn't look good on me. It's too late, though. Adam will be here in five minutes, and I'll never find a new outfit in time. Great. I get to go meet his coworkers and friends for the first time looking like a mess.

Staring at myself, I look deep into my own eyes. I wonder what it would be like to just disappear. To vanish. To not be here anymore. I wonder if anyone would miss me. If anyone would even notice.

My phone buzzes, shaking me back to reality.

Pulling up outside. I'll be up in a minute.

Crap. Hurrying into the bathroom, I squeeze a giant glob of toothpaste onto my toothbrush and jam it into my mouth, brushing my teeth as quickly as possible. There's a knock on the door as I spit, then rinse my mouth. Giving myself one last look in the mirror, I wish I hadn't. Even my makeup looks bad. What the hell was I thinking? I really wish Cara was here to help me tonight.

Slipping on a pair of flats sitting near the door, I grab my purse and shove my phone inside. With a deep breath, I open the door. And there he is.

Adam is definitely more pale than usual, which is probably why the bags under his eyes are so prominent. His hair is combed back, and he's dressed in uniform, but there's something different. I can't pinpoint what it is, but something doesn't feel right.

"You look nice," he says, holding the door as I pass through.

"Thanks," I say, ducking under his arm and turning to lock the door. My key slides easily into the lock, and I feel the resistance of the door locking. But pulling my key out, I start to doubt myself. What if when I turned my key to pull it out, I unlocked the door?

Giving the doorknob a jiggle. I know the door is locked, but what if when I jiggled the door, I shook it unlocked?

Taking the doorknob into my hand, I jiggle it again. Still locked.

Did I turn off the lights in the apartment? Crap.

"Let me check something real quick," I say, unlocking the door and hurrying back into the apartment. Sure enough, I've left the light in our bedroom on.

Did I unplug my straightener? Walking into the bathroom, I

can see it's unplugged. But is it really unplugged? What if my eyes are just playing tricks on me?

Running my hand over the iron, it's cool to the touch, meaning it can't possibly be plugged in. But what if I'm just imagining it's fine, but it's really not?

I slide my hand over the outlet on the wall. It's empty—but is it really?

Okay, I seriously have to get it together. It's unplugged, and Adam is waiting for me.

Walking back into the bedroom, I do a quick scan of the outlets in that room, checking that every light is off, everything is unplugged, and no blankets are sitting close enough to a plug to start a fire.

I do the same in the bathroom, shoving the straightener into the cabinet under the sink and trying to take a mental picture so I can reassure myself later that it is, in fact, unplugged and turned off.

Hurrying into the kitchen, I glance at the outlets there, unplugging the toaster and paying close attention to the stove. The burners are off. Everything is off and unplugged.

Passing through the living room, I pause. Everything was good in the bathroom. Everything was good in the bathroom . . . right? Everything had to be good in the bathroom. I wouldn't have walked out of the room if something was plugged in. Or would I?

Stepping into the bathroom for what I tell myself is the last time, I glance at the outlet. Empty. I open the cupboard to see my straightener sitting there unplugged. Okay, that is enough. Adam is waiting and we have to leave.

Reaching for the front doorknob, I hesitate again. Did I check everything? Or did I hurry through so fast I missed something? I can't leave anything turned on or plugged in because it might start a fire. And I don't want to be responsible for something like that.

"Molly?" Adam's still standing outside the front door, probably wondering what the hell is taking me so long.

"Coming," I say, opening the door and stepping out into the cool evening breeze. "Sorry about that, I almost forgot to grab something I need," I lie. What the heck is going on with me tonight? I mean, I know I'm a little anxious, but this is a bit extreme.

My stomach drops. No, that can't be it. It's got to be the nerves, nothing more.

Locking the front door, I jiggle the handle twice before forcing my hand off the doorknob and turning to face Adam. He has a bewildered look on his face, but I don't think it's because he suspects anything. He can't possibly know what's happening right now. What the hell *is* happening right now?

We walk down the stairs in silence, and Adam pushes the gate open before holding the passenger door of his patrol car and letting me slide in.

It feels so much smaller in here than it did the last time I rode with Adam. Like the space has shrunk. Or I grew. I'm not sure which is the more plausible explanation.

Adam slides in behind the steering wheel and looks over at me before shoving the key into the ignition and starting the car. Something is going on with him. And now I'm terrified he might know something is going on with me.

Neither of us talks the entire drive downtown to the beach. There are at least three dozen cars already in the parking lot when Adam backs into a spot near the boardwalk. Climbing out of the car, I stand at the front and wait for him to get out and adjust his uniform. I have no idea how he carries that duty belt around all day. It has to weigh at least fifty pounds. What they say is right, though—there is something about a man in uniform. Sunken eyes and sallow cheeks aside, he sure looks sexy all dressed up. Just seeing him like this makes me want to jump into his arms and lay one on him. But I refrain. This is neither the time nor the place for that.

The mood on the beach is solemn. A crowd of at least a hundred is gathering near a makeshift stage that's been brought in for this event. Giant picture frames stand beside the stage holding photographs of the fallen officer. Jared Hawthorne. He was my age. My age. And his life is over. I shudder at the thought of what that night must have been like for Adam watching someone get hit and die right in front of him. I can't even imagine.

Adam slides his hand into mine, and I look up to find him

heading toward a group of other officers. A few guys stand alone, others holding the hands of what are probably their wives. Instantly, I feel uncomfortable and out of place, like I've walked in on an intimate scene I have no place being a part of. I didn't know Jared. I don't know any of these officers. I met Adam only weeks ago. This all suddenly just feels wrong, and I really wish I hadn't come.

"Hey, bro," says an officer walking toward us, holding the hand of what I can only guess is his pregnant wife. She's adorable and looks amazing. I hope I look that good when I'm pregnant. If I'm ever pregnant.

Adam drops my hand as he reaches for the officer and they embrace.

"You doing okay?" he asks. Adam looks ahead and nods affirmatively. His eyes are glossy, and I really hope this guy doesn't pry any further for fear that Adam might completely break down.

After a few moments, Adam clears his throat and motions toward me. "Hernandez, this is Molly. Molly, this is my buddy Hernandez. We're on the same crew."

Hernandez extends his hand and I take it, returning his handshake. His hands are large and rough like Adam's. It must be a cop thing.

"It's nice to meet you, Molly," says Hernandez with a smile. "This is my wife, Alicia."

Turning my attention to her, I can now see just how glowing

she is. Pregnancy suits her. As she takes my hand, I find myself wishing she'd pull me toward her, put her arm around me, and pretend like we were old friends. She has an energy about her that makes me wish I knew her.

"It's wonderful to meet you," Alicia says in a singsong voice. "Adam never introduces us to the girls he dates, so you must be a big deal." She winks. I blush. Adam looks away.

"Thank you, everyone, for coming tonight," comes a voice through a large speaker not far from us. I'm a little relieved the service is starting and I won't have to try to make small talk with anyone.

The four of us turn to face the stage. There stands a tall, gray-haired man, his arm around a short, slender woman with a pixie cut. The woman keeps her eyes fixed on the ground in front of her, periodically wiping at the tears running down her cheeks.

My heart hurts. I never met this man, I don't know his family, and I really don't even know his friends. I know nothing about him. But I hurt for him. For all of them.

"We appreciate you all coming out to show your support for our family," says the man. "For our Jared."

Sniffles can be heard throughout the crowd with the occasional sound of noses blowing.

Glancing up at Adam, I see a tear trickle down his cheek and drop to the ground below. Stepping toward him, I hug his arm, hoping to offer some kind of comfort. What can I even say at a time like this? Nothing. There is nothing that can fix things.

Nothing to make anyone feel better. So I stand here, tears in my own eyes, trying to block out what's going on around me.

The man on the stage speaks for about five more minutes before trying to pass the microphone to the woman, who waves her hand in refusal. A young girl plays "Amazing Grace" on the flute, and then the police chief stands and says a few words. I try hard not to look at Adam again. I can see how hard this is for him. His body is rigid, his arm is stiff and still. Never once does he reach for my hand or make any kind of movement. Not even to wipe away the tears streaming down his face. Every now and again I feel a hot, salty droplet land on my arm or my hair, but I pretend not to notice.

Every word shared about Jared Hawthorne makes me wish I had known him in this life. It's true—the best die young.

When the speakers are done, a few young men start passing out floating lanterns. Adam holds on to ours and lights it when the signal is given. One by one, I watch as over a hundred lanterns slowly rise and make their way into the sky. Toward heaven. Toward Jared. If the purpose of these lanterns wasn't so tragic, I would say it's the most beautiful sight I've ever seen. The love in the crowd is strong. The sorrow heavy and unbearable. But watching these beautiful paper lanterns float up into the night sky gives me hope that somewhere, somehow, Jared is watching this scene. And maybe a lantern or two will actually make it up to him.

Once the last lantern has disappeared from view, the crowd

slowly begins to disperse. I stand with Adam, unsure of what to do or say. I'm glad he wanted me here with him to pay respects to this amazing man, but I still feel totally out of place and am terrified to talk to anyone for fear of saying something dumb and making not only myself but Adam look bad. It's nights like tonight I wish I could be like all the other girls. The ones who not only make everything look so easy but really seem to have it that way.

I hang back as Adam says goodbye to his crew. I met most of the guys and girls in his department tonight, with the exception of one. He's older than everyone else, which is maybe why he hung back and kept to himself. When I asked Adam about him, he seemed a little put out, like talking about this officer was the last thing he wanted to be doing. He did say his name is Sergeant Carlson, but that was all he said, and based on the look on his face, I knew better than to push any further. There were a few times I caught Sergeant Carlson watching Adam, but he seemed protective and concerned more than anything, so I'm not sure where the bad blood lies.

Adam holds tight to my hand as we walk back to his patrol car in silence. He's never struck me as a really talkative guy, but he is uncharacteristically quiet tonight. I'm sure it's just because of ton' ght and the fact that this is the one-year anniversary of a
'cer's death. Come to think of it, I've kept pretty quiet
guess the same could be said of me. But maybe it's
re.

The car roars to a start, and Adam pulls out of the parking lot.

"Thank you for inviting me here with you tonight," I say.

Adam nods but doesn't say anything.

"I'm truly so sorry for the loss of Officer Hawthorne. After tonight, I really wish I'd known him before he passed away. He sounds like an excellent officer and a wonderful friend."

Silent, Adam nods again and keeps his eyes fixed on the road in front of us.

I know I shouldn't let his lack of communication and interaction bother me given everything this day represents, but I can't help but wonder again if he's done with me. He asked me to attend the vigil with him days ago, so it's likely he felt like he couldn't get out of it. What if he only brought me because he felt like he had to?

My head is spinning once again, and there's that pit forming in my stomach. Here I am clutching his arm, and he's probably going to go into work tomorrow and discuss with his crew how bad he feels for me and how pathetic I am. There's a very good chance I've just made a fool of myself in front of a group of people I respect. Why am I such an idiot?

We finish our drive back to my apartment in silence. The streets are filled with students out and about by the time we get home, offering an added reminder that life goes on. I just spent two hours standing on the beach with over a hundred people mourning the loss of Officer Hawthorn, and back near campus, life is going on as though that never happened. It doesn't seem fair, but it is. I mean, this is life. And life goes on no matter what happens.

Adam pulls his car to the curb beside my apartment complex. He doesn't even look over at me as I say good night and close the car door behind me. Opening the gate to the complex, I turn back one last time to see him glance in my direction and then pull away from the curb. He's just having a rough night given everything going on. Right?

Music echoes through the courtyard as I slowly walk to the stairs and climb to the third floor. The closer I get to my apartment, the more clear it becomes that this is where the music blaring through the complex is originating. A party is the last thing I need to come home to right now.

But I am wrong. Todd is the last thing I need to come home to, yet here he is, stepping out of my front door, the girl from Sushi Ono in hand. Are you freaking kidding me?

"Hey, Mol!" he exclaims, nearly running right over me. He's clearly drunk already, as is his date, who's glaring at me with a look of disgusted recognition on her face.

"Hey," I say, pushing past him. I have got to find Cara and get this party shut down fast.

"Where you off to in such a hurry?" Todd shouts after me. Ignoring him, I step inside my apartment and instantly wish I had earplugs. The sound system is cranked up as high as it'll go, and there are at least twenty people dancing in the living room or slumped over on the couch. Scanning the crowd, I spot Cara in the kitchen beside a blender, holding the pitcher in hand as she flirts with some guy I know I've seen before but just can't place.

Dodging bodies, I make my way into the kitchen and finally reach her. "Hey," I say, trying to get her attention.

"Hey!" she shouts, throwing her arms around me. Her breath reeks of alcohol, and she nearly knocks me over when she leans all of her weight into the hug, catching me completely off guard.

"What's going on? Why are all of these people here?" I ask, wondering if it'll even be possible to convince her to cut the party short.

"I thought it would be fun to have some friends over," she yells, motioning to the people around us.

"Okay, well, what are the chances this party can be moved somewhere else? Maybe a house with a little more room?"

Cara frowns as she watches me. Her eyes are half closed, and her head keeps tipping forward like she's going to fall asleep at any moment. "Have some fun for a change, Molly!" she exclaims. Just then, a new song comes on the stereo, and she's screaming and throwing her hands in the air, turning around to dance up on the guy with his arms around her waist. The entire apartment erupts as the song gets started. It's so loud in here I can barely hear myself think. What the hell was Cara thinking inviting all of these people over on a Thursday night?

Turning back toward her, I can see Cara is a little too busy to talk, her tongue shoved down the unknown guy's throat. Mike? Mark? I'm pretty sure his name is Mike. He lived in the dorms beside ours during my freshman year. Yeah, that's where I know him from. Cara had such a crush on him then. I wonder how she reconnected with him after all these years. Although I'd prefer a quiet night at home, I can't be too mad at her. She's living out her freshman-year fantasy.

Touching her back, I try to grab her attention. She turns toward me slightly, then throws herself into my arms again as soon as she recognizes my face.

"You okay, Cara?" I ask.

"You know it!" she shouts, then squeals.

"Are you going to be okay if I leave?"

"Sure thing." She smiles. "I've got Mike here to keep me company." And with that, she's reattached herself to his mouth.

"Be safe. Call me if you need me," I say, patting her back before turning around and heading toward the door. I don't recognize any faces in my apartment, which is weird since we're all so connected in this little town. Our bedroom door is closed, which stops me in my tracks. I'm sure Cara closed the door when people started showing up, but what if she didn't? What if someone's in there? What if they're having sex on my bed? Or rifling through my stuff?

Walking toward the bedroom door, I hold my breath and turn the knob. One of three things is about to happen: either I walk in on someone hooking up, catch someone in the act of stealing my stuff, or throw the door open like a detective uncovering some big secret to find no one there. Looking around, it's obvious everyone is wasted. Even if I am overreacting, it's unlikely anyone in this house will remember it five minutes from now, let alone tomorrow.

Pushing the door open, I find a dark, empty room. *Oh, thank goodness.* Pulling the door closed behind me, I turn back toward the front door but stop again. Should I lock the door so no one can get in? If I do, I'll lock Cara out. But I really don't want anyone getting in there and messing with our stuff. Or stealing our computers. Or more importantly, our clothes. The only problem is, how the hell do I explain the locked door to Cara when she inevitably finds herself locked out of her own bedroom? What if instead of just crashing on the couch she decides to bust down the door? I don't want to have to purchase a new door.

I'm torn, rocking back and forth between the bedroom door and the front door. This could be bad either way.

Maybe locking the door is a worse idea. I don't want Cara mad at me. I'll leave it unlocked. I just need to make sure I hurry home when the party is likely to be breaking up to make sure no one walks away with any of our stuff. I'm not sure given her current condition that Cara would even notice someone carrying the oversized flat-screen out.

Okay, it's settled. I'm leaving and not locking the door. I turn back toward the front door just in time to watch Todd and his flavor of the month walk back in. Dammit.

With a deep breath and all the courage I can muster, I stand tall and brush past everyone until I reach the door. Turning the knob, I think I might actually be in the clear. That is until I feel the hand on my arm. Shit.

I don't even need to look to see that it's Todd, but I do anyway, and sure enough it is. The girl who was on his arm just moments before is now nowhere to be seen. While I'm pretty sure she'd like to rip my throat out, I feel more uneasy encountering Todd by himself. Without her, he has nothing to lose.

"You owe me a talk," he says, reaching for my arm and leaning in so close I can smell the vodka on his breath.

Pulling my arm away, I turn back toward the door. "Not a chance."

"Like hell there is," he says, tightening his grip.

"Let me go, Todd," I say, yanking my arm away, but before I can squirm free, he's squeezing me so tight he's cutting off circulation. The veins in my hand ache, and my entire arm is tingling.

His eyes are menacing, and I can tell he has no intention of carrying on a nice conversation with me.

"You're not leaving yet," he says, pulling me with him as he heads toward the bathroom. The music is loud, but there are enough people around I hope that making a scene will get him to leave me alone.

"Let me go!" I scream, yanking my arm away from him as

hard as I can. I know I've caught him off guard when he loosens his grip just enough I can finally free myself from his grasp. "Stay away from me and do not touch me!" I scream.

By now, at least ten people have stopped dancing and are watching us. Todd's face goes red, and I know it's not from embarrassment. He's furious. His jaw is set tight, and his eyes are hard.

"I never want to see you again, Todd." I lean in close to make sure he hears every single word. "You are disgusting and not worth my time. Do not talk to me, do not touch me, and get the hell out of my house."

By now the music has been turned down and everyone in the apartment is watching us.

"Molly?" I hear Cara's voice from the kitchen. I wonder how much of this she's seen.

"I'm okay," I shout back, raising my hand high in the air. "Todd was just leaving."

I turn back and glare at him. Who does this asshole think he is coming into my house, thinking he has some kind of control over me? Like he owns me? And that I owe him something?

Todd glares at me and won't budge.

"Dude, I think she told you to leave," says a guy with shaggy brown hair standing near us.

Todd stands like a statue, his eyes fixed on me, completely ignoring the guy.

"Hey, man," says the brown-haired guy, "I think it's time you leave."

Todd remains stiff. I've heard the phrase "if looks could kill" thrown around before but never fully grasped its meaning until now. If looks could kill, I'd be dead. I've never seen such hate in anyone's eyes before. Why is he here? Why did he come to a party at my house? Why does he hate me so much?

"Hey," says the shaggy-haired guy again, reaching out to grab Todd's arm. That one touch breaks Todd's death-stare and sends him swinging. It's like I'm watching my life happen in slow motion. Todd's fist cocks back before flying toward the shaggy-haired guy's face. I feel my body reacting, lunging forward to grab hold of his arm and prevent the inevitable, but I'm too slow. Todd's fist connects with the guy's jaw, sending him slowly flying backward through the air until he lands on his back on the carpet.

There's a collective gasp as everyone at the party watches the scene play out. In one solid motion, Todd flings himself back around and is stepping toward me. Is he going to punch me too?

I'm sure I look like a deer caught in the headlights of an oncoming car; I'm the deer, and the car is Todd, barreling down on me with all the force in his body. Protecting my head, I duck and turn, bracing myself for the freight train bearing down on me. But nothing hits me. I want to know what happened, why he's stopped, but I'm too afraid to look up and expose my face to his fist.

Head still protected, I shift my eyes as far left as possible to see if Todd's shoes are still there, but the shoes I spot don't belong to Todd. They look like army boots. Or duty boots. It can't be.

But it is. Adam. Standing there between me and Todd, twisting Todd's arms behind his back. I stand frozen, unsure of my next move. Part of me wants to reach over and deck Todd in the face, while another wants to jump into Adam's arms, and still another wants to turn to the person beside me and ask what the hell just happened.

There is chaos around me. An arm slides behind my back, and soon I'm sitting down on my bed, Cara beside me, Mike standing in front of us.

"What just happened?" I ask, slightly dazed.

"That asshole just tried to hit you, but this cop showed up and blocked him," says Mike. I don't know Mike other than his reputation from my freshman year, but he sure seems upset. I guess watching a guy try to punch a girl will do that to you.

"Yeah, Molly," says Cara, suddenly sober. "I don't even know what that douchebag was doing here. I thought I saw him across the apartment right before you got here, but I assumed I was mistaken. I thought he knew better than to ever show his face in our house again."

"Apparently not," I mumble.

I quickly rise to my feet, feeling light-headed as I try to fully grasp what just happened. Cara places her hand on my arm and gently pulls me back down beside her. I rest my head on her shoulder, and she wraps her arms around me.

"I can't believe he came here," I say, shaking my head. Why can't this guy just leave me alone? I mean, he has another girlfriend. Why can't he just move on already?

"He's lucky that cop grabbed him. If he'd hit you, I would have beat the hell out of him," says Mike. "I mean, who the hell tries to punch a girl?"

"I guess that's Todd for you," I say, forcing a very unconvincing laugh.

"What the hell happened to him?" he asks rhetorically, shaking his head. "He had it all going for him his freshman year. I remember him from the dorms. I just don't understand how someone can go from all that to this."

"He's just really good at putting up a front and shielding that side of him from the rest of the world, I guess," I say.

Adam appears in the doorway, rushing toward me.

"Are you all right?" he asks, taking hold of my arms like he needs to touch me to be sure I'm really okay.

"Well, he didn't hit me," I say. "And from what I understand, I have you to thank for that."

"Yeah, well, something didn't feel right, so I came up here to make sure you were okay and walked in at the right time, I guess." He wraps his arms around me and pulls me to him.

"So I'm guessing you two know each other?" asks Mike.

Cara shoots him a look as I nod in reply. "You could say that."

"Officer, I'm glad you got here when you did, or I may have ended up in cuffs tonight, too, after taking care of that dick bag out there."

Arms still around me, Adam extends his hand toward Mike, offering a handshake of appreciation, which Mike vigorously accepts.

"Do you have to take him in?" I ask.

"No," says Adam. "I called it in, and one of the on-duty guys is here to take him. Plus, I wasn't sure it was too ethical for me to take him to jail given our relationship."

"I understand." I pull back enough to see his face. This makes two times Adam has literally saved me from Todd. How did I get so lucky to find this guy? And how the hell did Todd turn into such a monster?

"Can we go somewhere and talk?" Adam whispers in my ear. Nodding, I tell Cara I'll be right back and thank Mike, then pull Adam out of my bedroom and through the front door, where a handful of officers are speaking with what's left of the party guests.

Stepping out into the cool night air, I'm shocked by how cold I suddenly am, then realize I'm covered in sweat. Shivering, I feel Adam wrap his arm around my shoulders, pulling me in tightly. Well, as tightly as he can. His duty belt and radio stick out far enough they keep a good three inches between us.

He pulls me toward the stairs, then stops at the top step. "Look, I'm really sorry about tonight. And Tuesday night. I've been feeling off the past few days. I'm glad I came when I did. I don't know what I would have done if he'd hit you. Walking in on that scene made me realize how much I care about you—not that I didn't know before."

I'm not sure if he has more to say, but I don't care. I pull him tightly against my body and press my lips to his. His hands are in my hair while mine are latched tightly behind his neck. Everything else just falls away—the party, Todd, my apartment complex—and it's just us in this moment, kissing each other feverishly as if no amount of kissing, no amount of time, will ever be enough. My hands are on his chest as he pulls me in even closer, and soon our bodies are pressed tightly together. Until I register the pain of his radio jamming into my collarbone and his duty belt in my stomach.

Pulling apart, we stare at each other, each of us struggling to catch our breath. I'm suddenly very aware that we're standing on a balcony in my apartment complex, in clear view of every unit. Not to mention Adam is dressed in uniform, and I'm not sure how good it is for his reputation to be spotted going at it with some college girl right after he's cuffed her ex-boyfriend. Come to think of it, this probably looks really bad.

"I should go," says Adam, leaning in to kiss my forehead. "It's been a long night, and I've got an early day tomorrow. I'll call you."

"Okay," I say, holding on to his hand until he's out of my reach. He looks back as he takes the stairs down to the courtyard, turning to wave as he reaches the last step.

Aside from the fact that this has been the weirdest and somehow most eventful night of my life, I am on cloud nine. I've spent the last several days worrying about Adam, thinking he was gearing up to end things with me, and then this happens. I came to realize a long time ago that my life is anything but normal, and tonight fits pretty well within that realm.

Walking back to my apartment, I can't help but smile. I helped honor a hero tonight and was nearly punched by my ex but ultimately rescued by my knight in shining armor. What more can a girl ask for?

CHAPTER 32

ADAM

It's six o'clock, and I'm idling in my patrol car here in my driveway. Everything about last night has taken it out of me, and I'm feeling completely exhausted today. Exhausted but somehow rejuvenated at the same time.

Officer Brown on the night shift took Todd to the drunk tank last night. Scanning the email he sent me along with a copy of the report he wrote, I can't get over what a giant piece of shit Todd is. He was booked on a domestic disturbance and assault but was bailed out only a few hours later, as soon as he sobered up enough to be let go. I guess it pays to have rich parents, especially when your dad is a lawyer.

The guy he hit is not pressing charges against him, so Todd will walk away from this scot-free. This asshole who seems to have it out for Molly is now on the streets again, and there's really nothing she can do about it. What if he hurts her? What if he takes things even further? I trust Molly to steer clear of this douchebag, but given my experience with him the past few weeks, he seems to be seeking her out.

I almost feel like I'd be able to protect her better if I wasn't a cop. As an officer, I must strictly adhere to the laws I'm sworn to protect. When an average citizen breaks the law, depending on the crime, some pardoning can occur if it's the first offense. Being as well versed as I am in the law, I know there is no way I can instigate a confrontation with this guy without it turning into breaking news plastered across the front page of the paper the next morning. I'm held to a higher standard and thus must maintain that to avoid harsh judgment and punishment.

Backing out of my driveway, I'm wracking my brain for ways to keep Todd away from Molly, to make sure she stays safe.

And then it hits me: Molly's mentioned she has successfully avoided Todd for months, up until that night he showed up on her doorstep. That was right after we met. Could this be inevitable? Am I toxic? Am I cursed? I mean, take Jake and Hawthorne—two people I've been closer to than nearly anyone else in my life, and look what happened to them. Now here I am starting a relationship with Molly, and all of a sudden bad things start happening to her. Is this my fault?

By now my head is spinning, and I'm struggling to focus on driving. Pulling to the side of the road, I feel like I'm on the verge of a panic attack. Or maybe a heart attack. What the hell is happening?

It all makes sense, though. Her life was fine until I stepped into the picture. She was clearly happy before we met, but now she's being harassed by Todd. Todd damn near attacked her last night after punching some guy who was trying to stand up for her. Oh, my gosh. This is my fault. This is all my fault.

My palms are sweating, and my heart is racing. This can't be happening. I haven't felt this way about anyone in so long—possibly ever. But I can't continue with a relationship knowing my bad luck might be poisoning her life. I care too much about her to put her through that. But how the hell am I supposed to tell her that? She'll think I'm crazy. Maybe I am crazy.

I drop my head and close my eyes. I have to focus on work. I cannot be thinking about Molly or worrying about this. Casualness creates casualties. I can't become complacent in my job or let my mind wander and expect to stay safe.

With a deep breath, I focus on clearing my head. I can do this. *Easier said than done.* But how am I supposed to tell her? I can't. I can't face her. I can't explain to her why it has to be this way. She'll never understand. But I have to keep her safe, and this is the only way.

* * *

MOLLY

It's been three days since I last heard from Adam. I'm not really sure what's going on, but I'm certain he's avoiding me. And why shouldn't he? I'm sure if I think long and hard enough, I'll remember some stupid thing I did or said that is undoubtedly what made him realize I'm not worth his time. I mean, how amazing can a girl be when her ex-boyfriend hates her so much he tries to punch her?

It just doesn't make sense, though. He saved me. He kissed me. He promised to call me. And then nothing. No text, no call, nothing.

My hands begin to shake, and I can feel my insides tightening up. This can't be happening. This isn't happening. This hasn't happened in over a week.

But it is happening, and there is nothing I can do to stop it. My heart pounds out a rhythm in my chest, threatening to explode. There is a giant pit in my stomach that makes me want to double over in pain. My breathing is becoming more shallow, so I try to focus on continuing to breathe in and out, but it's no use. I'm hyperventilating.

I. Can't. Breathe.

Panic is welling up from deep inside me, and I'm past the point of no return. I'm very aware of the beads of sweat forming on my forehead and the droplets dripping down my back. My face is burning hot and freezing cold all at once. Am I going to puke? Is that even possible when you can't breathe?

I'm going to pass out. I feel it. I'm watching myself from the outside. My mouth is open as I struggle to suck air into my lungs, but nothing's getting through. It's like I'm breathing through a coffee straw.

My vision is blurry. I can't even focus on my hands just inches in front of my face. Spots start popping up, making it even more impossible to see, so I stop trying and squeeze my eyes shut.

Please let this stop. Please let me be okay.

But no amount of pleading or prayer is going to save me now. My heart is pounding. My whole body is shaking. I wish I could call out for help, but I can't even breathe.

Am I dying? Could this be the end? Am I having a heart attack?

Yes, this must be what it feels like to die.

Just like the end of a scene in a play, a curtain slowly lowers, and everything fades to black.

CHAPTER 33

ADAM

For the past three days, all I've thought about is Molly. I wonder how she's doing. I'd really like to call and explain, but I just can't. I can't let her see how flawed I am and how messed up my mind has become. I don't want to hurt her, but I just don't know what else to do.

The morning after the party, she texted me a thank-you for saving her. All I could think about was how I was letting her down. None of this would have happened if she'd never met me. She thinks I'm her hero, but I'm the complete opposite. If it wasn't for me and this horrible curse I seem to carry, plaguing everyone I love with sadness and destruction, she wouldn't need saving.

If this is my life, if this is what I do, why does it happen to the people around me? Why can't it just happen to me? Why not just—

No, no, I can't go there. I can't even think about that. I'd never do that. I could never do that. Could I?

If I didn't exist, Jake might still be alive. If I didn't exist, Hawthorn could still be here. The heartache and pain my parents feel. The loss Hawthorn's family relives every single day. It's all my fault. If I hadn't been here, none of it would have happened.

So what if I wasn't? What if I wasn't here anymore? What if I could prevent anyone else from getting hurt? What if I could protect everyone from this horrible effect I have?

There is only one thing I can think of that would stop the damage my very existence seems to cause. There's only one answer.

I've never considered this before, but maybe I should. No more destruction, no more pain to those I love, and no more reliving memories from the worst days of my life every single day. It's getting worse. Life is getting harder. And I'm causing more pain.

I can't even bring myself to think the word, but it might be the best solution for all of us.

* * *

MOLLY

I am alone.

Someone quit at the coffee shop, throwing off the regular schedule. Cara has been trying to help cover open shifts, which means she's been working way more hours than usual. She was able to get off early this afternoon, but other than that, I've been alone. Walking to classes alone. Staring at a blank page in my notebook through every lecture alone. Then walking back to sit in my apartment alone. I have no one. My stress levels are at an all-time high, and I'm starting to think this is something more than just everything happening in my life. I'm starting to worry that it might be back. I know it's always been here, but for some reason, I thought I was cured. I know that's not possible, but I sure prayed for a miracle. A miracle I'm starting to realize I'll never see.

It's been almost two weeks since I stopped taking my meds, and I'm starting to think it was a bad idea. So what do I do? Do I go back on my meds and take them indefinitely? What if I have to take them for the rest of my life? What if I'm always crazy and can't live without the right prescription to balance out the imbalance in my brain? Is this truly a life sentence?

Life is hard, I know. It's not meant to be fair. But I'm not sure I can live the rest of my life with this, battling my demons every single day with no light at the end of the tunnel. How do people live like this? How the hell can I be expected to live like this?

It's like I'm being held captive in my own brain. I can't even trust my own thoughts because I never know which are from me and which are my brain fighting against me. How the hell do I trust anyone in my life when I can't even trust myself?

Halloween is two days away, and I still don't have a costume, so Cara and I are going shopping to see if there is anything left in the downtown boutiques. Shopping is usually a nice outlet when I'm feeling anxious, but today I'm dreading it. I was hoping to have a date for Halloween night. Maybe even wear coordinating costumes. Instead, I sit here in the passenger seat of Cara's Jeep, staring out the window as we make the drive downtown.

The reflection staring back at me in the window isn't someone I recognize. Just a week ago I was feeling confident and ready to take on the world, and now the thought of going to a party and being surrounded by a house full of people just makes me tired. And sad.

"Cheer up, Molly," says Cara, glancing in my direction as she steers the car toward the off-ramp that'll take us to the city's best shopping.

Forcing a smile, I nod, but I know Cara can see right through me. She's known me long enough to know when I'm faking it. What would she think if she knew everything?

"Do you want to start at the mall or farther down State Street? It's completely your call."

I don't care. Two days before Halloween and I'm pretty confident all of the cute costumes in my size are already sold out. "Wherever you think," I say, staring out the window.

What if Adam figured it out? What if he saw the signs and recognized my brand of crazy? What if he knows who I truly am and is rejecting me for it?

But that doesn't make any sense. There's no way he could know.

Or could he?

Oh, my gosh, he has to know. Maybe he has a relative with OCD and recognized the signs. Damn OCD. Those three letters will follow me around the rest of my life, haunting me, showing up just when I think I've finally rid myself of them.

If OCD is a mental illness and I have OCD, then I have a mental illness. I have a mental illness. How do I expect someone to react when they find out I am mentally ill? The term elicits thoughts of a person strapped up in a straightjacket screaming, yelling, and acting like the quintessential crazy person. That's what it means to be mentally ill, right? That's got to be the picture Adam has in his head now. Yeah, that explains everything. He knows I'm crazy and now wants to keep as far away from me as possible. Can I blame him?

Cara squeezes into a parking spot between two black BMWs, cuts the ignition, and sits still, staring straight ahead.

"I know what you're going through, Molly," she says. "I figured it out and wish you would have told me."

Wait, what? What is Cara talking about? I didn't say any of that out loud, did I? How the hell did she figure it out?

I stare at her in silence, unsure how to respond.

"It's okay, Molly. You can tell me, you know. I won't think you're crazy."

Silence. I can't find the words to respond. How do I respond to that?

I finally blurt out "What?" and just stare at Cara.

"It's obvious, Molly," she says. "Just say it."

My hands are shaking, and my palms are sweaty. That knot has returned to my stomach, and I'm positive my face is now as white as a picket fence. My breathing is getting shaky, and I'm suddenly worried I might have a panic attack right here in Cara's passenger seat.

"Say what?" I squeak out.

She's watching me, looking confused now. What the hell does she think I'm not telling her?

"Just admit it, Molly, you are in love with Adam. I could see it the first time I saw you two together and can hear it in your voice every time you mention him. How else do you explain why you've been so torn up over not hearing from him?"

Color rushes back into my face as I process what she's said. She's talking about Adam, not the current status of my mental health.

"Yeah," I say, sounding almost relieved. "I mean, yeah, I really care for him. Maybe I even love him, but none of that

264

matters anymore. You can't make someone love you back, which is obviously the case in this situation."

Cara frowns. I know she wants me to be happy, but right now I just can't be. And there's no point in sugarcoating what's happening. It is what it is, right?

Opening her door, Cara squeezes between the two cars, stopping to wait for me near her trunk. Taking a deep breath, I open the door and suck in as much as possible to fit between Cara's car and the car parked on my side, meeting her at the bumper.

We spend the next two hours scouring every store on State Street, trying to find something, anything, that will work for a costume. Thank goodness I have Cara with me. She is the queen of throwing together cute outfits, and her ability to piece together an adorable Halloween costume out of thin air is pretty remarkable. Unfortunately, my heart just isn't in it. Halloween has been my favorite holiday since I've lived in this small town, but this year I don't really care if I go out or not.

"You have your pick of about a dozen costumes, Molly," Cara says as we begin our trek back up to the car. "You're going to have to choose something."

"I know," I say, shoving the straw from my cup into my mouth. This guava smoothie can usually cure any funk I'm in, but today it's lost its magic.

"Okay, let's narrow this down to make it easier," she says, holding up her hand. "My three favorites were the pirate wench,

Little Bo Peep, and the angel. What do you say? Do you like one of those better than the others?"

Thinking for a moment, I consider Cara's costume. She's dressing up like a sexy referee this year and is seriously rocking her costume. She looks amazing in anything she puts on, but the dress she got coupled with her perfect figure make for a costume that's going to get her a lot of free drinks that night.

"Um," I say, trying to delay making a decision. "I guess I'll go with the angel."

"Yay," says Cara, clapping her hands. "That's the one I was hoping you'd choose. You look fantastic in that white dress. Plus, I have the perfect makeup to make you absolutely glow."

At least one of us is excited about this.

We walk back to the boutique where Cara's pieced together the angel costume, and she retrieves the short white sundress, the silver stilettos, and the package containing a crystal-encrusted set of angel wings. This is definitely the most beautiful costume I've ever worn.

On the drive home, Cara speaks quickly, listing off our itinerary for Thursday night. "Then after Jorge's house, we'll stop by Veronica's party and finish up the night at Mike's. Sound good?" She looks at me, anxiously awaiting my response. Any other year, I would be thrilled to pieces about our lineup. The sheer number of parties we have to hit up and all the people we'll see on the last Halloween of our college careers would have been enough to leave pre-Adam Molly counting down the days and anxious beyond belief. Post-Adam Molly is anxious but for completely different reasons. I dread having to make small talk and can think of nothing worse than being surrounded by that many people all night.

"Sounds good," I say, trying to sound convincing.

I must be a better actress than I think because Cara buys my response and goes right back to talking about how epic Thursday night will be. I'm losing the ability to really care about much of anything, especially Halloween night, even if this is my last one here. I really don't want to go out and have to deal with guys trying to rub up on me while they do something that only partially resembles dancing.

Staring out the window, I watch house after house pass by, each no doubt filled with a happy family living out their perfect lives in this beachside town. It's just another reminder that no matter what I do, no matter where I go, I'll never have a normal life. I will never be normal. Because even with the proper medication, I'll never rid myself of the mental illness controlling my brain.

I will never be normal.

CHAPTER 34

ADAM

Six days. It's been six days since I last saw Molly. I've spent the whole last week trying to shake her from my mind, but where I normally would find solace in running, that's turning out to be far from the case now. Every time I run, I see things that remind me of her. The bright-pink peonies in the yard down the street, the waves crashing on the beach. I hold my breath every time I pass a female runner, wondering if it's her. It never is. I'm not sure what I'll do if one day I do encounter her on the jogging path, but for now, I hold out hope and worry that I'll see her there one day.

The past two days have been overcast, the sun never managing to get hot or bright enough to burn off the marine layer, leaving the town in an uneasy shadow that's quite fitting for my current mood.

Halloween is the busiest night of the year around here, and given that I have nothing else to do, I've volunteered to work a double shift and help cover the chaos with the night crew.

I haven't received a text from Molly in days, and I assume she must have gotten the picture and decided to leave me alone. I hope she knows this isn't her fault. I hope one day she realizes how much better off she is without me.

Since running isn't offering any relief lately, I'm headed to the gym this morning to lift weights and push myself until I can't feel my arms or legs anymore. Maybe if I have a physical pain to focus on, I won't have to think about the constant pain in my gut.

The gym is relatively empty today, just a few of what I can only guess are stay-at-home moms on some of the machines and a handful of guys lifting in the corner. And as always, there's that one guy who's not really working out—mostly just checking himself out in the mirrors. Yeah, he's here too, and he sure does enjoy looking at himself. What a cheese dick.

Scouring the room, I locate an open bench as far away from everyone else as possible. The last thing I need right now is anyone trying to talk to me.

Dropping my bag beside the bench, I adjust the weights to do some bench presses. Two hundred pounds. I typically lift more, but sticking with my theme of being alone, I'd rather not need a spotter while working out today.

Lying on my back, I adjust my position beneath the bar and make sure my grip is secure. Then, just like so many times before, I lift the bar from its resting place and bring it down to my chest, then lift it again. *Five, six, seven, eight, nine, ten, down.*

Resting for a minute before starting the next rep, I force my mind to stay focused on the weights. I haven't lifted in a while, so I can already feel the ache in my muscles. It's good, though. I welcome the pain. Sometimes that's the only way I know it's working. The only way I know I'm still here.

Resuming my grip on the bar, I lift it, lower it, then press it straight up ten times, lowering it back down again before taking another rest. One minute rest. Ten presses. One minute rest. Ten presses.

By the fifth rep, the muscles in my arms are burning, but I don't care. I push through it. Beads of sweat gather on my forehead, my chest, and my back. My shirt is moist and sticking to my body, but I don't give it a second thought.

Returning my hands to the bar, I get ready for my last set of reps. Lifting the bar from the rest, I take a deep breath in and my world comes crashing down.

Hopscotch. Bikes. Jump rope. The giggles of small children. The screeching of tires. The thud of a body hitting the car. Screams, most of which are mine. Standing on the side of the road, frozen. Running to the car. Pushing with all my might to lift it off him. He's not breathing. He's turning blue. And blood. So much blood. I'm pushing as hard as I can but nothing happens. He's still stuck there. I'm screaming. Then someone's grabbing my shoulders and pulling me back, yanking me away from the car. Away from him. I was supposed to hold his hand. I should have. I let go to grab a quarter from the sidewalk. A quarter. Is that all his life was worth to me? Twenty-five cents? Twenty-five shitty cents. Nothing. And now he's gone.

Everything is black. I can't see. Are my eyes open?

Voices around me. The guys from the other bench? The douche prancing around in front of the mirror? The ladies on the treadmills? I don't recognize the voices, but they're there. Something is happening. *What the hell is happening?*

Lights. Bright lights beating down on me. My eyes open, and I'm surrounded by seven people. There's concern in their eyes. Or is that pity? Fear?

Someone is yelling. Screaming, in fact. Did I drop the bar on myself? Who the hell is screaming? Is that me?

I try to sit up but can't. Is the bar on me? I dropped the bar on myself, didn't I?

Shifting my head slightly, I can see the bar resting safely above me. Why can't I sit up?

Hands. There are hands on me. Who the hell is touching me? What the hell is happening?

Then it hits me. I must have been screaming. These people

must think I'm having some kind of psychotic episode. Shit. Shit. Shit.

"I'm okay," I whisper. It takes all I have to get those words out. Why can't I talk?

"Dude, are you okay?" asks the douche.

"Yes," I croak.

"Did you just have a seizure?" asks the woman using the StairMaster nearest my bench.

I shake my head. "No, no, I'm fine," I say, my voice a little stronger.

"Just lie still," says one of the guys who was lifting across the gym. His hands are on my left arm, holding me down. There's another set of hands on my right arm. This must be another of the guys lifting.

Struggling to free my arms, I try to convince them I'm okay, but they aren't buying it. "Lie still and wait here until the ambulance arrives," says another woman I don't recognize.

The ambulance? I cannot let the paramedics get here and see me. We work together. They know me. Five minutes after they get here I can expect everyone in my department to know what's happened.

"I'm really okay," I say. "I must have dropped the bar or strained something. I'm so sorry for making you all worry."

The grip on my left arm lets up, and I retrieve my arm, rubbing my wrist with my right hand as soon as the guy on that side lets go. Sitting up, I look at the strangers surrounding me and feel the humiliation welling inside. How did this just happen? How the hell did this happen?

Lifting my bag from the floor, I stand, praying my legs won't give out. Thankfully, they don't. With wobbly knees, I thank the people surrounding me one more time and head toward the front doors. They all stand there staring. I think they might be in shock. Maybe confused? Or terrified? They don't understand what just happened, and they seem unsure of what to do.

Pushing through the door, I stumble to my car and slide behind the driver's seat, starting the ignition and backing out of my spot. I'm turning out into traffic when I hear sirens in the distance. Just in time.

Five minutes later, I'm pulling into my driveway, climbing out of my car, and walking up the driveway to my house. Once I'm inside, I'll be okay. I'll feel okay. I can deal with this.

Before I can reach the front door, I see Mrs. Mitchell standing in her front yard with a hose, watching me. This is definitely not what I need right now.

I force the best smile I can, plaster it across my face, and wave at Mrs. Mitchell. "Hello, Mrs. Mitchell. Beautiful day today, huh?"

She scowls at me, then turns her back and continues watering her lawn.

"Have a great day!" I shout as cheerily as possible before turning to open my front door. If I didn't know better, I'm pretty sure I heard an expletive leave her mouth. So much for the sweet old lady down the street.

Dropping my bag in the entryway, I take the few necessary steps to reach the couch and drop down onto it. Closing my eyes, I lie back and rest my head on a pillow.

Seventeen years. It's been seventeen years since the accident. Seventeen years tomorrow. How has it been seventeen years since I last saw Jake? Since I last spoke with him?

Some days my life feels like a nightmare I'll never wake up from, even more so the past few weeks. It's like everything is crumbling around me.

I'll never be able to show my face at the gym again after today. I'll need to find a new place to go or stick with running and workouts I can do here at home. My world is shrinking. Just thinking that feels dramatic, but it's true. Piece by piece, I'm losing control of my life. First it was certain running paths that triggered flashbacks. Now it's the gym. What next? How much more can I lose before I completely lose myself?

The house is silent even if my mind isn't. Maybe if I hold my breath or try hard enough, I can clear my mind and relax. Who am I kidding? The only way to clear my mind completely would be to stop the thoughts from coming. And the only way to do that is to make a very permanent decision I'm still not sure I'm ready to make.

My limbs are slowly feeling heavier, and my body is finally relaxing. My brain is spinning, but I can feel myself slipping into sleep. With any luck, I'll sleep until Friday so I can bypass

Thursday completely.

If only it were that easy.

CHAPTER 35

MOLLY

Halloween. It's finally here. The day I used to count down to each year. Cara and I did a practice run of our costumes and makeup last night, which kind of helped get me into the mood for the holiday, but my heart still isn't there. Hopefully by the time tonight rolls around, I'll be feeling better and ready to party.

Thursdays are a slow day. I only have two classes to attend today. It feels like the day is dragging on. The minutes feel like hours, the hours like lifetimes.

After my classes, I head back to our apartment to take a nap so I'll be well rested for tonight. Hopefully with enough sleep, I'll feel less overwhelmed and more ready to have a good time. Hopefully.

As soon as I'm through the front door, I lock it behind me. Then I double-check it. Then check it again just to be sure.

Dropping my book bag beside my desk chair, I open my laptop and log into my email. When I turned in my application for the Professional Writing distinction in my major, they told me they'd send out an email to let us know if we were accepted the last week in October. Well, it's October 31, and I have yet to receive anything. I'm not sure if that's a good or bad thing. Probably a bad thing.

Aside from a few emails from online boutiques I like to shop, there's nothing new in my inbox. Dang it. I was hoping to get my answer today. Maybe they're running behind in making their decision. Or maybe I didn't receive one because I didn't get in.

I have reading to do, but I'm not in the mood. In fact, I've lost interest in doing schoolwork of any kind. I'm on track to graduate, and I know I need to pass these classes in order to do so, but right now I really don't care. Whatever happens, happens.

Walking into the kitchen, I fill a glass with water from the fridge and stand there, trying to decide if I want anything to eat. I'm not really hungry. Did I eat breakfast this morning? I can't even remember.

Turning around, I head back toward the bedroom. Maybe a nap will help me snap out of this. I haven't been sleeping well lately anyway, so taking a nap definitely can't do any harm. Come to think about it, I am pretty tired.

Passing the front door, I make my way toward the bedroom, then stop. I know I locked that door when I came home. Right? Yeah, I did. But am I sure? Um, yes. Maybe? Crap. No, I'm not sure. What if when I jiggled the handle the door unlocked? What if I unlocked it without realizing what I was doing and now it's just sitting there unlocked? I'll never be able to sleep unless I know that door is locked.

The door is locked. I locked it when I came home. I even checked it twice. It's locked.

Yeah, but what if it's not? What is checking it going to hurt? At least I'll have peace of mind that everything is okay so I don't have to lie in bed worrying about it.

No, I can do this. The door is locked.

Okay, so maybe you thought you locked it. But have you ever thought you locked it just to realize you didn't? You can't trust yourself. You're not perfect. You forget things all the time. Just check it.

I'm confident I locked the door, but there's enough doubt in my mind. If checking it means peace of mind, why not just do it and be done with the whole thing? Yeah, I'll check it and then take a nap.

Walking to the door, I can see the lock is flipped into the locked position, but I still reach out and jiggle the handle. Okay, it's locked. I stand staring at the lock for a good ten seconds just to be sure. Yes, it's locked.

Okay, I did what I had to do, now I'm going to sleep.

Walking into my bedroom, I stop once more. I did make sure it was locked, right? I mean, I know I wouldn't have walked away from it if it wasn't. But I did lock it, didn't I?

If I stand just right, I can see the front door from my room. The lock is flipped up, which means it's locked. Locked. LOCKED! *Now stop thinking about it and just go to sleep.*

Closing my eyes, I do my best to relax my body. It's actually not that hard—I'm exhausted. It's my brain I'm having trouble shutting off. As soon as my head hits the pillow, a huge to-do list starts running through my mind. Will I have time to get it all done?

Going through my mental checklist, I try to be rational. Clearly, vacuuming the apartment can wait until tomorrow or this weekend, as can ironing my little black dress.

Calm down. Focus on slowing down your heart rate. Breathe in. Breathe out.

It's useless. My heart is racing just as fast as my mind. Should ·I take a melatonin to help me along? No, that has bad idea written all over it.

I really want to text Adam and see what he's doing. I wonder if he's going out tonight. No way. I bet he's working.

Stop thinking about him. It just makes things worse. Get him out of your head.

Sitting up, I swing my legs over the side of the bed and drop my head into my hands. I am mentally and physically exhausted.

I don't even know what to do with myself at this point. It's like my body is shutting down, starting with my ability to reason. And my ability to care. So then is my body shutting down, or is it my brain?

I slide off of my bed and cross the room to my desk, flipping open my laptop and pulling up my email. There's a new one at the top from the English department. This is it.

Clicking on the email, it opens, and I scan down quickly in search of the words I've been waiting three years to read. Only they're not there.

Dear Miss Taylor,

We appreciate your interest in our program and recognize all of your hard work; however, we regret to inform you that due to a high number of overly qualified applicants, we are unable to accept you into our program at this time.

I can't read anymore. I can't believe this is happening. How is this happening? All my hard work, all for nothing? Everything was riding on me being accepted into this specific program and receiving this distinction.

My whole world is crashing down around me. What am I going to do now? My tentative job—gone. Everything I've planned for is over. What do I do now?

There's a sound at the door. Jingling keys? The door opens,

and there's Cara. Thank everything holy.

"Hey, girl," she says, dropping her bag beside the front door. "Are you about ready to get this party started?"

With everything I have, I force a smile. *Try harder. She's never going to believe that.*

"Let's do this," I say, hoping that if I try hard enough, I can salvage the night after all.

* * *

Three hours later, we're decked out in our costumes and ready to go. Cara's legs have never looked longer, thanks to her short skirt and knee-high socks. Complete with her hair pulled back into a baseball cap and a whistle around her neck, she is poised to be the life of any party we attend. That's Cara for you—always the showstopper. Tonight more than ever, I'm feeling like her sidekick. We might as well roll up to all these parties on a motorcycle with me in the sidecar.

With Cara's help, my makeup is absolutely flawless tonight. My eyelids are covered in silver sparkles with tiny crystals dotting the corners of my eyes. Fake eyelashes make my eyes pop bright, and the perfect red hue makes my lips look extra kissable. I just wish there was someone who wanted to kiss these lips.

My white dress, hitting midway to my knees, fits me like a glove and accentuates my curves. And the silver stilettos match perfectly with my eyeshadow, adding to my sparkle. And these angel wings. They are definitely the most beautiful piece of this costume. Encrusted with crystals, they sparkle brightly in even the faintest light, giving the illusion that I'm actually glowing. On second thought, maybe I'll be the one to steal the show tonight.

"Wow," says Cara as I step into the living room, clutch in hand, ready to go. "You look amazing!"

"Thanks," I say, still a little unsure of myself, but I'm determined to have fun tonight, no matter what it takes. So starting now, I'm plastering a smile across my face and going to fake it till I make it. "Are you ready to do this thing?"

With a whoop, whoop, Cara throws her hands in the air and screams. "To the best night of our college careers!"

Yeah, one can only wish.

As we step out into the moonlight, it's clear there is already a lot of foot traffic out in the neighborhood. There is loud laughing coupled with excited voices and the intermittent whistle and catcall. This is Halloween in our small town—everyone's favorite night of the year.

Cara links her arm through mine, giggling as we pass people on the street. The girl dressed as a witch must be a freshman and not have gotten the memo that tonight is about looking good, not scary. We pass a handful of sexy Little Bo Peeps, a girl dressed like a butterfly, another dressed like a mobster, and still another dressed in a thigh-high dress and tall white boots—a go-go dancer, maybe? Guys don't have to worry so much about their costumes. I see a James Bond, someone who's clearly from *Magic*

Mike, and a guy I can only guess is supposed to be Al Capone.

The scene is chaos walking the streets, but somehow there's order here. Everyone is smiling and happy, some obviously drunk already. As we pass a frat house, we see a guy puking in the bushes while a girl dressed in lingerie with a set of ears on her head (a mouse, maybe?) pats his back. Red cups held upside down, people pass from party to party, making sure to see and be seen. This is the night people wait all year for around here. There's almost a magical feeling in the air, like anything can happen.

I allow myself to get caught up in the excitement, laughing along with Cara at the costumes we deem pathetic, trying to guess what some people are, and picking out the Halloween greenies. They're easy to spot since they're the ones who seem a little too excited to be out and about.

Turning down the street, we head toward a brown house three doors down. Music is blaring from every direction, making it difficult to identify where the parties are. To be honest, there's probably some kind of party at every house on this block.

"This one," says Cara, pointing toward a house with six different silver cars crammed into the driveway. Nodding my head, I keep my arm linked with hers and take a deep breath. I can do this.

The door opens right in front of us, and a group of people files out, laughing and chugging what's left in their cups before opening the gate and stepping out onto the street.

As soon as we're inside, I can feel the bass from the song boom through my body. Cara waves at someone, and we beeline for the keg in the kitchen. Grabbing a cup, Cara passes it to a guy dressed like a cowboy. He fills it up using the proper technique to ensure it's more beer than fizz, then hands it to her. He's clearly not a freshman. He's done this before.

He points to me, then motions toward the cups, asking if I'd like a drink too. I shake my head and wave my hands to make sure he knows my answer is no. I've never had a drink in my twenty-one years, and don't intend on starting tonight.

Nodding his head in understanding, he turns his attention to a girl dressed like a bird—a parrot maybe—and fills her cup with the foaming liquid.

Cara grabs my arm and pulls me toward the living-room dance floor. A new song starts on the sound system, and everyone lets out a shout of excitement before starting to dance. Cara joins in, holding her full cup high in the air before lowering it to her mouth and taking a large gulp. Within minutes she's in need of a refill, so we push our way back into the kitchen and pass her cup to the designated filler.

Twenty minutes later, we've made our way through the party and said hi to everyone we need to see there, Cara is three drinks in, and it's obvious she's feeling good. She's laughing and smiling and carrying on with anyone and everyone she sees. Guys are literally flocking to us, hoping for a chance to talk with her, or, God willing, dance with her. She takes it all in stride, acknowledging each guy but maintaining a tight grip on my arm.

Watching her, I can't help but feel jealous. She's having so much fun. She's making memories she'll never forget on our last Halloween here, and I'm tagging along, struggling to keep a smile on my face, while no guy in this place has given me even the slightest acknowledgment. What does she have that I don't? Well, other than the model-perfect looks and legs that go on for miles.

Her laughter is infectious. Her inhibitions gone, she's letting the night carry her where it will. I want that.

"Let's head over to Veronica's now," she shouts even though she's standing about two inches away from me. Nodding in approval, I grab her hand and follow her toward the front door. Out in the cool night air, I realize how freaking hot it was in there. I'm pretty sure half of what I thought were sparkles covering my body are actually beads of sweat.

We head down the block toward the bluffs, the crowds lining the sidewalk growing thicker and spilling out into the streets. This is where the police tend to set up shop and try to keep students from getting hit by cars, weeding out those too intoxicated to be left to their own devices.

Cara is nearly skipping down the street. "It's that white house right there," she says, pointing about halfway down the block to a front yard crammed full of people.

Pushing our way through bodies, we reach the front door and step inside. Just like the last house, this house is hot and filled with people. Between the music and the voices, there is an almost constant roar in the air, making it hard to hear anything less than a scream.

"This way," Cara mouths, pulling me toward the kitchen. As always, it's easy to spot the professional keg tapper filling cups on demand. Cara grabs a cup and shoves it at him, happily retrieving it when it's full. The guy looks at me, and I start to shake my head. Then I stop.

What if I just let go tonight? What if I just let it all go and take a chance? I've lost Adam, and I don't really care what happens from here. I've never felt this way before, and I just want to stop feeling. I've said I'll do whatever it takes to have the best night ever, and maybe this is what it takes.

Grabbing a cup from the counter, I hand it to the guy, who accepts it and fills it with brown liquid. I can feel Cara's eyes on me as I take it back from him without looking at her.

"Umm, excuse me!" she shouts, motioning toward the cup. "What the hell is this about?"

Shrugging my shoulders, I stare at the cup. Here goes nothing.

Holding the cup to my lips, I tip it back and feel the carbonated contents hit my tongue. This is not at all what I expect beer to taste like. I hear constantly how delicious it is. Maybe this is the wrong kind because this is freaking disgusting. I'd really like to hold my nose, but even I know that goes against party etiquette.

Cara's eyes are wide. She's known me for over three years now. I don't drink. I'm sure she's wondering why the hell I've just up and grabbed a cup tonight.

"To the best night ever, right?" I shout. Cara smiles and lifts her cup to meet mine. "Bottoms up!"

Tilting my head back, I open my throat and let the fizzy liquid roll down, trying my best not to taste it. When my cup is empty, I hand it back to the guy at the keg and wait for him to refill it.

Cara is obviously in shock but I think a little excited at the same time. She finally has a drinking buddy.

"Let's do this!" she screams, pulling me toward the dance floor.

Maybe this is extra-potent beer, or maybe it's because I haven't eaten much of anything today, but within twenty minutes, my head is buzzing. The smile on my face is no longer forced as I sway back and forth, channeling the music blaring out over the sound system.

Forty minutes and two more cups later, the room is spinning in the best way. I've suddenly become the world's best dancer, sashaying my hips around. All eyes are on me, and I know it. I'm glowing and floating and can see every guy around us watching. I'm amazing. For the first time in my life, I feel amazing. I'm free. I don't have to worry about anyone else, just myself. I'm going to be happy.

Cara grabs my arm and pulls me toward the front door,

where we're met by a group of people pushing their way into the party. I'm pretty sure a guy grabbed my butt, but I can't really be sure. It's like there's a strobe light following me around and everything is happening in intermittent flashes. Some guy winks at me—that's got to be who grabbed me. He's cute, but I'm not sure how I feel about the unwelcome touching.

Back on the sidewalk, Cara and I strut our stuff down the street. I'm flying high. Why have I waited so long to give this drinking thing a try?

Two blocks over we've finally reached the line of houses sitting high on the bluffs. The waves breaking on the beach below echo up and down the street. They must be crashing hard if I can hear them over the sound of the thousands of people filling the street tonight.

This must be Mike's house. I don't know what time it is, but it feels late, and I know this is where we're supposed to end the night. Also, I've never been to this house before, so it seems logical it's Mike's.

Reaching for my hand, Cara pulls me toward the house. This party is definitely more packed than all the others, most likely due to location. We have to fight our way in, but most of the guys we pass lift their arms in retreat, stepping back to give us a good once-over before moving out of the way and letting us through. Given their disgusted looks, it's obvious all the other girls hate us. This is amazing. This must be what it feels like to be Cara every night.

As we walk through the door, we're greeted by hundreds of people who by the end of the night will be our best friends. Dancing our way to the kitchen, we locate the keg, get a drink, and take to the dance floor.

Lights flash to the beat of the music. Mike and his roommates have pulled out all the stops on this party. In every direction, I spot people I recognize. I remember him from the dorms, her from that drama class I took my sophomore year, and those two from my English discussion group last year. This party is amazing! It's like a walk down memory lane. It's late enough that everyone is pretty buzzed. I hear two girls behind us talking, their speech slurred. Surely we don't sound that sloppy.

Leaning in so her lips are practically touching my ear, Cara shouts that she sees Mike and asks if I want to go with her. Do I want to go and watch them make out? No, thanks.

"I'll stay here," I yell, throwing my arms in the air and spinning around.

Cara laughs and points to her wrist, signaling she'll be back in a few minutes. Nodding my head, I let my body move to the beat of the music. I'm light and floating, soaring above the party with my angel wings. But somehow I'm also heavy and empty. I feel my smile fading as I remember what I have to be sad about. Adam. The writing program. Just when things were going so well, they've crashed down like broken windows all around me, trapping me with shattered glass. What am I going to do now?

I didn't watch where Cara went, and I can't spot her

anywhere right now. My vision is blurry, and everything is happening in those broken strobe-light-like increments. I see faces around me smiling and laughing. Why do they get to be so happy and I don't?

Turning in a circle, I instantly feel dizzy and begin to lose my balance.

"Whoa," says a voice from behind me as I feel a pair of warm hands grab hold of my waist and help me regain my balance.

"Thanks," I say, turning around to see who's rescued me, hoping it's someone I know.

It's definitely someone from my past, but not at all who I expect to see.

"Don't touch me," I say, stepping backward and crashing into someone dancing behind me. A girl dressed like a skanky peacock turns around and glares at me before turning back to dance with her friends.

I'm surrounded by hundreds of people, but suddenly feel like I'm completely alone. It's only me and Todd.

Todd standing in front of me, his hands reaching for me again.

I'm dizzy and think I might fall down or throw up. Am I having a panic attack? Am I just imagining this? This can't really be happening.

Todd's mouth is turned up in a smile, and I can see he's genuinely pleased to have found me. And just his luck—I'm drunk and alone with no help in sight.

"I was hoping I'd find you here tonight," he hisses. The smile remains, only it's twisted into something sinister. A sneer?

"Leave me alone, Todd," I say, turning around to go somewhere, anywhere, that he's not.

"Hey, hey, Mol," he says, grabbing hold of my right arm. "Where are you running off to so quickly? I believe we have some unfinished business."

My head is spinning so fast I can't keep my balance any longer. My legs give out, and suddenly I'm crashing toward the ground. Reaching out to grab hold of anyone and anything I can, I come up empty-handed and know I'm going to hit the ground. Just then, I see the guy dancing behind me throw his arm back in some weird dance move and feel a pain in my left temple as everything goes black.

CHAPTER 36

ADAM

In true Halloween fashion, there has not been a reprieve in the chaos tonight. If I'm not stopping someone for carrying an open container of alcohol, I'm cuffing the guy peeing in the bushes or helping steady the arm of a coed clearly too drunk to be out walking. We have a van out here tonight transporting people to the jail to sit in the drunk tank since it's impossible for us to drive through the overwhelming crowds in our patrol cars.

I've been stationed at my post on this block for the past five hours, and there appears to be no end to the craziness. I remember my first Halloween on these streets when I was in high school and snuck over here to check it out. It was insane and wonderful all at once, and I couldn't wait for my freshman year of college so I could really be a part of it all. There's something magical about Halloween here that makes the chaos infectious.

My first Halloween as an officer was much different. I still had friends attending the university and ended up arresting a handful of them for drunk and disorderly conduct. Needless to say, I haven't spoken to those guys since.

It took me becoming an officer to realize how dangerous this night really is. Girls walking around wasted, unable to protect themselves from the predators among them who want nothing more than to take advantage of them. Guys thinking it's a good idea to ride their bikes while intoxicated, crashing into groups on the sidewalk, leaving multiple people injured and the girl riding on the handlebars in the hospital. And don't get me started on alcohol poisoning.

As an officer, I'm responsible for the safety of this community and everyone in it. It's unfortunate the college students see our presence here as a buzzkill and inconvenience rather than an added measure of safety. Maybe someday they'll be grateful we were here to stop them from getting behind the wheel of that car or going home with the wrong guy, but until then, we continue to flood the streets every October 31 in hopes of protecting them from themselves.

There's a party down the block I've had my eye on that seems to be getting a little out of hand. We're nearing the two-o'clock curfew, when all music has to shut off and parties must end, so I've decided to station myself closer to the house in case things don't go smoothly when the residents shut things down.

Girls in short skirts and shirtless guys with oiled-up muscles pass by. It's pretty comical, actually, like everyone is trying to rev up their pheromones on this night in hopes of attracting the opposite sex. Come to think of it, that's basically what every night in this small town is, but Halloween is when they can get away with anything.

Checking my watch, I note the time: 1:58 Two more minutes and things will get worse before they get better as people stumble down the street, heading home from wherever they've ended the night.

Glancing down the street, I can already see an increase in the foot traffic on the sidewalks. Hernandez is one block east of me working traffic control, preventing any cars from getting back this far. Smith is a block south of me, cuffing a guy with a nosebleed who's yelling at another guy sitting on the sidewalk bleeding from a head wound.

As two o'clock hits, the music shuts off and the streets go silent, the only sounds the crashing waves and the partygoers slowly emptying into the streets and starting their long walk home.

Guests begin filtering out of the house I've had my eye on, falling in line with everyone else on the streets. One by one, I see the bloodshot eyes of the drunk, tired students who pass me, some glaring at me, others trying to pretend they're sober, while still others are completely oblivious to the fact I'm even here.

After ten minutes, the last few stragglers exit the house. That was definitely easier than I thought it would be.

A girl steps through the front door, frantically looks through the yard, then walks back into the house. She's wearing a striped dress, baseball cap, and knee-high white socks, and if I didn't know any better, I'd say it was Cara, Molly's roommate. But I'm sure it isn't.

Maintaining my post, I watch the streets slowly empty as everyone goes home. The girl steps back out onto the front steps, shouting something. She has a guy with her now, and they're both shouting.

Taking steps toward the house, I listen to pick up on what they're yelling. Is that a name?

Walking up the driveway, I watch both go back into the house, the girl screaming now.

"Molly!"

Molly? Maybe that was Cara.

Quickening my pace, I reach the front door and knock. It takes a minute for someone to open the door, and they don't look too excited to see me.

"I just saw a man and woman out here looking for someone. Do you guys need some help?" I ask.

The guy stares at me blankly—definitely drunk, probably high, and very much confused.

"Is Cara here?" I ask.

The guy turns around and motions toward the girl in the striped dress.

"Cara?" I shout. The girl turns around, looking confused at first, then relieved.

"Oh, my gosh, Adam, is that you?" she asks, rushing toward me.

"Yeah, is something wrong?"

"I lost Molly," she says. Her mouth is moving a mile a minute as she spits out a story about leaving Molly on the dance floor to find Mike, then not being able to find her and not knowing where she went. She tells me that Molly was drunk—that she's never had alcohol before—and didn't know if she was okay. With every word, she grows increasingly more panicked. Grabbing her shoulders, I try to bring her back to reality.

"Hey, Cara, we are going to find Molly."

She nods gratefully, tears in her eyes. "I just have a feeling something bad's happened to her."

"I understand," I say. My heart is racing, but I'm trying to keep my head straight. "Can I come in?"

"Yes, of course," Cara says, holding the door open for me. The guys left in the house look at me nervously.

"Have any of you seen Molly?" I ask them. Each shakes their head, looking away and avoiding eye contact.

Turning back to Cara, I ask if they've checked all of the rooms in the house.

"No," she says. "We checked the ones down here but not upstairs."

"Let's go up and check them," I say.

Cara is visibly shaking, so I put my hand on her arm and turn her to face me. "I promise we are going to find her, okay? We are going to find her, and she's going to be okay."

"Okay," she says, nodding as if trying to convince herself to believe me.

We start the climb up the stairs, kicking beer cans and empty cups out of the way on each step. At the landing, I can see that there are four bedrooms, two on either side, with a bathroom at the end of the hall. Starting on the left, we open the first two bedroom doors, finding them empty.

The bathroom is empty. Bedroom three is empty. Reaching for the doorknob on bedroom four, I think I hear movement inside. The knob won't turn—it's locked. Knocking on the door, I announce myself and ask whoever's inside to please open the door. No response. The movement within stops. Someone doesn't want me to know they're in there.

Knocking again, I tell the person inside to open the door, asking if Molly Taylor is in the room. Again, no answer.

"Cara, go find out who's room this is and have them open the door for me, please," I say. It's likely the resident of the room is inside smoking pot or having sex, but if he's not, this might be where Molly is.

Cara runs down the stairs as fast as she can, returning

297

moments later with a guy in tow, saying he's the owner of the room.

"Do you have a key?" I ask.

"Not out here," he says. "I only lock my room when I go out of town and leave the key inside the rest of the time."

"Did anyone ask to use your room?"

"No," he says. "I have no idea why anyone would lock themselves in my room. Nothing I own is worth enough for someone to waste their time stealing from me."

Knocking again, I still get no response.

Stepping back and getting into position, I slam my shoulder into the door as hard as I can. It doesn't budge. Winding up again, I hit the door one more time. This time it pops and the door swings open. There's a dark figure across the room on top of the bed. He looks over at me as I enter the room and jumps up as fast as he can. There's someone on the bed who's either asleep or passed out.

"What the hell is going on in here?" I ask the person jumping up from the bed.

As he steps toward me, the light from the hall crosses his face and I know who he is. And based on that, I know exactly who's lying motionless on the bed.

Rushing toward Todd, I drop him to his knees and cuff him before he even knows what hit him. He's yelling at me, calling me a stupid pig, saying his dad will fry me up like bacon in the courtroom if I don't let him go immediately. Ignoring him, I step toward the bed to find Molly with her eyes closed, unmoving. There's a bump on her head.

"What the hell happened to her?" I ask Todd.

He says nothing but just smiles at me.

"What the hell did you do to her?" I yell.

Bending down, I cradle Molly in my arms. I can see her dress has been torn and her underwear is exposed but still up over her hips and intact. Looking at Todd, I notice that his belt is undone, the top button on his jeans unbuttoned.

Yanking him up off of the ground, I give him one more chance. "You tell me right now what was going on here, or I'll throw your ass in jail."

Todd stares at me defiantly. He doesn't have to say anything. I already know what he was doing. From the looks of it, we stopped him before he achieved his intended goal, but I can't be sure.

"Molly," I say, shaking her gently. "Molly, it's Adam. Are you okay?"

Her eyelids flutter a bit before her eyes open slightly. "Where am I?" she asks, trying to sit up. She reaches for her head. "What happened to me?"

"What do you remember from tonight?" I ask.

"Cara went to find Mike. I was dancing alone. I tripped, and someone caught me." Her face goes white as she remembers what happened next. "It was Todd. Todd was there. He wanted to talk to me. I said no. I tried to get away. I don't know what happened next. What happened? What did he do to me?"

Keying up on my radio, I call dispatch. "Tango 587, I've got a 10-44 at 1048 Beach Street. Roll me one or two more, please."

Copy that, Tango 587. All units be advised we need 10-94 at 1048 Beach Street.

Several officers on the street respond, and within moments, Hernandez and Smith are in the room with me.

"What do we have here?" asks Hernandez, looking from Molly to Todd to me.

"The victim was knocked out when we found her. This guy was on top of her in what appears to be an attempt at a sexual assault."

At this point, tears are streaming down Molly's cheeks. She is starting to piece together what's happened to her, and I know it can't be easy. Someone she once trusted, someone she once loved, even, was just found over her lifeless body, preparing to assault her. That, in and of itself, is going to take her some time to process.

Todd sits on the floor, hands cuffed behind his back, staring at his feet. He's said nothing since we burst into the room. He just sits there looking either angry, void of emotion, or almost pleased with himself. There is something seriously wrong with this guy. I hope he can get the help he needs. And I hope this is the final straw in keeping him the hell away from Molly.

Molly stares at me in silence, and I wish I could read her mind. There is so much behind her eyes I feel like I should look away. But I can't. She's watching me with those eyes. Those deep-green eyes. She's looking for answers. But I've got nothing for her. Nothing but guilt. If I hadn't pushed her away, maybe she wouldn't have even been here tonight. Heaven knows she never would have been alone with Todd if I'd been here. And Todd never would have been in the picture had I not met her.

This is my fault. Completely my fault. And she knows it.

* * *

MOLLY

I'm lying on the bed in a room I don't recognize, surrounded by people I don't know, with Cara hunched over in the corner and Adam somewhere beside me. My eyes are closed as I struggle to process what's happened.

I was dancing. I know I was dancing. Cara said she needed to find Mike and left. Someone grabbed me. Todd. Todd grabbed me from behind. Then I got hit. Something hit me in the head.

Reaching my hand up, I gingerly touch the lump near my left temple and wonder what on earth hit me hard enough to do that.

Todd is in a heap on the floor, hands cuffed behind his back. An officer is preparing to load him into his car and take him to jail.

I was dancing, Todd grabbed me, something hit me, and now I'm here. With my dress flipped up, underwear intact, Todd's pants unbuckled.

I don't trust Todd at all to have done the right thing. I know if he'd had the chance, he would have raped me. I think that was probably his plan all along. He never got what he wanted from me, and this was his final attempt to take what he wanted. How did he go from someone I loved to this? How bad is my judgment that I actually cared about someone capable of something like this?

Adam stands across the room, barely looking at me.

I'm not sure if it's the hit to the head or all the beer I drank earlier, but my head is pounding, my stomach is doing flip-flops, and I'd really like to puke right now. Unfortunately, I'm lying on an unfamiliar bed, surrounded by strangers, and don't think any of them would appreciate watching me vomit.

Why did I decide to drink? Todd attacking me is not my fault—I know that. But maybe if I'd been sober, I could have fought back. I could have avoided him altogether. I feel like I've let myself and everyone else down. His actions are not my fault, but I feel at least partially responsible for what happened to me.

I wonder if Adam thinks that too. Or if now that this happened to me, I'm damaged goods and he's 100 percent done with me. He won't look at me because he's disgusted. This is all my fault. All my fault.

My breathing is getting faster, and I know there's no stopping it. No breathing exercises are going to slow this down. The freight train has left the station, and there's no stopping it now.

My throat is closing up. I'm breathing through a straw. I can feel eyes on me, but I can't do anything to stop what's about to happen.

My heart beats hard and fast in my chest, so much so I'm afraid it might pop right out of me. It hurts. It's beating too fast. What if this time I really do have a heart attack?

Cara is beside me, saying something, but I can't hear her. All I can hear is my racing heart and strained breathing. I sound like I'm drowning. Maybe I am drowning. Maybe this is it. Maybe this is the last time. Maybe this time my heart and breathing won't go back to normal and all of this will end. Is it bad that this thought is actually comforting?

Maybe it would be better if it all ended. If I was gone. Adam wouldn't have to be ashamed of dating me. Cara wouldn't have to worry about fixing my awkwardness. My parents wouldn't have to worry about my mental health and whether or not I'm ever going to be okay. And I wouldn't have to worry about anything. Ever again. I could finally be at peace.

I'm surrounded by every person in the room. Someone's calling for an ambulance. There are voices all around me, but I can't make out any words. Cara's face is frantic. Adam is once again beside me, his face so close to mine that if I lean forward ever so slightly, we'll be kissing. A goodbye kiss, perhaps?

My eyelids are heavy. My heart won't slow down. My breathing grows increasingly more shallow until nothing is getting through. Nothing.

Maybe this time I will die. Maybe this can finally be the last time.

And maybe, just maybe, this is my own personal yellow wallpaper. What if I'm the creeping woman and this is my chance to break free from the putrid yellow wallpaper once and for all? Yes, that must be it. I'm breaking through the bars. I'm finally free.

Here comes that curtain again, slowly falling and covering everything in darkness. Suddenly, all I see is black. And then I see nothing. It's over. It's really over. This is the end.

CHAPTER 37

ADAM

I'm calling out for an ambulance, trying to figure out what the hell is happening. Molly was okay, and then she wasn't. Her face went white, she started hyperventilating, and then she suddenly she passed out. I was standing beside her. I was right there. But it didn't matter.

Sirens blare in the distance. The ambulance is in front of the house. More police units pull up outside. Red and blue lights flash. She's not breathing. I'm pressing down on her ribs, trying desperately to keep her heart beating and bring her back. I can't lose her. Why is this happening? Why did I have to do this to her?

The heavy footfalls of steel-toed boots sound on the stairs, and in what feels like slow motion, the paramedics burst into the room. They push me to the side, asking for vitals. I'm watching myself from outside of my body as I choke out the words. "She started breathing fast, she was panicked, and then she was gone." What the hell is going on? This can't be real life.

She's on a stretcher, unresponsive. They're carrying her down the stairs, one medic on either end of the gurney. She looks so tiny. How have I never realized how small and helpless she is?

Staring down the stairway where I watch Molly disappear from view, I'm suddenly on my feet and moving. Bounding down the stairs, I hit the bottom and am out the door before I can even process what I'm doing. They're closing the doors to the ambulance, and it's pulling away. I'm not fast enough. I need to know she's okay. I need to be there when she wakes up. I need her to know I'm sorry.

Rushing to my patrol car down the street, I turn on my lights and siren and attempt to part the Red Sea as I weave through the party-going stragglers still wandering the streets of this small town. A few people look dazed as I drive by, my lights flooding their faces with red and blue flashes. It's the middle of the night, and most people are home by now, passed out, resting peacefully, or trying not to throw up. And here I am in my patrol vehicle, racing through the streets, trying to catch up to an ambulance on its way to the hospital. How did I get here? How is this my life right now?

Pulling up in front of the hospital, I throw my car into park and rush inside. Molly's been taken back to the ER, where they're working to stabilize her. She regained consciousness once in the ambulance but quickly passed out again. They're hopeful, but there are no guarantees.

No guarantees.

What the hell is happening? This was supposed to be a typical Halloween night, and now here I am standing in the emergency room at the hospital, wondering if someone I care very much about is going to survive.

She was fine. She was fine until she wasn't.

Collapsing into a chair in the waiting room, I let my head fall into my hands. Everything is happening in broken pieces, like shattered glass. Everything is shattering around me. Everything. I screwed up and pushed her away to protect her, and here she is in the hospital, fighting to live. What have I done? What the hell have I done?

A doctor appears, covered in scrubs and a hairnet, with a mask pulled down below his chin.

"She's going to be okay," I hear him say. "She's stabilized . . . some kind of traumatic incident . . . loss of consciousness . . . period of time without oxygen to her brain . . . no permanent damage . . . lucky you were there . . ."

Nodding in disbelief, I'm still trying to wrap my head around what the hell happened tonight. Todd. Molly. Emergency room.

My head is spinning.

Sarge shows up at the hospital to see how I'm doing and to check on Molly, then sends me home to get some sleep.

* * *

It's four in the morning, and I'm lying here with my eyes open, staring at the patterns on the ceiling. I couldn't do anything to help her. I left her in harm's way. What happened is my fault. It's all my fault. Jake. Hawthorne. Molly.

Would anyone miss me if I was gone? Would it make a difference? There will always be another young, eager officer ready and willing to fill my spot at the department. One who won't make decisions that lead to the death of another officer. My parents already act like they have no children left. I overheard my mom speaking on the phone one afternoon years ago, telling her friend how even though I'm here, it feels like I'm not. It's like they lost two sons that day. And I guess that's true. I'm not sure you can ever really come back from that. The pain, the guilt. It's never-ending. It's all-encompassing. It haunts every moment of my day, then comes back in horrible vivid flashbacks just to be sure I haven't forgotten what happened. What I am responsible for.

And Molly. Molly trusted me. I'm sure she figured spending time with a cop meant she'd be safe. But she was wrong. Look what it did for her—getting her assaulted by her ex-boyfriend, then admitted to the hospital after a touch-and-go ambulance ride. All my fault. It's all my fault. If I hadn't been around, this never would have happened. I am the common denominator between all these people, all these horrific events.

Hawthorne's family swears they don't blame me for what happened. But I know the truth, and I know they know too. It was my decision that put him in a position to be hit. If I hadn't been the officer in charge of the scene and given him bad directions, he'd still be here. He wouldn't have ended up a sitting duck, just waiting to be hit. Waiting to die.

It should have been me. It should have been me.

Damn it all to hell. It should have been me.

My feet hit the floor before I realize my body is moving. I'm shirtless and in gym shorts, but I don't care. I slap tennis shoes on my bare feet and fly out the front door, my legs moving as fast as they can, my feet pounding the pavement. No music today. Just the sound of the waves crashing on the beach in the distance, crickets chirping, and birds preparing for the morning.

Did I even lace up my shoes? Does it even matter?

I've run three miles before I start to feel the burning in my chest. My face is sweaty. I can feel it dripping down my back and neck, but I welcome the moisture. The cool, wet feeling. It should be refreshing, but today it's like every droplet of sweat is carving a path through my skin, cutting me to my core. Somehow I feel like I'm becoming even hotter from the sweat. Maybe they're really droplets of fire. That would explain the pain.

Dandelions. Yellow flowers. Yellow roses. It's happening again.

Run faster. Push harder. DO NOT STOP.

My body is screaming, but I can't slow down. I won't slow down. My lungs were burning only minutes ago, but now I feel nothing. Have I pushed past the threshold, or is my body shutting down?

Who the hell cares? Just keep running.

Lights are turning on in houses along my path, and people are backing cars out of their driveways to start another normal Friday morning at the office. I should be working, but it's not going to happen today. Sarge already knows. He knows I can't. I just can't do it today.

Car after car passes me on the street, but I hear nothing. Turning to watch one pass, I see the driver flip me off. Is he honking his horn? It must be broken because I can't hear a thing. Except for the ringing. Is that ringing in my ears? Can the drivers on the street hear it too?

Suddenly I'm aware that I'm in the middle of the road. I'm running in the middle of the road. How the hell did I get here? I was on the sidewalk only moments ago. Wasn't I?

Veering to the right, I step up onto the sidewalk, pushing myself to keep moving. My legs are like limp noodles, but as long as they're moving, I'll keep going. Is my breath getting stuck in my chest? I recognize this feeling. There's not enough oxygen getting into my lungs. I. Can't. Breathe.

My feet keep moving, but I think they might be slowing. I can't tell. Something is happening.

Cars pass me. They're all watching me. Everyone is looking. Waiting for me to crack. Waiting for me to slow down. Waiting for something to happen. And something is happening. What the hell is happening? What the hell is happening to me? Has my brain finally shut down? Have I run myself into such exhaustion that my body has given up?

No, that can't be possible. My legs are still moving. Fiery sweat cuts paths down my skin. Rivers and roads. Carving a map. A map of my pain. A map of my regrets. There is no reason for me to keep going. It doesn't matter anymore. Nothing matters anymore. It's all my fault. That's all that matters. It has to be over. I can't live with this anymore. I can't live like this anymore. I can't live anymore.

* * *

MOLLY

Where am I?

My eyes are closed, but I know I'm not in my own bed. There are too many beeps, too many voices to be alone in my room.

With eyelids fluttering, I will my eyes to open. My vision is blurred, and I can't really focus on anything, but my assumptions about not being in my own room are definitely true. I don't recognize anything here. Turning to my left, I try to pinpoint the source of the incessant beeping and realize I'm staring at a monitor keeping track of my heart rate and breathing. Am I in the hospital? What happened to me?

Struggling to sit up, I reach for my forehead and find a large bump. Did I hit my head? Have I lost my memory?

The monitor beside me begins beeping faster as the panic sets in. Am I hurt? Where is everyone?

Groping around on the bed, I finally locate what feels like a remote and start pressing buttons. Finally, I must have hit the right one, because a woman's voice comes through the speakers in the railing beside me.

"I'll send a nurse in now for you, Molly."

"Um, okay," I say quietly, hoping the nurse can give me some insight into what the hell is going on.

Moments later, a short, dark-haired woman enters the room. She has a full, hourglass figure that is somehow complemented by her scrubs and wears glasses with bright-blue frames that accentuate her bold-blue eyeshadow and vividly red lips.

"Hi, Molly," she says pleasantly as she enters the room. "How are you feeling?"

"I don't know," I stutter. "My head hurts, and I have no idea how I got here. What happened to me? Why am I here?"

"Sweetheart, you passed out at a party last night," she says with what sounds like genuine concern in her voice.

"Passed out?" I repeat. "Like I fainted?"

"No, honey," she says, shaking her head from side to side so her short dark curls bounce around her face. "You were hit in the head and knocked out. An officer found you locked in a room, at which point you woke up, hyperventilated, and passed out again."

"Where's Cara?" I ask, trying again to sit up until I feel a pulsing pain in my temple.

"Cara's your roommate, right?" she asks. "She's been sitting out in the waiting room all night, waiting for you to wake up. Do you want me to get her for you?"

"Yes, please," I say. Every word is like torture. My head really hurts. "Did she call my parents?"

"Yes," she says. "And from what I understand, they should be here anytime."

I'm not really sure what else to say. I want to ask her a million questions, but I'm not sure she can give me the answers I need.

"Can Cara come in here?"

"Sure, sweetie," says the nurse. "I'll go get her now. You sit back and take it easy. You sustained a really hard hit to your head and went through some pretty serious stuff last night. Right now, you really need your rest."

"Wait," I say, hoping to catch her before she's too far out of the room. She pops her head back in through the door and waits for me to go on. "Pretty serious stuff? What does that mean?"

"Maybe it's best if I send the doctor in to speak with you," she says.

"Why can't you tell me?"

"I'll go get the doctor," she says, and with that, she's gone.

Five minutes later, Cara rushes through the door and practically throws herself on me.

"Molly, I am so sorry!" she exclaims. "It's all my fault. I shouldn't have left you to find Mike. I'm sorry I was so selfish. I should have stayed with you. I'm so sorry. I'm so—"

"What are you talking about?" I ask, cutting her off.

Cara's mouth hangs open like she's searching for the right words to say but just can't find them.

A tall, thin woman with red hair walks through the door, the porcelain-like skin of her face and arms dotted with a handful of freckles. Cara startles as she enters the room and steps to the far side of the room to avoid getting in her way.

"Molly," says the doctor as she glances at my monitors. "I'm glad to see you're awake. Julie said you have some questions for me about what happened last night."

"Yeah, I do," I say, irritated that no one is telling me anything.

"From what we understand, you were drinking at a party with friends." She motions toward Cara, who looks down at the floor.

Drinking? Drinking. Oh, my gosh, that's right. I was drinking last night.

"You were left alone at one point," she continues, "and were approached by your ex-boyfriend, Todd."

Todd? I don't remember seeing—Oh, my gosh, it's all coming back to me. I saw Todd. He wanted to talk. I said no. Then something hit me in the head and everything went black.

"He claims he didn't hit you, that someone dancing near you swung their hand back while dancing and smacked you in the head. At any rate, you were hit on the head and knocked out, at which time he took you up to a bedroom. From what we understand, Cara went searching for you and located a police officer outside who came in and found you in the house. He knocked down the bedroom door, possibly stopping Todd from assaulting you."

"Assaulting me?" I ask, my voice shaking. "Like hitting me?"

"No," she says, glancing at my monitors again, probably so she doesn't have to look me in the eye while she explains this to me. "When the officer and other witnesses found you, your dress was hiked up, and his pants were undone."

"What?" I ask, my voice a shrill croak I don't recognize.

I look to Cara for answers, but her eyes remain on the floor, tears splattering her boots.

"We did an exam and tested for fluids, but from what we can see here, you were not raped. Your hymen is still intact, and no fluids were present."

My heart and mind are racing. How the hell did I go from a fun night out with friends to lying in a hospital bed with some doctor I've never met explaining to me the status of my hymen? This isn't happening. This can't be happening.

"You are lucky the officer found you when he did," she says, choosing not to further explain her point. No explanation is necessary.

With shaky hands, I push my hair behind my ears and try to focus on the happenings of the last few hours. Glancing at the clock, I see it's seven in the morning. The party ended at two. This must have happened at the end of the night. I can't remember anything well enough to paint a clear picture for myself. I knew Todd was an idiot, but I never imagined he'd resort to this.

"Where is Todd now?" I ask, very aware that he could be lurking the halls of the hospital.

"You don't need to worry," she says, taking a step toward me with her hand extended. "He's being held in the county jail. I doubt he'll be able to make bond."

Yeah, you clearly don't know his father.

"And my mom and dad are almost here?" I ask.

The doctor pauses for a moment, listening to what looks like a mini walkie-talkie, then looks at me with relief in her eyes. "They just checked in at the front desk and are on their way up now."

Nodding, I hold back the tears. I need my mom right now.

Moments later, my mom is bursting into the room, practically running to get to me. She throws her arms around me and holds me tight—tighter than she ever has before. Her chest rises and falls, and it's obvious she's crying; that's all it takes to send the silent tears streaming down my face. I hate that my parents have to go through this. I hate that my poor choices are resulting in their pain.

Dad stands beside my bed, awaiting his turn for a hug, then finally giving up on my mom ever letting go, wrapping his arms around both of us.

"I'm sorry," I whisper, choking on my tears. "I'm so sorry."

My dad pulls back abruptly and grabs hold of both of my arms, looking me straight in the eye. "None of this is your fault," he says firmly. "None of this. You understand that, right?"

I nod but am unsure how much I really believe it. I shouldn't have gone out feeling so lost. I shouldn't have chosen to drink. I should have stuck with Cara. Any and all of these separate events led up to what happened.

Where do I go from here? How am I expected to just go home and back to my classes like nothing ever happened?

"Can I speak with you for a moment?" asks Julie, stepping silently into the room.

"Um, sure," I say, pulling away from my parents.

"Would you mind stepping outside for a moment?" Julie asks, looking at my dad.

My parents exchange a confused look, and I'm pretty certain my face is mirroring that look. What does she have to say to me that she can't say in front of my parents?

"Do you want us to stay?" my mom asks with a furrowed brow.

Looking at Julie, then back to them, I shake my head. "No,

317

go ahead and go out," I say in an attempt to sound confident. "I'm okay."

Cara steps out of the room first, then my dad exits with my mom lingering behind a bit, clearly unsure whether she's comfortable leaving me here alone. I force a smile and nod, hoping it's enough to reassure her. It must be. She gives me one last look, then steps through the doorway into the hall.

Closing the door behind them, Julie turns toward me, her expressions serious. Now I'm scared.

"I need to ask you something," she says. "I wasn't sure if it was something you'd want to discuss in front of your parents. We ran some blood work when you first arrived to try to pinpoint what was causing your episode. When the results came back, they showed Prozac in your system, but only at about half a typical dose, signaling to me that you perhaps stopped taking a prescription recently. Is that correct?"

Looking down at the ground, I can't bring myself to make eye contact with her. I know the second she looks into my eyes she'll know everything. The secret will be out. And then I'll have to tell my parents and face the reality of what I did.

"Molly?" says Julie after what feels like an eternity. "Honey, you can tell me the truth. I want to help you."

It takes me another minute to muster the courage to focus on her and, through tears, I nod my head.

"Did you stop taking your prescription on the advice of a doctor, or did you stop taking it on your own?"

I wish I could lie. But lying won't change what happened. Lying won't change anything. I'm in too deep and know I need help. This is my chance. *Tell her the truth. Tell her everything.*

Tears continue to roll down my cheeks as the words roll out of my mouth. I can't stop them. I'm not sure I want to. Maybe I've been looking for an excuse to finally let it all out.

Adam. Todd. OCD. The pills. Everything.

Julie sits in silence, letting me purge my secrets until all that's left are tears. She doesn't look disappointed. She doesn't even look surprised. She's just watching me, letting me rid myself of the truth.

"It's all right, dear," she says, stepping toward me, her eyes kind. "I'll talk to Dr. O'Brien and see what she wants to do, and we'll go from there."

Nodding, all I can get out is a whispered thank-you. For years I've worried about being judged if anyone ever found out about my OCD. I've been terrified of the moment I would have to come clean about going off my pills. But I'm not scared anymore. For the first time in my life, I'm not afraid of what might happen and who I might lose because of my secret. I need help. I can't do this alone. I'm ready to get help.

CHAPTER 38

ADAM

It's eleven o'clock. I should be asleep because they're expecting me to show up and work my shift tomorrow, but I just can't. Thoughts swirl around in my head like a tornado, leaving a wake of destruction in my mind. I haven't slept in over thirty-six hours, but I don't dare close my eyes. Every time I do, I see it all play out again. Jake and the car. Hawthorne and the semi. Molly and Todd.

I've seen too much and caused too much pain.

My eyes ache, but I don't dare blink. I can't see it again. Smell the smells. Hear the sounds. It's all too much. Everything is too much.

Sitting up in bed, I place my hands tightly over my ears and rock back and forth. I know it's silent in my house—logically I know that. But these scenes of my life are playing out like a broken record. The thud of the car on his tiny body. The call out for an officer down. The cracking sound the door made when I kicked it in and found Todd on Molly.

I wish I could bang my head against the wall and knock these memories out. What have I done that's so horrible I have to live in this constant hell, plagued by these scenes? Haunted by the faces of people I've loved. People I've let down. Tears streaming down my mother's cheeks. The scream she let out when they told her what happened. The wailing of the sirens as the ambulance showed up to take Hawthorne to the hospital. Flashing lights. Red and blue. His mother's cries. The fear in Molly's eyes right before she passed out. The look on her face. As long as I live, I'll never forget it and I'll never forgive myself.

I'm dizzy.

Struggling to steady myself on my feet, I make my way to the bathroom, hoping a splash of cold water on my face will help. Freezing cold, burning hot—it doesn't make a difference. I feel nothing. My skin has stopped feeling. Is this my body's way of shutting down?

I stare at my reflection in the mirror. Although the bathroom is dark, the slightest hint of light from the streetlamp behind my house shines through the window, allowing me to see the shadow stretching across my face. And it's the truth. I'm a shadow of the man I used to be. But honestly, was I ever really that man?

Spinning. Everything is spinning. My shoulders slam back against the wall, but I don't lose my footing.

I'm exhausted but can't sleep. I can't stop these pictures from swirling around in my head. I can't do this anymore. I just can't do this anymore.

Throwing myself forward, I pull open the door to the medicine cabinet and jam my hand in, searching for any pills I have in there. I know I had a prescription for pain pills two years ago after I broke my hand on the job, but where are they? Okay, here they are. Damnit—expired. Are they still potent enough if they're expired?

No. That's not how I want to go. I can't wait for the pills to take hold. I need this to end. It needs to be over now.

Stumbling back into my bedroom, I make my way toward the gun safe. With shaky fingers, I enter the code to unlock it. My go-to code for everything: 021490. Jake's birthday. It's no wonder I'm so screwed up. I make myself relive his death every time I enter a password.

But not for much longer.

The lock clicks, and I pull the lever to open the door. Sliding my hand across the cool metal of the safe, I feel around until I touch the polymer frame that tells me I've found my gun. Slowly, I pull it out of the safe, feeling how perfectly it fits in my hand. Bringing it down, I turn it to the side and admire its craftsmanship. I was assigned this firearm as my primary duty weapon my first day on patrol, and I've carried it with me every day since. It's fitting this beautiful piece of metal that brought me into the police life will be the same one that takes me out and sets me free.

The safety is off, and there's one in the barrel.

Lifting the gun, I raise it toward my forehead. Is there a right way to do this? Is it possible to have bad aim when the ice-cold barrel is touching my skin?

Closing my eyes, I allow myself one more thought. It's of Jake running toward me through the field beside our childhood home. We played tag in that field every day in the summertime, but I haven't thought of it in years. Until now. I imagine this is what Jake will look like when we're finally reunited. He'll run toward me. Greeting me. Welcoming me home.

Sweat is dripping from my forehead, but my hands are surprisingly still. This must be like the eye of the storm. The calm in the chaos. This is my opportunity.

My only regret is the mess I'll leave behind for my fellow officers to comb through for evidence and the reports that will undoubtedly need to be written.

"Please, God, forgive me," I whisper into the darkness.

Placing my finger on the trigger, I begin to squeeze until—

What was that?

There it is again. Knocking. Is someone at the front door?

Who the hell is outside my house at this hour?

Holding my breath, I pray they'll go away. But they don't. The knocking continues on and off for the next several minutes. I can't pull the trigger with someone standing outside my door. Please just go away.

I'd like to punch a hole through the wall, but I put my gun down on a shelf in the closet and take calculated steps toward the door.

The knocking comes and goes in waves, but it's clear that whoever's at the door is not giving up and not going away.

With a deep breath, I peer through the peephole. Readjusting myself, I strain to see the face of the person covered in darkness standing on my front porch. Is that Carlson? It can't be. What the hell is he doing at my house?

Taking a step back, I turn the lock and open the door.

Letting out a long sigh, Sergeant Carlson pushes past me and walks into my living room. "I thought I was too late," he says, his voice shaking.

I stare at him in silence. He stares right back at me.

He's dressed in his uniform and must be working an overtime shift tonight. I still don't understand why the hell he's banging on my door in the middle of the night, though.

"Adam, I know," he says, staring at me hard, willing me to look at him. I can feel his eyes burning holes into my forehead, but I can't bring my eyes to meet his.

"Adam," he says, stepping toward me. He grabs hold of my arm and shakes me slightly, then a little harder. Finally, I look up to meet his eyes.

"How do you know?" I whisper, my voice cracking.

"Because I've been there," he says, shifting his hand to my shoulder and gripping it tightly. "I know the look in your eyes because I've seen it in my own. I've lived what you're living. I've been there."

"No, you haven't," I say, feeling the anger and pain in every word that tumbles out of my mouth and into the darkness.

"Yes, I have," he says. "I've watched friends killed in the line of duty take their last breath. I've picked up the pieces of innocent victims from the side of the road after a horrendous accident with a drunk driver who walks away from the scene unscathed. I've held toddlers crying for their moms or dads whose lifeless bodies are slumped in the driver's seat of the family car, trying to convince them and myself that it will be okay. I've cried silently in my room at night as I've relived those painful images over and over again. The smell of burning rubber is enough to cause a flashback. So is the smell of blood on the pavement. I know because I still live it every day of my life. It's hell, but it gets better. I promise, Adam, this is not worth giving up."

I'm not sure if I'm angry or sad, but my hands are balled into fists, and I'm on the verge of letting them connect with Sergeant Carlson's face.

"You don't have to believe me. Honestly, I doubt I'd believe myself if I were you. But I can help you. I know how to help you get through this."

"No, you don't," I say.

"Yes, I do. I'm not leaving here tonight, and I'll be damned if you're going to die on my watch."

His posture is stiff, and I can tell he's set on holding his ground.

"I just want it to stop," I whisper.

"I know," he says. "You need to talk to someone who can help you deal with the flashbacks. It is possible to get a handle on them. They'll never go away, but you can regain control of your life. This doesn't have to be the end. This is *not* the end. Your story isn't over."

I'm not sure if I believe him or not, but I know I can't last another sleepless night reliving these memories.

"I can't sleep," I say, pretty sure I sound like a whiney bitch but not really caring too much what Sergeant Carlson thinks about me right now. This is me at my worst. I have nothing to hide.

"You're going to think I'm full of it, but listening to books on tape helped me out a lot. Got any of those lying around?"

"No," I say.

"All right, then you're shit out of luck because I'm going to have to read to you."

Walking over to the bookshelf, he runs his thumb over the spine of each book from left to right, then stops on a small one toward the end. I know it before he holds it up for me to see. *The*

Yellow Wallpaper.

Sitting down on a chair, Carlson motions for me to lie down on the couch. I'm exhausted. I'm drained. I have nothing left to fight him, so I give in, staring at the ceiling from the couch.

"Sergeant Carlson," I say before he starts reading. "How did you know to come here?"

"I just had a feeling I had to get here, so I listened. I don't get these feelings often, but they're never wrong. You can bet your ass that's why I'm here. Your life isn't meant to end tonight. I was just the messenger to help you see that. The sun will rise tomorrow. Life will go one. Your life will go on."

My life will go on.

Fifteen minutes ago I felt more alone than I ever have, tormented by my living nightmares, and now here I lie on my couch as Sergeant Carlson begins reading to me.

"It is very seldom that mere ordinary people like John and myself secure ancestral halls for the summer," he begins.

Closing my eyes, I envision the estate, the room with yellow wallpaper the color of the madness that takes over the main character's mind. Maybe she wasn't so mad after all. When I really think about it, this isn't a terrifying story, it's rather sad, actually. This poor woman isn't crazy. She's just overwhelmed by her thoughts. Terrifying thoughts that won't leave her alone. We're not so different, she and I. Only I answered the door when someone came to save me from myself. I'll let the help inside rather than throwing the key out the window and creeping about

327

the room. I'll learn to move beyond the room and find a way to live outside these walls. Outside of my thoughts. This is my life, and I am in control. How will I ever repay Carlson for showing up when he did and saving me from my own terrible nightmare? I'm not ready for that permanent a solution. I do have people who care. I do have something to live for. I need help. And I can't do this alone.

CHAPTER 39

MOLLY

Life is like a nightmare I can't wake up from.

I was finally discharged from the hospital but only after seeing the psychiatrist on staff. The last time I met with someone was toward the end of my senior year of high school when OCD really took over my life. Before that, I thought only crazy people saw therapists. Normal people could handle their emotions on their own, right? Something has to be seriously wrong with you to need help from a professional. Might as well lock you up in a mental institution.

There is so much no one understands. And most people never

will. Not unless it happens to them. The feelings of failure. The inability to trust your own mind, and as a result, a difficulty really trusting anyone else.

Now my secret is out. Cara knows. There's no doubt Adam knows—not that it makes much of a difference. I haven't seen him since that night after the party. I thought for sure he'd come see me in the hospital, but he never did. He hasn't called, texted, or stopped by. So I guess it's official. He's done with me.

Cara is walking on eggshells around me, worried she'll say or do something that will trigger me or send me into a panic attack. I can't say I blame her after the way things went down that night. Watching your best friend stop breathing right in front of you cannot be easy. But somehow I feel like having my secret out in the open has made us closer. She finally knows the real me—all of me—and she still wants to be my friend. I'm not sure I'd tell her earlier if I could go back in time, but I sure am glad she knows now.

News of Todd's arrest spread quickly. The outing of my OCD has been overshadowed by what he did, which is totally fine with me. There's enough attention on my life right now I'd like to deflect as much away as possible. I've had what seems like a constant string of people reaching out. Everyone seems to want to show their support. While I appreciate it, I really would rather be left alone right now. I'm still trying to process what happened to me. My memory of that night is still gone, something I consider a blessing in disguise, and I pray it remains that way for the rest of my life.

The case is strong enough against Todd that the officers working it say they don't think they'll need me to testify to get a conviction. A conviction. Todd. All the time and effort he's put into earning his degree thrown right out the window. It doesn't matter how good of a lawyer his dad is—this town, this state, as a matter of fact—does not hold kindly to men assaulting women. But he's innocent until proven guilty, right?

Well, he's already been tried in the court of opinion in our small beachside community, and things have not gone in his favor. He will forever be known for what he did to me. What a waste to throw your entire life away in one moment of anger. I don't understand it, and as mad as I am at him for what he did to me, I feel sorry for him. His life is over. Mine is just beginning.

I'm meeting with my therapist this afternoon for the second time this week, and I'm actually kind of looking forward to it. She is a nice but no-nonsense kind of person, something I appreciate. She doesn't sugarcoat things, and I can tell she is going to push me to face my fears. Although OCD is something I know I'll never get rid of, never be cured of, maybe there's a chance for me to take back my life and regain some control. It's time I finally find some peace in my life.

Dr. Sanji's office is on the outskirts of town in a cute little beach cottage that's been converted into a workspace. Two other doctors share the space with her, both also specializing in mental illness.

Mental illness. It's still hard for me to accept that phrase applies to me, but the more I'm learning about myself and my illness, the more I'm beginning to feel a sort of pride. No, I don't intend to walk around wearing a shirt with big thumbs on it that says "This Girl Has OCD," but I'm finding it easier to stop being ashamed. Yes, there are people I know who sidestep me or pretend they don't see me on campus now, but you know what? Most are people I don't talk to much anyway, and, honestly, I shouldn't care what they think of me, right?

I live in hell every day with a brain that makes me doubt everything about myself, all the way down to every thought that passes through my head. Double-checking doorknobs, electrical outlets, and light switches has been a part of my life for as long as I can remember. It's who I am. With the help of Dr. Sanji, I'm finally starting to see my OCD for what it really is—a part of me that doesn't define me. I am not OCD. I just have it.

Because you know what? *I* define myself. Not others and what they think of me. Not what happened to me that night. Not what Todd thinks of me or the fact that Adam has completely distanced himself from me. I am defined by the way I view myself, and from now on, I'm not going to be ashamed. I have nothing to be ashamed of. I am strong—maybe stronger than anyone else I know. I am smart, even if I wasn't accepted into the program for a distinction in my major. There is so much more life to live, and I am going to hold on tight and do my best to enjoy the ride. I've seen how precious life can be. Everything can change in an instant. I want to be happy and healthy. And I want to live.

Pulling up in front of the small whitewashed house, I park my car on the street. Closing my eyes, I take a deep breath. I've got this.

Closing the car door behind me, I click the button on my key fob and hear the doors lock and the alarm set. Tossing the keys into a pocket in my purse, I remind myself that I locked the doors, I know I locked the doors, and I don't need to check again. *I've got this.*

Walking up the flower-lined cobblestone path to the front door, I can't help but take in the beauty of this home. It's small and simple but so welcoming. This place is like my lighthouse, guiding me through the darkest days of my life. I know I can always come here and find my way home.

Opening the blue front door, I step into the waiting room, which must have been the living room at one point. It's large and open, with beautiful walnut hardwood floors and light-blue walls the color of the sky on the clearest sunny day. White leather chairs and sofas line the walls of the room, and the oversized coffee table in the center of the room is stacked high with books and magazines. I smile and wave at Brenda sitting behind the front desk.

"I'll let her know you're here, honey," she says, smiling.

"Thanks," I say, taking a seat in the corner of the room. The waiting room is typically empty at this time of day but in the next five minutes will fill up with one or two other patients as the start of a new hour draws near.

Looking around, a book with a yellow cover sitting on the coffee table catches my eye. I know what it is before I even pick it up. *The Yellow Wallpaper.*

This short story has had a huge effect on me throughout my life, inspiring me to write and helping me to feel empowered as a woman, but now I feel an even stronger connection with the main character and with Charlotte Perkins Gilman. Charlotte dealt with depression in her life and was told to take it easy and do less—even social interaction might be too taxing for her. She felt the "cure" for her depression, or as most referred to it at the time, "female hysteria," was ridiculous, and she used this short story to make a statement. She knew this so-called cure, not her depression, would be what drove her crazy.

I can relate so much to Charlotte and her main character. I always thought I was crazy, but it turns out I wasn't. The only thing making me crazy was trying to hide who I really am. But no more. It's time to be free and creep around.

"Molly," comes a bright voice. Dr. Sanji waves me in from the doorway of her office.

Standing, I adjust my skirt and step toward her, smiling as she greets me at her door.

"And how are you doing today, Molly?" she asks, closing the door behind us.

Dropping down onto the oversized navy-blue couch in her

office, I set my purse on the ground and tell her I'm fine. The couch is made of soft microfiber, so it almost feels like I'm sitting on a cloud it's so puffy and comforting. Pillows of a variety of textures and colors line the back cushions, some covered in sequins, others in faux animal hair, others still looking like someone skinned a muppet to make them. It's a mishmash of colors, styles, and textures, but here in this office, it makes me feel safe.

"How are you feeling about your current dosage?" she asks, sitting down behind her laptop.

"Okay, I guess." If I'd known the consequences of going off Prozac and then resuming it, I never would have gone off it in the first place. Readjusting to the right dosage has been absolute hell.

"My appetite is back a little now, but I'm still pretty nauseous most of the time. My anxiety levels have decreased by maybe 50 percent, but I still feel really anxious most of the time."

Dr. Sanji nods as she types on her keyboard, looking up at me when she's finished. "Do you feel comfortable keeping your dosage at forty milligrams, or do you think you'd like to try sixty to see how that goes?"

Given how difficult it's been adjusting to the side effects of forty milligrams, I really dread the thought of upping my dose and having to start over. The constant headaches leave me in bed most days, but I can't shake the feeling that a higher dose might help me feel better.

"I think I'd like to try sixty," I say, wiping my sweaty palms on my skirt.

"Okay, I think you'll see a large improvement in upping your dose, but I want to make sure it's something you're comfortable with," she says, giving me a serious look.

"I understand," I say, nodding.

"I'll be sure to get this prescription sent over to the drugstore," she says, jotting down a note on the pad of paper beside her laptop. "How has your sleep been lately? Is the melatonin working again, or do you need me to write you a prescription for a sleep aid?"

"Well, I basically take a handful of melatonin every night, but I think I've found a dose that's working," I say, watching as she types more notes into her computer.

"Good," she says. "It's important to keep you sleeping well so the Prozac continues to work. Now," she says, closing her laptop screen. "How are your classes going?"

"Classes are okay, I guess," I say. I'm a little embarrassed by how much my grades have slipped this semester, but there are only a few weeks until winter break, and then I can spend some time with my family, reset, and come back ready to get it done the last semester of my college career.

"How are you doing with your other classmates? Are you still running into people who are avoiding you or acting overly sensitive to your situation? Do you feel like you're handling all the extra attention a little better now? Or should we work on more skills to use when you're feeling overwhelmed?"

"You know how small this town is," I say, rolling my eyes. "I think it's getting better. People are starting to find other things to focus on. But I still feel like a total freak. 'The girl who almost died having a panic attack after being assaulted by her ex-boyfriend.' I really can't wait for the school year to be over so I can move on and start over somewhere new, where no one knows me."

"Yes, this town can feel pretty small sometimes," she says, slightly furrowing her brow. "Has Todd tried contacting you at all?"

Looking down at my hands, I really just want to cry. Todd. At one point I honestly thought he was the one. I considered spending my life with him. How the hell can someone be so wrong about a person? How awful is my judgment that I dated him? That I loved him? How can you misjudge someone so badly?

"Molly?"

"Oh, um, no, he hasn't. Not since his last letter."

A week after everything happened, I received a letter without a return address, but I didn't need an address to know who sent it. I'd know that handwriting anywhere.

Molly,

I'm sorry for what happened. My future is riding on how this all turns out. If you dropped the charges, it would all go away and we could both just go back to life like none of this ever happened. I was angry, but now I'm just sad. I hope you'll consider the impact this will have on my life.

Love, Todd

I thought I'd at least receive some half-ass apology, but I didn't even get that. All he cares about is himself. It's always about him. I feel so much pain over wasting even a minute of my life on him. But you can't go back in time. And really, what does living with regret get me? A whole lot more opportunities for anxiety. All I can focus on now is my life moving forward because that's all that there is—a fresh beginning laid out in front of me.

"What about Adam?" she asks. "Has he reached out to you at all since that night?"

I shake my head but keep my eyes fixed on the desk in front of me. Nothing. I've heard nothing from Adam. Once again, me and my horrible judgment. I've tried to reach out to him a few times, but he never calls or texts me back. If nothing else, I'd like the opportunity to tell him thank you—I mean, if it wasn't for him, things could have (and no doubt would have) turned out very differently. It's time for me to let it go—let him go—and focus on myself and getting through this last part of school before I spread my wings and fly far away. Far, far away.

"Can we talk about that for a minute? Because I sense some

unfinished business and perhaps an anxiety trigger there," says Dr. Sanji.

"Yeah, he could very well be a trigger for me. I feel so sad every time I think of him. I just don't know what went wrong, Well, I mean, I do. But I just don't understand. It's really hard to accept the fact that, once again, I misjudged someone so badly. I thought he was this wonderful person, and he just turned out to be someone else to let me down. I don't know. I mean, I'll move on and be okay. Eventually. I guess maybe it's just that I don't feel like I have any closure. Things were going well, but then it all stopped so abruptly. I'm not sure how much of this is normal emotion and how much is my OCD forcing me to fixate on something that was never mine. Something I'd like to have but never will. Honestly, I feel like my world has crashed around me and shrunk so small I'm being suffocated.

It's like I don't know which thoughts are mine and which belong to OCD. I mean, will I ever be able to differentiate? Right now I feel so broken in every single way. Some days I feel like I want to give up. Honestly, had it all ended that night, I would have been okay with it. Life is hard and living with a broken brain feels like too much some days. How will I ever find someone to love me for me? Someone who can look past this broken piece of me and see me for who I am? Really, at this point, I don't even know who that is. But I need someone to see me. How will I ever handle being a wife? A mother? A normal functioning human in society? I just feel so lost."

I drop my head and stare at my hands again.

Dr. Sanji is quiet for several minutes before she speaks.

"Molly, what you are feeling is totally normal for someone dealing with a mental illness. As you learn new tools to manage the obsessions and get your compulsions under control, you'll feel more confident in your abilities to manage in life. Your life will always be a struggle with anxiety and your OCD, but that doesn't mean it's over. You have a lot to offer society. You just need to decide what you want to do with your life, then start setting goals to get there. Keep working hard like you have been, and your life will eventually fall into place, whatever it may be."

"I've lost interest in so many things because I feel like they don't matter anymore. Some days I just feel like it's all hopeless, that I'll never break free from this cycle of obsessions and compulsions."

"It can take a few months for Prozac to start fighting the feelings of depression, but you can expect that loss of interest to disappear when it does. I know it's hard, but with time, you'll start to feel whole again. You've been through a lot, and what you are feeling is completely normal."

"Okay," I say, watching her open the laptop and type in a few more notes.

"All right, well, our time is almost up," she says, looking up at me. "Is there anything else you'd like to talk about?"

I shake my head.

"Okay," she says, turning her attention to the oversized

calendar covering a portion of her desk. "Let's see, I'm scheduled to see you back here next week. Does that work for you? Or would you like to meet again before then?"

"Let's just plan on next week," I say, meeting her eyes. Although I don't know her well yet, I trust her. There's something in her eyes that puts me at ease and lets me know she's not here to judge me and really does want to help me. I've dealt with my fair share of psychologists and psychiatrists. I've met with ones who had no patience for my compulsions, ones who didn't have the first clue about OCD, and still others who seemed genuine but really just couldn't help me. Dr. Sanji, on the other hand, I feel really lucky to have found. She is one of the only things that makes me feel grateful I'm trapped in this town for another five months. I truly believe she is going to help me acquire the tools I need to fight OCD and come out on top.

"All right," she says, rising from her seat. "You call me if you need anything. And if you decide you'd like to meet again before next week, let me know, and I'll find a way to squeeze you in."

Nodding, I thank her as she shakes my hand and walks me to the door. Stepping out into the waiting room, I can see three patients seated throughout but don't want to make eye contact. There's a kind of unwritten rule in a psychiatrist's office that you don't look at each other. We all know we're dealing with our own kind of crazy, so there's no need to stare to try to figure out what brand anyone else is.

Passing the front desk, I tell Brenda I'll see her next week and continue toward the main exit. My phone begins vibrating in my purse, so I stop to dig for it amid the mess of chaos that includes my wallet, receipts, a hairbrush, lip gloss, gum, pens, a notepad, and myriad odds and ends, hoping to grab it before it stops ringing. Most people think a person with OCD is overly organized. This is clearly not the case for me.

Feeling around, I locate my phone just in time to see "Home" flash off the screen, replaced by a missed-call warning. Shoot.

"Excuse me, miss," comes a voice from below me. I glance down to see a hand holding a tiny vile of perfume that must have dropped from my bag as I dug for my phone.

"Thanks," I say, retrieving it from the hand and shoving it back into my purse. Looking down at his face to smile before stepping out the front door, I stop dead in my tracks, and my face flushes red. Maybe it goes white because I feel like I've seen a ghost.

It's Adam.

* * *

ADAM

It's been over a month since everything came crashing down around me and I was ready to end it all with the business end of my duty weapon. I can still feel the cold metal pressed against my forehead. Just the thought of it makes me shudder.

Life is still anything but easy. The flashbacks are coming in full force, but at least now I understand them a little more. And I have a name for what's happening to me—something more than that losing my mind. PTSD. I thought this was something only members of the armed forces experienced—certainly the things they've seen and heard are infinitely more traumatic than my experiences. But somehow, starting with the death of my little brother, there have been traumatic events in my life I haven't processed correctly and have somehow become trapped in my brain so they can easily be brought back to the forefront of my mind with a specific smell, sight, or sound.

My department partners with a local therapist to offer counseling and therapy for those of us who have experienced something traumatic on the job. I've seen a lot of bad stuff in my four short years on the force, but nothing has hit me as hard as witnessing the death of Hawthorn last year. From what I've learned about myself and PTSD, that event compounded with Jake's death sent my mind into some kind of overdrive and made processing both events even more difficult.

I haven't spoken with Carlson since the night he showed up at my house. I never thought much of him—he was always such a loose cannon—but now I feel something more. Sympathy? Empathy, maybe. He was there for me in my absolute darkest hour. He stayed until his shift ended in the morning and then stayed a little longer to make sure I was okay. Things seem to be better in the light of day. Most of the time.

I met with Dr. Simms for the first time last week, and he

seems to really understand PTSD and the effect it can have on your life. He's mentioned Eye Movement Desensitization and Reprocessing, also known as EMDR, but I'm not sure it's a good fit for me. I've heard positive things and can definitely see the merit in this therapy, but for now, I'm going to focus on talking through the issues and trying to get some of my thoughts and emotions under control. This has gone on for so long I can't imagine life without these tormenting thoughts.

Sitting here in the psychiatrist's office, I glance nervously around the room at the two other patients waiting for their appointments to begin. I'm struggling to figure out how I got here, but understanding what causes these upsetting memories to be dredged up is helping me put my pride away and ask for help.

Feeling a vibration in my pocket, I pull out my cell phone to see a text message from Hernandez. Alicia went into labor two weeks early, and their baby boy was born just a few hours ago. Diego Sanchez Hernandez, named after his grandpa. Accompanying the information is a picture of one of the cutest, chubbiest little babies I've ever seen. Dark hair, peach fuzz around his face. He's perfect.

Congratulations to you both. Give Alicia and that little guy a hug for me. I'll stop by to visit after my shift ends tomorrow.

Sounds great. We're so happy. Life is complete. See you then.

Life is complete. I wonder what that must feel like. My life has never been complete. I doubt it ever will be. I'm working toward that now, though, right? Isn't that what this is all about? Maybe someday.

Shoving my phone back into my pocket, I hear a door open and see the feet of one of last session's patients passing by. They stop beside me, and a small vial falls down and hits the floor. Perfume, maybe?

Picking it up, I try to get the attention of the girl who's dropped it. "Excuse me, miss," I say. When she looks down at me, I don't know what to say. I hand her the vial, my eyes fixed on her face. I'm not sure if I should get up and run or stand up and throw my arms around her. She looks down at me, the hint of a smile on her lips—until she sees my face.

"Adam," she whispers, more like she's talking to herself than to me.

"Hey, Molly," I say, shifting uncomfortably in my seat.

"Uh, what are you doing here?" It's obvious she's embarrassed to see me, especially in the waiting room of a psychiatrist's office. It doesn't occur to me until then that perhaps I should be a little embarrassed for her to find me here too.

My face burns hot as I tell her I'm waiting for an appointment.

"Oh, okay," she says, looking around then room, then toward the door. "Well, nice to see you," she says, forcing a smile before turning back toward the door.

My appointment is set to begin in five minutes, and I can't miss it. But I'm not sure I can miss this opportunity to explain myself either.

"Molly, hold on a second," I say, reaching for her hand. She stops dead in her tracks and just stands there. I can't tell if she's angry, nervous, sad, or what, but she keeps her back to me, letting her hand rest in mine for a moment. Finally, she turns back toward me.

"I've really got to get going," she says, a look of sadness on her face. I know I must have hurt her, but I need her to know why. Not that her knowing will justify anything. I just need her to know that it was me, not her. Well, actually, I guess it *was* her. I wanted to keep her safe from me.

"Are you busy tonight?" I ask.

"Um, I'm not sure. When?"

"In an hour, maybe?" I hadn't given much thought to how things would go when I saw her again, but I knew an encounter was inevitable. This town is far too small to ever completely disappear. This is just not the place I'd envisioned us running into each other.

"Um, yeah, I guess you can give me a call and see," she says. "Well, that is if you still have my number."

Ouch. But I deserve it. "Yes, I do. I'll call you when I'm done here, and maybe we can go get some ice cream or something and talk for a bit?"

"That could maybe work," she says. "See you later." And with that, she walks straight for the door and exits, never looking back.

CHAPTER 40

MOLLY

I'm sitting alone at the table in my apartment, staring at my phone. I've spent the last hour trying to keep myself busy so I don't end up doing this, but alas, here I am. Seeing him at Dr. Sanji's office has thrown me for a loop. I feel my anxiety levels rising and am grateful that as of tomorrow morning, I'll be upping my dose of medication, hopefully completely getting rid of these feelings.

One hour and one minute after seeing him in the doctor's office, my phone begins to vibrate, the name Adam popping up on the screen. I've been waiting for this for the last hour. Who am I kidding? I've been waiting for this for the past month. But here I am now, staring at my phone, wondering if I really want to hear what he has to say. What kind of explanation can he possibly have that will excuse him blowing me off completely?

Grabbing my phone at the last second, I slide my finger across the screen and answer the call.

"Hello," I say, trying to sound as aloof and uninterested as possible. What I really want to do is follow up my hello with "Now go ahead and explain yourself" and rapid fire about fifty questions I've been dying to know the answer to. But rather than giving in, I leave it at hello.

"Hi," comes his voice from the other end of the line.

There's a pause. After being left to wait with no answers for so long, I feel the need to make him wait and work for it a little. Awkward silence has got nothing on me today.

"Are you home?" he asks.

"Yeah," I say, unwilling to give up anything more than that.

"Can you come downstairs?" he asks.

I'm stunned for a moment, not expecting to find him sitting in his car outside my apartment complex, but sure enough, a quick peek out the window confirms that he is, in fact, downstairs.

"Um, yeah," I say, glancing around to make sure everything is unplugged and locked so I can run down. "Give me a second."

After a quick sweep through the house, I make my way to the front door, grabbing a sweater and my purse, then locking the front door behind me. Then double-checking. And triple-checking. My anxiety must be flying high right now because OCD is really rearing its ugly head.

Giving myself a few moments to relax and calm down, I take the stairs slowly, counting each one as I step on it. Twenty-three. Before I realize it, I'm at the gate and leaving the safety of my home to step into the unknown, which I'm fairly certain will be full of a lot of stupid excuses.

Adam waves me over when he sees me emerge from the gate. I know he was having a hard time with the anniversary of Officer Hawthorne's death the last time I saw him, but he looks a little worse for wear. There are bags under his eyes, stubble on his chin, and he's in dire need of a haircut. His gray hoodie is zipped up almost all the way to his chin. When was the last time he combed that hair of his? He usually keeps it so short I'm not sure he even owns a comb. I'm surprised I didn't notice how unkempt he was back at Dr. Sanji's office.

Taking calculated steps toward him, I see him try to force a smile but to no avail. He's watching me closely as I close the gap between us, and it's making me a little uncomfortable.

"Hey," he says. "Want to go for a drive?"

"Sure," I say, making my way to the passenger side of the car and letting myself in. He reaches the door just as I'm doing up my seat belt.

"Sorry, I would have got that for you."

"Don't worry about it. I've got it." It definitely came out more bitchy than I'd intended, but whatever. He's lucky I'm even giving him the time of day.

Sliding in behind the steering wheel, Adam sits there staring out the windshield for a few seconds before starting the car. Turning to me, he says, "Anywhere you want to go?"

What kind of question is that? I have no idea what he wants to tell me or how long I'm going to want to be around him after I hear this so-called explanation.

Shrugging my shoulders, I say, "Down to the pier, maybe?" The pier is typically pretty empty. For some reason, not many people like to go down there. Plus, it's not far from my apartment, so it'll be a quick drive home, just in case.

"You got it," he says, turning the steering wheel and pulling out into traffic. He keeps his eyes focused out the windshield for the five-minute drive while I take sideways glances at him, trying to get a read on his mood and some idea of what he's planning on telling me. Sickness? Broken bone? Alien abduction?

Pulling into the empty parking lot, Adam parks in a spot directly in front of the walkway to the pier. He cuts the ignition and turns to look at me for the first time since he's climbed into the car. "Shall we?" he asks, opening his door and hurrying around to my side to open mine before I can.

"Thanks," I say, pulling my sweater on and wrapping my arms around myself.

Closing the door behind me, he places his hand on the small of my back to lead me down the path—quite a presumptuous move for a guy I haven't seen or heard from in weeks.

We're both quiet until we reach the wooden bridge of the pier and begin our walk toward the water.

"So, I told you I want to explain myself," he begins. Nodding, I glance in his direction long enough to see him watching me closely. "Well, this is pretty difficult for me to talk about, so I'm not going to go into too much detail, but I've been going through a pretty rough time the last year. Things continued to spiral out of control in my personal life after we met, but I didn't dare say anything for fear that I'd scare you off. And also because, at the time, I didn't know what the hell was happening to me."

He looks down at his hands before continuing. "I was in Dr. Simm's office this afternoon to meet with him for help dealing with PTSD."

I stop for a second and look at him, but he keeps walking forward, so I quickly try to keep up.

"I still don't completely understand what's happening, but I've been having these flashbacks of the accident that took Hawthorne's life." He swallows hard, rubbing his hands together. "And the one that claimed my brother's life."

He's never told me about what happened to his brother. I knew he'd passed away, but that's about it. I suddenly feel like the worst person in the world for ever being upset with him.

"There were so many similarities between the two accidents, the largest of which was me and the part I played in things. I've held on to a lot of guilt and anger for a very long time. Everything built up until Halloween night, when I went into a tailspin."

He's silent again for a minute, and I can't tell if he's considering whether or not to go on or trying to figure out how to say what he wants to tell me. He stops short of the end of the pier and turns to face me. I stop walking and stand silently, giving him time to work out his thoughts before he goes on. His head is down, and I think he must be staring at his hands again, but when he lifts his face to look at me, there are tears on his cheeks.

"I've thought for so long that these two accidents were my fault. That if I had done something differently, or had I not been there at all, they could have been avoided completely. I started to see myself as the common thread of horribly bad luck between everyone and all the sorrow caused by these events, and I started to worry I might have the same effect on your life. That was confirmed to me the night of Hawthorne's vigil when Todd attacked you. I pulled away because I thought it was my presence in your life that was causing these horrible things. Then Halloween happened, and I realized that by pushing you away, I was once again responsible for what happened to you."

Grabbing my hand, he continues. "I do care about you, Molly, and that's what makes this so hard. I blame myself for the bad that's happened in the lives of everyone I care about, and I worried my bad luck would drag you down too. Then it did. And the flashbacks became unbearable—until I just couldn't take it anymore."

He's silent, and I don't request any kind of explanation. I can only imagine what he's trying to tell me.

"Thankfully, the night I hit my lowest low, a sergeant in my department showed up on my doorstep and stayed with me until morning. That was when I finally decided to get help. And when I was given the diagnosis of PTSD. I know it's kind of a scary thing, but I hope you can look beyond it and not see me as crazy or broken."

He stands staring at me, maintaining his hold on my hand. Slowly, I pull my hand away. I can see the pain in his eyes until I lean forward and wrap my arms around him. His body is tense and rigid at first, but then he gives in and relaxes against me.

"I'm so sorry you've been going through this," I say, feeling like a jerk for the way I treated him when he first picked me up.

Pulling away, I grab his hand again. As much as I'd like to be mad at him for blowing me off and never calling me back, I can't help but feel a connection to him. And how can I stay mad at him when I have my own secret? If he's brave enough to share his, maybe I'm brave enough to share mine.

* * *

ADAM

I'm having a hard time getting a read on what Molly's thinking. She's standing here, holding my hand, staring at me. She's clearly gearing up to say something, and I brace myself, expecting the worst. What kind of person wants to knowingly take on a person with mental illness?

"There's something I need to tell you," she says, taking a step backward and removing her hand from my grasp. Her eyes shift as she refuses to make eye contact with me. "I'm not sure if you already heard, but there is a reason I had that panic attack Halloween night."

Panic attack? I thought she'd hyperventilated. I tried to keep my distance from the investigation so as not to cause her any more harm, so I never followed up on anything or read through the completed police report.

"Since high school—well, my whole life, actually—I've been dealing with OCD. It got really bad in high school, and I sought help before coming to college. With the right medication, I've been able to keep most of my obsessions and compulsions in check, maintaining a relatively normal level of anxiety."

She looks up at me, perhaps for validation. I'm not sure what to say or what she's looking for from me. How is it possible she has OCD? I've never noticed her washing her hands a ridiculous number of times. Her apartment wasn't exceptionally clean. It doesn't make sense.

Taking a deep breath, she continues. "When we first started seeing each other, I missed a dose of medication. I felt better than I have in years and thought maybe going off my meds was a good idea. I misdiagnosed my withdrawals for the flu and didn't realize what a bad idea it was to stop taking my medication cold turkey until the compulsions returned, my anxiety came back with a vengeance, and it felt like my world had come crashing down. Halloween night was the culmination of a lot of bad decisions that ultimately ended in that massive panic attack."

She refuses to make eye contact, but I can't take my eyes off of her. I had no idea she was struggling. She always seemed so pulled together. I guess we're both pretty good liars.

"It was a blessing in disguise, I guess, because my stay in the hospital resulted in some pretty extensive psychiatric evaluations that ultimately landed me back on my meds and in therapy with Dr. Sanji. Which brings us to today—I was leaving my appointment with her when I ran into you."

"I guess we've come full circle, huh?" I say, trying to force a laugh but finding myself unsuccessful. Nothing about any of this is funny. I didn't assume to know everything about Molly, and I'm sure she felt the same about me, but as it turns out, we really know nothing about each other. Nothing at all. So many secrets. And for what? To avoid being seen for who we really are? Because we were both too afraid of being judged? What kind of life am I choosing to live?

Molly nods and looks out over the water. I hadn't noticed before, but she's wearing very little makeup, and her hair is pulled back in a ponytail. This is clearly a much different Molly than the one I met that first night. But if I'm being honest, I'm a much different person than I was that night too.

Turning toward her, I take her hand firmly in mine. "Well,

Molly, I'm Adam. It sure is nice to meet you."

Smiling, she returns my grip. Perhaps this doesn't have to be the end. Maybe every ending is only a new beginning. A few weeks ago, I stood at the edge of the end, but I've ultimately found a new reason to be here. What happened wasn't my fault. As hard as it is for me to admit that, it's the truth. We all make choices we think are the best for a situation, then deal with the consequences. For most people, however, the consequences don't involve life or death.

My life is not normal, nor will it ever be what most people consider normal. I'm an officer. I'm a brother. I've lived through loss, but I've also experienced much happiness associated with my job. PTSD will be a part of me for the rest of my life, but that doesn't mean my life is over. Every day is a choice, and I can choose to be here and make a difference. To honor the lives of the people I've loved and lost. And to work every day to make the world a better, safer place. *Normal* is such a relative term. Are any of us really normal?

CHAPTER 41

MOLLY

It all started with two white pills, so it's fitting it ends with them too. Only this time I put my pill bottle back up on my desk, in clear view of anyone who might pass by. I won't let fear drive me anymore, and I won't let it hold me back. I am me—OCD and all—and I'm happy to be me.

I heard once that if we all put our own issues and problems into a pot and were given the chance to choose someone else's, we'd likely pick the ones we were originally given. Why? Because we were given the difficulties and trials in life that would help refine us and make each of us stronger. I don't know why OCD is a part of my life, but it is. Sure, there are days I wish I was someone else. When I wish I didn't have to fight to remain rational every second. To take medication to keep my anxiety levels manageable. But it's all part of me. What I've come to understand is that it is only *part* of me. It does not define me. I am not OCD. It's just something I have.

While my future is uncertain, I do know this: I am not alone. I have people who support me. People who advocate for me. And I have Adam. With him, I know I can face anything OCD throws at me.

Life is hard. Life's not fair. But going through hell has made me see that all I am is me. And I think I'm pretty okay with that.

THE END

ACKNOWLEDGMENTS

This book never would have come around if it weren't for the inspiration I receive every day from my sons. Joshua, Caleb, Jacob, Lucas—you make life worth living.

To my husband, Greg, thank you for supporting me and believing in me through this process. You are my favorite sounding board.

To my mom and dad: what can I say? I wouldn't be who I am or where I am without you. The way you raised me, the ideals you instilled in me, and the seed of motivation you've nurtured within me to never give up. I'm proud to call you my parents and hope to make you equally as proud.

I so appreciate the team at Eschler Editing, particularly Michele Priesendorf who completed the final edit on my manuscript. And Angela who took the time to speak with me after the Storymakers Conference last year and help me find new direction.

Jessica, my friend, my editor, my favorite person to eat dessert with. You were one of my first readers and you've been that writerly support I needed when I felt like I was losing my mind.

To all of my family and friends who have given me the courage to keep on going, thank you. To all of the writers who have supported me and encouraged me along the way, thank you. Words can never fully express my thanks and appreciation. Not everyone has the same level of support I have received in my life, and I will forever be grateful for those who take a vested interest in both myself and my family.

AUTHOR'S NOTE

How many times have you heard someone say, "I'm so OCD"? How many times have you yourself said it?

Growing up, I could never quite pinpoint why certain things were so hard for me. I mean, I had friends, I did well in school, and I was a nice person—why wasn't I always as comfortable in social situations as everyone else?

In college I started referring to certain elements of my personality as "so OCD". The compulsion to double check a burning candle, the need to make sure my hair straightener was unplugged. When I got married and became a mom, the joke started to be less funny. My view on life shifted from "I'm so OCD" to "Maybe this really is OCD." It took nearly another decade for me to finally be diagnosed with OCD, and when I was, it was one of the most freeing events of my life. I no longer had to wonder what was wrong with me. I no longer had to wonder if what I was experiencing was OCD. No, I finally had a definite answer. And after deciding to go on medication to help get my increasingly life-consuming obsessive thoughts and compulsions under control, I could finally start living the life I loved again.

OCD is a mental illness that should be taken seriously, not turned into a joke. Obsessions and compulsions are nothing to take lightly. No, when your mind is a constant tornado of the worst-case scenario, it doesn't seem like such a joke anymore.

Although one in five people in the United States experience mental illness of some form, there remains a misrepresentation of mental illness not only in literature, but in society in general. I understand how difficult it is to find a true representation of what I go through. No matter who you are, now is the time to speak up and share your truth.

As a society, we need to do better. We need to be more understanding. We need to find ways to reach out and empathize with each other. I wrote this story in hopes of helping spread awareness not only of OCD, but also PTSD, and mental illness is general. It's time we bring the topic of mental illness out of the darkness and into the light. We can all do better.

If you live with mental illness, I want you to know you're not alone. You are here for a reason. You are needed. And you are loved. Find someone you can talk to about the thoughts going on in your head—bringing these thoughts out of the dark and into the light decreases the shame and can help you feel less alone. This is something I have to remind myself of each day. Find a family member, a friend, a doctor, or other health care professional. If you need more information or tips on how to find help, check out the resources shared by the National Alliance on Mental Illness (NAMI) on NAMI.org.

You are strong. You are worthy of love. Never stop fighting the good fight. We need you here. You deserve to be here.

For everyone with mental illness, their family members and friends, this is for you.

I see you.

ABOUT THE AUTHOR

Kelli Thalman is looking for a way to change how the world views mental illness. Struggling with OCD herself, and living in a household with a husband and four sons who all have some diagnosable form of anxiety, this fight is one that she doesn't take lightly. A graduate from UC Santa Barbara, Kelli spends the majority of her time homeschooling her kids, supporting her husband, and squeezing the joy out of every moment. When she's not trying to figure out how her house is in a constant state of chaos and where all of these never-ending piles of laundry came from, you'll find Kelli sneaking away to write while shoveling peanut butter M&Ms into her mouth until her stomach hurts. *Two White Pills* is her first novel. Follow along with what she's doing at kellithalman.com.

Made in the USA
Las Vegas, NV
04 November 2022

58740042R00210